VIRGINIA FOX
ROCKY MOUNTAIN SECRETS

DRAGONBOOKS
PUBLISHING HOUSE

DRAGONBOOKS
PUBLISHING HOUSE

Copyright © 2023 by Virginia Fox.

All rights reserved. No part of this publication may be reproduced, stored in a retrieval system, or transmitted, in any form or by any means, without the prior written permission of the author, or as expressly permitted by law.

This book is a work of fiction and, except in the case of historical fact any resemblance to actual persons, living or dead, is purely coincidental.

Names: Fox, Virginia, author.

Title: Rocky Mountain Secrets (Rocky Mountain Romances, Book 5)/ by Virginia Fox.

Description: First Edition. | Boulder, Colorado: Dragonbooks, 2023.

Summary: Assigned to track down a smalltown serial killer, FBI Agent Aviary Wilkinson is paired with hunky Cole Carter— but he's her brother's best friend. Helped by Avery's partner, a pet rat named Miss Marple, the pair struggle to navigate their feelings, solve the case, and save a town wedding in the process.

Subjects: BISAC: FICTION / Romance / General. | FICTION / Romance / Contemporary. | FICTION / Women.

ISBN 979-8-9862800-1-1 (Paperback) | ISBN 979-8-9862800-0-4 (eBook)
LCCN: On file.

Editor: John Palisano
Associate Editor: Eric Guignard
Cover Design: Juliane Schneeweiss
Interior Design: Jennifer Thomas

JOIN ME!

Sign up for my newsletter to get insider information, and receive a FREE digital download of my Rocky Mountain Romances prequel, *Rocky Mountain Diner.*

Dive into a little romance, a dab of suspense,
and a whole lot of fun!

https://books.virginiafox.com/rmdiner_novella

ROCKY MOUNTAIN SECRETS

CHAPTER ONE

Avery Wilkinson stepped from one foot to the other, seemingly bored. She'd worked undercover for five months, which felt like an eternity. Sometimes, she had trouble remembering where fiction ended and reality began. She scratched the right side of her half-shaved head. Her long black hair fell smoothly down her left shoulder. Her hair had been cut in irregular steps with tips dyed bright red. Black kohl framed her eyes. Her flawless skin and slender, boyish physique took years off her and no one suspected anything amiss. Each element helped to create her cover as a youthful punk rocker.

Even with all that hard work though, she'd soon be too old to pass.

She raised her arm and the rivets on her black leather jacket clinked. The clinks signaled Miss Marple, her companion rat, who lived inside Avery's jacket. Like Avery, Miss Marple worked for the U.S. Drug Enforcement Administration. She stuck out her nose and blinked her black beady eyes.

Avery stroked her head and fed her a sunflower seed from the bag in her pocket.

"Go on. Go back inside. It's not time yet." The rat grabbed the seed and disappeared back into the jacket pocket.

Over the past few months, Avery had infiltrated the Monsanto clan, a family loosely tied to the Mafia.

Despite the work of two previous teams, the DEA had zero proof of any illegal activities.

Avery was brought in because she specialized in money laundering and drugs. She brought along a very special partner; Miss Marple was trained like a drug-sniffing dog, only better because she was so little. She could be snuck in places a big dog couldn't normally go.

Well trained, excluding "sit", "down", and "heel", she had naturally impeccable manners. Born in the Netherlands, she'd been kicked out of the police force's test program because her success rate was too low.

Avery suspected the problem was more that Miss Marple was very sensitive and, unlike many of her peers, enjoyed human contact. If she was locked up and brought out only for training, she shut down. It took a good deal of TLC and Miss Marple had to trust you.

Of course, Avery was thrilled with her little helper's work; the rat had never let her down. Trained in four scents, Miss Marple's repertoire could be expanded as needed.

If everything goes smoothly, she'll prove herself...and her nose...again today, Avery thought.

She knew the deal with the Monsanto brothers—they had a huge soft spot when it came to homeless children. Probably because they had worked their way up from the streets themselves, Avery bet. Ironic, really, that they were also dealing drugs, which were often the reason kids ended up on the streets in the first place.

Avery thought about her friend Paula back home in Independence, Colorado, who had taken in one such runaway into her home that past year. *I wonder how they've been over the past few months?*

As exciting as her job was, Paula felt herself getting tired of the daily charade. Just being herself seemed more and more tempting each day. *If I even remember who I am anymore.*

She shooed away the negative thoughts and focused on Tony and Alberto's conversation. Tony had taken Avery under his wing after their first encounter and treated her like his little sister. Alberto didn't go quite that far, but at least he tolerated her as if she were Tony's little project. "My little sister," he'd say.

Fine with me, so long as no one tries to get in my pants. Just want to do my job and forget the rest.

Little sister or not, Tony had long been very careful about where he took her or what conversations he let her overhear. She had perfected the brash emo-punk-rocker-teenager act and spread a convincing *I-don't-care-about-anything-maybe-I'll-die-today* mood, so Tony concluded Avery was harmless. In principle, she was. Almost. Except for her black belt in karate. And the knife in her boot. And Miss Marple.

Speaking of? Miss Marple always went along for the ride. "Rats are unsanitary and disgusting," Tony said, but Avery wasn't having it, so he had to accept they came as a package deal.

Avery patted her pocket, checking to see that the mouse was still in the house. She was. Her mind eased, and she took in the scenery of the large warehouse. *This is the first time he's taken me to a business meeting with his brother. Make sure you don't slip up.*

They made it to the office on the top floor of the large warehouse on the San Diego waterfront.

Avery would have loved to send Miss Marple on a tour of the long corridors with the wooden pallets but Tony had insisted she go with him to the office. "Make sure you don't leave my side," he said.

"Got it," she agreed. *Too bad. This would have been a once-in-a-lifetime opportunity to get some real evidence.*

"What time is the delivery going to be today?" Tony asked.

Alberto put up a hand. "Don't worry about it. The goods will be here."

"Just need to know a time so I can plan accordingly," Tony said.

"You have to be here at ten o'clock sharp. Five minutes later and they'll be gone again," Alberto said. "You think you can remember that?"

Poor Tony. Even in a gangster family, being the youngest wasn't easy. She didn't know if she was suffering from a weird version of Stockholm syndrome, but she actually felt some sympathy for him. She sighed. The world was rarely black or white, after all.

She popped her gum bubble. "Are we almost done here?" she asked in the same brash manner she'd perfected over the past few months.

"In a minute, honey. I still have work to do here." Tony shook his head.

Avery cringed at the mention of his nickname for her, even though it was just a crude way to express his affection for her. She had to live with it. Anything that might confirm her suspect's perception of her role, she had to let go. Well. Almost anything. At least he only seemed to have brotherly feelings for her, and nothing romantic.

"Can I at least walk around a little?" she tried her luck.

"No way," Alberto said before Tony registered the question.

She would have to keep an eye on Alberto. He was the more perceptive of the brothers. He was also the only one around whom she regularly had an uneasy feeling about. She'd catch him studying her as if he couldn't quite figure her out. Smart guy. Just inconvenient for her. She had no illusions—blood was definitely thicker than water in these circles. Especially if the water turned out to be a snitch.

She contorted her face, making a convincing pouting teenager, and sat on the floor. Out of sheer boredom, and to upset Alberto, she took Miss Marple out of her jacket and sat her on the floor. The rat sat on its hind legs and curiously sniffed the air. Miss Marple liked strange places and always blossomed when she got the opportunity to explore.

Alberto seemed annoyed when he saw Miss Marple and turned back to his brother. "Make sure you're on time," he urged.

When he turned away, Tony rolled his eyes and winked at her.

She bit her lips and had to stifle a laugh. Sometimes he could be quite charming.

"You receive the goods, check them, and have them supplied to the designated containers. You have five men available. And leave your appendage at home," Alberto instructed with a nod in her direction.

Avery took note and kept a straight face.

Miss Marple sat under Alberto's desk, cluing Avery that something was amiss there. Avery clicked the little tin frog, which she carried everywhere and disguised as something she used to channel nervous energy. Fortunately, none of the brothers knew what clicker training was. Otherwise, they may have figured out the ruse.

Once Miss Marple made it back to Avery, she picked up another sunflower seed as a reward. Avery wasn't surprised Miss Marple sensed something. She suspected Alberto had money or cocaine hidden inside the desk. The quantities would likely be too small to be of any use as evidence. Not much more than could be used for personal use. Such a little quantity would only get him a slap on the wrist, a fine, and maybe a few hours of community service. *Probably not even that, with the lawyers he could afford*, Avery knew.

She held out her jacket to Miss Marple and let the rat slip into her safe haven. *Hope they're done soon. If we have to be back by ten o'clock tonight, that doesn't give me much time to prepare.*

Cole checked his pistol. Safety on. The clip clicked in tight. Everything was in order and ready to go so he slid it back into his holster. He picked up a heavy

Kevlar vest and strapped it on. Next, the headphones and microphone. He was ready for action.

According to his supervisor, the FBI had received a tip that a major shipment was due to arrive later that night. A raid was planned on one of the warehouses near the docks. Info about the nature of the shipment had been vague; it could be anything from drugs to guns, to women and stolen art.

He didn't like assignments where he didn't know exactly where he stood. With such incomplete information, it was difficult to assess risks, like the possibility of violence.

His partner Ali, who everyone called Big A because of his size, slapped Cole on the shoulders as he passed. When Big A gave out such pats on the back, normal men went down on their knees, but Cole was nearly his size. "It'll be a piece of cake. You'll see. We'll be in and out in twenty minutes. And if we're lucky? We'll get a big haul."

"Right. Sure. As if it would ever be that easy," Cole said.

After several years of undercover assignments and a subsequent burnout, he'd switched to inside work as a computer specialist, commonly known as a hacker. That had been intellectually very exciting, but after a while, he'd missed the adrenaline rush of working in the field.

But by then his boss didn't trust his mental stability to return to field work. What had the FBI psychologist told him? Weren't the sessions supposed to be confidential, anyway? They complied with his request for field work only to the extent that he was allowed to sit in on team assignments. *Yay.* He would much rather work and solve real-life cases from start to finish, working with Ali as his partner. It didn't look like he would get the chance anytime soon.

The director of operations called them. Cole hurried inside and took his seat in the large, nondescript FBI van. He leaned his head against the headrest and shut his eyes, mentally going over the course of the raid one more time.

Half an hour later, the time for the raid came. Everyone stood at their assigned position. They coordinated prearranged steps using hand signals.

After a few minutes, the raid was over. Big A held the leader, Tony Monsanto, at bay. The culprit, who couldn't be much older than twenty-five, sweated profusely.

Cole had caught a suspected accomplice of Tony's hiding behind a container and pushed the person forward one-handed. The prisoner fought like a lion and let out a torrent of obscenities. "Well, at least your vocabulary's impressive," Cole said.

He waved a hand in the air toward Big A who was keeping Tony in line. "What about the folks other than these two?"

"The others are all employees of the freighter," Big A said. "We've sent them back to their ship until we can figure out what we're dealing with."

"It's all a big misunderstanding," Tony said.

"I'm sure it is. But we'll let the prosecutor decide that, okay?" said Big A kindly.

Cole pushed his prisoner into the light. Tony gasped.

"Time to take a closer look," Cole said. "Look familiar?"

"Let her go," Tony said. "She has nothing to do with the business side of our family."

"Come on." Cole turned his prisoner around, resulting in another barrage of curses. *Creative*, he admitted. He was about to comment when he saw the face and froze.

The night had become much more interesting when it dawned on him who he had in his hands. *What the heck is she doing here!? And dressed like this!?*

The woman in his hands wriggled. A warning flashed in her unmistakable eyes. Before he had time to interpret it, however, the expression disappeared and she spat in his face.

Stunned, he stared at her, silently wiping her spittle from his face.

"Maria, don't do that," Tony said.

Maria?

Tony continued, addressing Avery's alter-ego. "You'll only get yourself into trouble. Just talk to the policeman and you'll be back home in bed in no time, where you should have stayed from the start."

Avery was fighting for her survival in the Monsanto family. *Time to show some loyalty.* She kicked Cole in the shin with the toe of her heavy motorcycle boots. Not with all her might, but just enough to make him wince convincingly.

Cole yelped. "Hey! Don't do that!"

Across the room, Big A grinned seeing the prisoner—*a girl*—hurt Cole.

Avery, on the other hand, had reached the end of her rope. If she wanted to have the slightest chance of keeping her cover intact, Cole needed to act appropriately. Arrest her, preferably. Hell, as far as she knew, he'd been undercover himself for years. He should know how to play this game.

"Cuff me already," she hissed at him through clenched teeth.

"If you insist," Cole said, and roughly turned her around. He twisted both arms behind her back.

She hoped Miss Marple survived all the turbulence in her jacket, poor thing.

While Cole locked handcuffs around her wrists, he leaned over and murmured, "If you'd asked, I would have brought handcuffs last time."

He was referring to their last run-in in Independence when his sister had been kidnapped and she, as a profiler, and he, as a computer expert, helped to recover her. The great relief and, naturally, the undeniable, highly explosive attraction between them, had led to them ending up in bed together after a successful rescue. And not for the first time. Furious he'd brought up the subject at such an inopportune time, she stomped on his foot. "In your dreams," she said angrily, glaring at him over her shoulder.

She could tell Cole suppressed a yell as he pulled on the handcuffs. "Is that how it's going to be?"

Miss Marple picked that moment to get some fresh air and wriggled out from Avery's collar.

Startled, Cole jumped back. "What the heck is that?"

He was already about to reach for the rodent to hurl it into the nearest corner when Avery sobbed loudly. Miss Marple, sensing the impending danger, disappeared once again back into hiding.

Tony chimed in. "Hey, what are you doing with her? I'm reporting you for the disproportionate use of force. It's not necessary to scare my sister like that and treat her so rough."

Cole gritted his teeth, raised an eyebrow mockingly, and asked, "Your sister? Is that what they call it these days?"

Tony stared at him darkly.

"You can explain that to the judge. Let's go." Cole pushed Maria/Avery out of the warehouse and toward the squad car.

Avery felt overcome with relief once they were outside and wanted to sink into Cole's arms. *Come on. Use your last reserves of strength. Can't let any weakness show. Not a good idea in an environment dominated by testosterone. You learned that early on. Don't forget it now.*

"His sister? A handcuff fetish? Anything else you want to tell me?" Cole asked, amused.

"Do me a favor?" she asked.

"What's that?"

"Be quiet."

CHAPTER TWO

Avery leaned against the wall of the festively decorated barn. She recalled it'd been converted into an exercise room at one point, but was being used now as a reception hall.

Try not to look too bored. You haven't been back here in a while and this christening means a lot to Grandpa. Remember, you're not on assignment and this is supposed to be fun.

"It's Jaz and Jake's daughter," Grandpa had told her. "Camelia. Cammie for short. It'll be a great weekend, and I'd love to see you."

Her grandfather never asked anything of her, so she booked her ticket to Independence as soon as she'd put down the phone. *Not sure why he feels presence is necessary, though. He'll just be flirting equally with Miss Minnie and Miss Daisy and barely even paying attention to me. Those sisters don't seem to mind either, which is weird. What are they doing...?*

Avery spotted a pair of new teenage girls she hadn't met, so she tried to figure them out—a habit born from being a Federal agent. Always trying to profile people as fast as possible.

The older one was probably Leslie, Paula's adopted or foster daughter. Avery wasn't sure what part of the adoption process they'd reached. She deduced the girl near Paula had to be her friend Shauna, Nate's daughter.

The girls rushed around the room, filming and taking photos with their phones.

As they passed by her, she tapped one of their hoodies, which they had pulled over their clothes due to the crisp temperatures. "Hi. What are you two up to?"

Leslie gave Shauna a furtive, guilty look.

Shauna did not suffer the same bias. "We're kind of like the court photographers."

"Court photographers?" Avery cast a quick glance around. "Did I miss the arrival of the royal family or something?"

"She means that we have a job to take as many pictures as possible," Leslie said.

A plausible explanation. So, why was Leslie squirming? *Strange.* "Well then," Avery said. "I'll let you get on with it, then."

The girls shared a puzzled look. Avery could have sworn there was more to it but without evidence, there wasn't much to go on. She shrugged. It didn't matter. In twenty-four hours, she'd be out of the cold-ass Colorado mountains and back in California, soaking up the sun.

Although California might not have been the best idea; she didn't want to run into Tony.

With her left hand, she grabbed the chin-length bob she'd had cut after finishing the job. While she doubted Tony would recognize her as "Maria", his awkward teenage "sister" who was supposed to be in juvie, she didn't want to risk it. Florida was a better plan. She had enough vacation days accumulated to kick back and lay low for at least two weeks.

Avery shifted her weight from her left foot to her right. The dress and matching shoes she had chosen for the occasion made her look fabulously good, as she had to admit, but were anything but comfortable! The high-cut pencil skirt accentuated her slender waist, the blouse, and her petite and well-proportioned torso, and the shoes made her legs look twice as long.

Only it looked like her carefully planned efforts had been in vain. *He* wasn't here. *Cole.* Which she was also very relieved about, she reminded herself. *Right.* Which was why she was so calm and relaxed. *Sure. Yeah right.*

She had never been good at fooling herself. She sighed. That was probably the root of all her issues. If she saw something she liked, she saw no reason to deny herself such pleasure. Be it brownies or a man, but while she loved brownies in all their variations, when it came to men, she seemed to have settled on one man over the years. A man who, until now, hadn't felt the need to show up at his niece's christening. She snorted in a less-than-ladylike manner. *How typical of him?* She tried to be angry, but couldn't. They were just too much alike. Probably an important job had gotten in the way. The job came first. Period. That was just the way it was.

She was about to pull out Miss Marple, which she had smuggled in her roomy purse, so she could get some fresh air when Paula sauntered over with Cammie in her arms. Hastily, she tried to maneuver the rodent back into the depths of her bag. Most people didn't react very well to her little companion. As completely incomprehensible as it was to her, she learned to live with it.

Miss Marple, on the other hand, had not. She was understandably unhappy about being locked up again, having already spent the previous hour in hiding. It probably hadn't been one of her best ideas to bring Miss Marple to a christening.

Paula, who watched the whole show, raised an eyebrow in amusement. "You don't have to make Miss Marple disappear because of me. How about we go outside for a bit? You can let her run around a little without offending the sensibilities of our more delicate guests."

"Good idea," Avery said, laughing.

When they were outside, she asked, "Where are the dogs? They weren't invited to this? I miss them."

Paula grinned. "I'm sure you do but don't worry. Rambo is with Kat. He thinks he sees his friend Rocky too much, anyway. The dogs are safe at home. Nessie keeps them company."

"Who's Nessie?"

"Nessie is Nate's pubescent and very greedy Newfoundland. Trust me, you don't want him around with an open buffet. He can't help himself! The first thing he'll do is run full speed into it to make sure everything falls off. He'll help clean it up, though."

Avery laughed at the image, but couldn't help herself from profiling her friend. Quite uncharacteristically, Paula's voice had softened when she spoke about her boyfriend. Usually, she only spoke of men as vague subordinates, if at all. The Nate thing had to be serious.

Carefully, she set Miss Marple down on the grass. The rat sat and sniffed the air. She settled on a direction and scampered off.

"How do you find her?" Paula asked

"Miss Marple comes when I whistle," Avery said. "Nate, huh?"

"Yes. Nate and I," Paula said with a happy grin. "And Leslie and Shauna."

Avery pointed to the sleeping Cammie in Paula's arm. "I guess there'll be a third one soon, then?"

Paula shuddered. "Just don't. I like to leave the incubation and the first rearing phase to other people. I prefer to take them on after they've been housebroken and can talk. I think Cammie is adorable and I like to take care of her, of course, especially knowing I can give her back in the evening."

"Does Nate see it that way?"

"Fortunately, yes. We both feel that, with the girls, we have two wonderful children who keep us busy enough." She turned. "I don't know how much you know about Leslie's history. She's been through quite a bit. One foster home after another until, by some lucky chance, she ended up with me. And Shauna hasn't had it any easier with a mother who suffers from a borderline personality disorder."

"Oh. I didn't know that," Avery said, concerned. "I can understand why it's more important for you to take special care of those two rather than bring another Carter into the world."

"How would you know? You're always on the road saving the world."

Avery squirmed in embarrassment. "It's not like your brother isn't doing the same thing as me," she said before she could stop herself. Great. She'd fallen into the trap nicely. Where was the nearest wall to bang her head against?

"Ah yes, my lovely brother. Speak of the devil…"

Avery recalled her training and forced herself not to blush or show any reaction when she turned around.

With big, lithe strides, Cole sauntered toward her. *Like a panther, deadly and beautiful,* Avery thought. She preemptively bit her tongue so as not to blurt it out. His confidence really was plentiful without her help. She stared as he approached. There was no way she couldn't.

Cole was glad to finally be in Independence. Halfway from the airport, he had a flat tire and had to call a towing service because there'd not been a spare in his rental car. What should have been a matter of fifteen minutes had taken over two hours. He was tired, hungry, and his mood was in the basement. Until he saw who stood in front of the barn.

His sister Paula stood with the guest of honor, Cammie, on her arm. At least he hoped it was Cammie. If he missed Paula's pregnancy and baby, all insanity would break loose. His mother wouldn't talk to him for another twenty years.

He recognized the woman next to Paula. Was it really Avery? If so, her wardrobe choices had improved one hundred and fifty percent since they last met.

Cole's mouth went dry, his pulse quickened, and he felt his lust stirring inside him, as it did every time he ran into her. *Too bad we never manage to be in the same place for more than forty-eight hours. Maybe we're both simply migratory birds. Or maybe there's a deeper reason for this?*

Her gaze captivated him and he decided to postpone his philosophical questions for another time. Without realizing it, he strutted over to her; it was like his body was on automatic.

Cole was sure she couldn't take her eyes off him, either. *She recognizes me, all right.* Ha. He hadn't expected to see her there, that was for sure. *Wow. She's looking good. Real good.*

Glad I wore this outfit. Avery knew it caught Cole's attention; she felt a serious pang of satisfaction. *Gotcha!* She'd never seen his eyes wider or his body look tenser. All her work paid off.

Paula looked back and forth between the two. She knew they were once an item, for sure, but she seemed a little surprised. "I'd better get home soon," she said as she tried to stifle a laugh. Avery paid no further attention to her because Miss Marple clambered up her leg, obviously having had enough of her exploring. Quickly, Avery bent down, picked up the rat with a gentle grip and placed it in her pocket. Miss Marple poked her head out and looked at Avery in wonder, twitched her whiskers indecisively, and then disappeared inside the bag.

Paula shrugged. "Nice seeing you again, my wonderful brother Cole. Maybe call me when all your blood returns to your brain."

Avery cringed at Paula's teasing.

Cole just replied to her with a grunt.

"Okay, then," Paula said and hurried away. "Sheesh. Get a room, you two."

"Wilkinson," Cole said. "What a nice surprise. I didn't know you'd be here." He usually teased her whenever he had the chance. This wasn't one of those times, he believed.

Avery had no such qualms. Still, she refrained from her usual sassy self. *Damn socialization,* she thought, annoyed. It was the first time they'd crossed paths at an official event. Usually, their paths only crossed after a job where it was easy to chalk up the mutual attraction and its consequences as just blowing off some steam. She tried to be polite. "I thought you were stuck on an assignment."

He shook his head. "For once, no. My mother would tear my head off if I missed the christening of her first grandchild."

"Cammie really is an adorable kid," Avery said. She wished they were somewhere else, ripping off their clothes like usual. The small talk felt weird. They'd never needed to resort to it before.

Avery noticed him stepping from one leg to the other. Was he nervous, too? She had not considered such a possibility. She watched him carefully as he ran his hand through his short hair and averted his eyes. *Yes. He is nervous. Point for me. Now just keep it together and don't think you've won before you cross the finish line. Remember, this was supposed to be a vacation and now work.*

"Cammie, you say? Whew, I'm glad. I was afraid Paula had done the same to Jaz and produced a baby, too, without me noticing." He looked relieved.

Avery laughed.

The corners of Cole's mouth twitched. He gave in and joined in her deep rolling laughter. *He always did say my laughter was irresistible, didn't he?* A picture of them curled up on a couch after one of their hookups crossed her mind.

The laughing broke the odd mood, it seemed. "Good to see you," he said, his laughs settling down.

Avery nodded and wrapped her arms around his waist in a deep embrace. *Happy to see him without arguing or getting naked within the next two minutes.*

Miss Marple, on the other hand, was less than impressed with their courtship. She nimbly climbed up Avery's blouse, onto her shoulder where Cole's head was, and bit him on the earlobe.

"Ouch!" he cried, tearing himself away and jumping back a step.

Miss Marple was at least as frightened and scurried back inside the safety of the bag.

Avery, on the other hand, held her stomach from laughing and couldn't stop.

Cole's face turned beet red. "I don't know what's so funny about that. And anyway, who takes a rat to a christening?"

"Now don't be like that. Paula was chill about it. You're not going to believe the old horror stories about rats eating little kids, are you?"

"Well, she did just try to eat me," he said.

"Yes, because you invaded her comfort zone. She doesn't know you, after all."

"Of course we know each other. I still have the scars from the last time we met."

Avery rolled her eyes. "You never took the time to befriend her back then, either."

His lips twisted into a lazy smile. "I was too busy getting to know her owner better at the time."

She waved him off, the flirt. "I know. I was there but Miss Marple doesn't care about that, though. Come on, let's go inside. The ceremony is about to begin."

"Fine," he said and followed Avery.

As they passed a mirror she caught him trying not to stare too conspicuously at her rear end. Caught, he averted his gaze at the several flower arrangements placed on the reception table. "Sheesh. Did my brother rob a flower store?"

"These are all Camellia's that Lily rounded up. A gift from the residents of Independence. The Diner Sisters have once again emptied their betting pool and decided to use some of the proceeds to give little Camelia a worthy welcome."

"How did they even come up with that name?" he asked.

"I imagine they wanted to carry on the tradition of naming children after flowers. Rose, Jasmine...and now Camellia. Would be interesting to know what Jaz's mother's name is."

He shrugged. "It would because I have no idea."

"Are they actually married?" she whispered. "Do you know?"

"Yes. Just before she gave birth, I think Jake was finally able to convince Jaz. At least that's the story. I wasn't there when it went down, though."

"Oh, yeah. The work always takes priority."

"Exactly. You know the deal."

They hushed as the background music began. Jaz saw them and waved them over where they stood in a circle around Jaz and Jake, who held Cammie in their arms.

Avery gleaned from their invitation that neither belonged to a church, and they'd opted for an non-denominational baptism that included elements of other traditions.

Surprised, she watched someone light a charcoal brazier. Others hurried over and put their hands over the small grill-like object to warm their hands. *What is this going to be?* Her mother had been a Lakota but she was very skeptical of all the hocus-pocus, as she secretly thought of the rituals. Avery suspected it had more to do with the strained relationship she had with her mother than with displaying Native American culture.

Cole took her hand and gave it a quick squeeze. Immediately, her tension melted away.

She needn't have worried. The ceremony was short and very loving. Jaz and Jake welcomed their daughter into their life with few heartfelt words.

At the conclusion, the minister, an amazingly patient-looking woman, lit a large pine branch and circled the little family three times.

Avery wasn't sure of the ceremony's meaning and thought she'd ask Jaz later. She was strangely touched. The smoke from the burning pine needles gave off a pleasant aroma. For her, the smell of pine was associated with the region. Since most of the houses in the area were built of the same pine, the resin's scent, which liquefied in the summer months, could be smelled everywhere. She sighed deep.

Miss Marple seemingly sensed the relaxed and happy mood in the room and poked her head out with curiosity. Avery ran her hand over the silky fur.

"Come on," Cole said. "Let's go congratulate the happy parents."

Embarrassed that she was still holding his hand—*what am I, a little girl?*—Avery let go and took Miss Marple out of her pocket. "You go ahead. I have to feed Miss Marple before she gets ornery."

He shot her an incredulous look, so she gave him a shove toward Jake. "What are you waiting for? It's your family, after all, not mine. I'm just an acquaintance."

"Fine," he said and hurried away.

When he was out of earshot, she breathed a sigh of relief. The night had almost become a bit too cozy. She'd likely see him later that evening at Rocky Mountain Diner, the only place where there was something to drink, good music, billiards, and darts. Once there, it'd be easy to put their strange relationship, or whatever you wanted to call it, in place.

The night shook her. All the unfamiliar hand-holding and empathetic looks led to things she couldn't deal with. Especially with him. Soon, she'd have to go back to San Diego and to work. She couldn't be burdened with missing anyone while on an assignment.

Forget all this romance stuff. She tugged her jacket, signaling Miss Marple. "How does some oatmeal sound? You can do my comfort eating for me!"

Miss Marple, for her part, was more than happy to oblige.

"Are you going away again so soon?" asked Avery's grandfather, George Wilkinson, sitting in the living room next to the fireplace. "You just got here."

"Yeah," Avery said. "I'm meeting Tyler and the others. Will you watch my little one until then? Food's on the table."

She slipped on her leather jacket, tied a turquoise scarf of thick wool around herself, and fished Miss Marple off the kitchen counter. With the rat in her hand, Avery walked over and placed her in her grandfather's lap. He grinned from ear to ear. With an affirmative nod, he picked up the rodent and laughed softly. "Of course. You're seeing Tyler and the others. Would the others include her brother, by chance?"

Mischievously, she smiled. "Jake? I don't think so. If he's not on duty, he's probably home with his wife and kid. Or were you talking about Sam?"

"Your avoidance tactics are pretty obvious," he teased.

"I've never been able to fool you." Amused, she shook her head. "I don't know what Cole's plans are. We haven't coordinated but, yeah, I hope he'll be there."

"Just don't be disappointed if, contrary to expectations, he's not."

Surprised, she lifted her gaze from the boots she had just slipped into and looked up. "Where did you get that idea?"

"Oh, I don't know. I'm probably just imagining things," he said, still petting a very appreciative Miss Marple.

Avery knew all too well how accurate his powers of observation were. "You have to tell me what you were imagining, then. Only fair."

He nodded. "Fine. I saw him trying not to look at you when you left the reception in such a hurry."

"Meaning?"

Her grandfather said, "He looked like someone looking for a change. I don't think he's very happy with his current situation. Grass is always greener and all."

Avery felt her face flush with anger. "A change?" she said. "In what way?"

Her grandfather snorted. "Am I a psychic? You'll have to ask him yourself."

She walked to the door and rolled her eyes. "Fine." She'd have to meet him first. She just hoped her grandfather was wrong.

CHAPTER THREE

Sᴡᴇᴀᴛʏ ᴀɴᴅ ᴛɪʀᴇᴅ, Avery landed at the San Diego airport. The restorative effect of her vacation had already disappeared after the long, tedious flight in economy class. The seat felt like she was sitting on a wooden board.

While waiting for her luggage, she remembered the last time she was at the airport, waiting for her flight to Denver, and then to encounter Cole and what happened between them during the baptism in Independence.

For the first time in ten years, they hadn't ended up in bed together. She couldn't explain how or why. Despite her grandfather's teasing, she'd expected to meet Cole in the evening at the diner and then go home with him. *Or he could have come home with me. I just love waiting past midnight for someone to not show up. Sure could have used the company. Would have hit just the right spot after everything. Guess he wasn't interested.*

Avery watched the baggage carousel make what felt like the hundredth round with no sign of her suitcase. *Hopefully the travel gods haven't banned my suitcase to Alaska.*

She didn't know why her boss had insisted on ordering her back to San Diego after only two weeks. *I'd understand if he told me my cover was blown, but everything'd gone to plan, as far as I know, and they're thinking I'm still serving time in juvenile hall somewhere. Hopefully for a long time.*

Avery didn't want to miss Tyler and Pat's visit to California. Pat had an interesting construction project in

Carlsbad. The coastal town was about forty miles north of San Diego. Close enough that Avery could hopefully visit frequently. Since she moved from place to place a lot in her job, she didn't have many opportunities to make friends. Especially not when undercover. She looked forward to hearing what Tyler was dreaming about. The last time they spoke, she mentioned starting a dance theater for children and teens. Avery hoped her friend would succeed. Anything keeping young people from ending up on the streets or getting into alcohol and drugs was a good idea. Of course, she'd offer her support again. It was always surprising how cooperative unwilling communities or schools suddenly became when a Federal agency got involved. Even if unofficially.

Finally, she caught sight of her suitcase. She hoisted it from the baggage carousel onto the trolley and pushed it with long strides to the terminal where she could pick up animals.

Once there, Avery was met by a sleepy Miss Marple.

Half an hour later, she arrived at her rental car. She stowed her luggage and Miss Marple in her transport box in the back seat before plopping down in the driver's seat, relieved.

She glanced at her cell phone and confirmed she had forty-five minutes left to reach the DEA office downtown. She groaned. No time to check into the hotel and freshen up. She needed to put on something other than a tee-shirt. Shorts and spaghetti straps were not dress code. *I miss being goth girl Maria. Her outfits would have totally freaked out my boss.* Laughing at the idea, she backed out of the parking space and headed for the freeway.

After a two-week vacation spent fishing and whitewater canoeing, Cole arrived at the office. He felt refreshed and rested but he was glad to be back with his colleagues. A little distraction would do him good. The past two weeks allowed too much time to think about why he hadn't taken the chance to spend a few hours with Avery. He wasn't sure, but for some reason, he hadn't felt right that night. *Because you're a blooming idiot*, his libido said. "Quite possibly," he said. "Quite possibly."

There were good signs, though. He'd been informed after the last raid that he would once more be cleared to work on his own cases with his favorite partner. His mood lifted thinking about it. Maybe he could talk Big A into going to the shooting range with him after work, too. A little competition among friends would help take his mind off things.

Big A approached him with a big grin. "There's our renegade."

"Renegade?" asked Cole as they hugged and patted each other on the back. "I was just gone on vacation for two weeks. Might do you some good, too, partner."

"You can save the 'partner' thing for the next few weeks," Big A said.

"Save? For what? Don't tell me Jerry has insisted on another idiotic team-building exercise."

The last time their boss Jerry had such an idea, Cole had been assigned a complete rookie named Aloisious. It was still a mystery to Cole what he was doing on active duty. The guy couldn't take two steps without tripping over his own feet. Granted, he was a genius at computers. Cole could learn a trick or two from him, and that was saying something, but why anyone would have thought it worth entrusting a weapon to this guy, he couldn't understand. Since Al, as they nick-named him, almost shot his toes off during their first mission because he forgot to put the safety on, Cole unceremoniously took away his ammunition. Al was quite happy about that.

Thank God he had an experienced partner in Big A.

"Now let's get serious. What's going on?" Cole asked.

Big A ducked his head so that it almost disappeared between his massive shoulders. "*UH-UH*. If you don't know yet, let Jerry explain it to you."

Cole gave up. When Big A had one of his moods, there was nothing you could do.

"Then I guess I'd better get back to Jerry and find out what's going on because you're not telling. Save a donut for me, okay?"

Big A grunted in agreement.

Shaking his head, Cole stowed his things in his locker. *You were gone for two weeks and everyone went crazy.*

Ten minutes later, he stood outside Jerry's office. He knocked and entered. The first thing that caught his eye was a woman standing by the window. Dark pants, light polo shirt, chin-length bob. Avery? What was she doing here?

Convinced his vivid imagination was playing tricks on him, he stepped back to check the nameplate next to the door. *Jerry Smith. Special Agent in Charge, FBI.* He blinked and continued his way into the room.

Avery watched him silently from across the room. He recognized the telltale twitch at the left corner of her mouth. *She's silently laughing at me.* Even though it annoyed him a little, he got it. If the roles were reversed, he wouldn't have felt different.

Jerry cleared his throat. "Special Agent Carter, may I introduce Special Agent Avery Wilkinson of the DEA. I understand you already know each other."

Cole nodded and shook her hand. "Wilkinson."

"Carter."

After the formal greeting, he had to stifle a laugh. He had no idea what she was doing there, but maybe there was an opportunity to make up for what he'd missed at their last encounter. Or so he wished, until he saw her expression. Mild amusement, but with a certain wariness and reserve she'd never shown toward him in the past. *Great. I did a great job of that, didn't I?*

He nodded toward Jerry, "Yes, we've met. It's a small world." He cast a questioning glance. "I don't mean to be rude, but what is she doing here? I didn't know there were plans to work with the DEA."

"I'm assigning you a new case. Special Agent Wilkinson will be your new partner. Big A and Special Agent Garcia will be at your disposal should you need additional assistance." Jerry handed Cole a file.

Speechless, Cole accepted the file. *New case?* Did anything Jerry said explain Avery's presence?

"If I may, I'd like to give Special Agent Carter a brief overview of the case and my cooperation," Avery addressed Jerry professionally.

Jerry nodded and shooed her out of his office. "Of course, of course. The main goal is solving the case quickly. Now get lost. I still have work to do."

Once they were outside, Cole fixed her with a look. "Will you please tell me what this is all about?"

"Oh my goodness. So much excitement over my presence. You're acting like I've been itching to get involved in this case," Avery said. "Just so you know, I would have loved to have done without it. I was hoping to be transferred somewhere else."

Avery reached into her bag, which she casually carried over her shoulder, and unearthed Miss Marple. The rat looked around curiously before quickly climbing over her tee-shirt and onto her shoulder.

Cole ignored the rodent. After all, she'd had the good sense not to introduce Jerry to the newest team member. "Where did you want to be transferred to?" he asked. *Does she want to get away from me that much?*

"To Boston. Or anywhere else on the East Coast. The farther from California, the better."

He looked down at his shoes, surprised at the news.

"Don't worry. This has nothing to do with you, so you can stop looking like I just kicked your imaginary puppy."

Usually very taken with her dry humor, he couldn't smile. "Then why?"

"You don't give up so easily, do you? Actually, I figured you'd be the one person on this planet who understands my situation best."

Surprised, he looked her in the eye. "Situation?"

"My God, you're really on a roll today, aren't you? The raid four weeks ago? At the warehouse in the Port of San Diego? I was there undercover, you must have realized that much."

Cole scratched the back of his head. "Oh yeah. That's right. I forgot all about that."

"Sure. I understand. For you, it was just a normal raid. Everyday life. But for me? Three months of undercover work went down the drain. If the Monsanto family found out I was a snitch, I'd like to be far, far away. Especially not living inside their territory."

"Oh."

"Yeah. 'Oh.' So, if you're planning on giving me a hard time for supposedly intruding on your sacred investigation, think again."

He raised his hands. "It's all right. I get it. Didn't mean it that way. Can we start over?"

She gave him a deliberate look and smiled reservedly. "Fine by me. After all, we have a case to solve."

Relieved, he returned the smile. "Well then, let's get going. I'll call the other two. The conference room is just up ahead, third door on the left."

"Here," Cole said. "I brought you a coffee. Black with two sugars."

Surprised, Avery looked up and accepted the coffee Cole held out to her. At the same time, she noticed a tall man raising his eyebrows speculatively and letting his gaze wander back and forth between her and Cole. She assumed the tall man was Big A. *Oh great. The rumor mill has already started.*

"You'll have to tell me that trick. What did you use to blackmail him into bringing you coffee?" Big A winked.

Before she could say anything, a tall, slender woman hurried into the room. Her long, copper-colored hair was braided into a tight braid. Her gold-colored eyes flashed. "I'm sure she didn't have to look too far for that. After all, our new boss's record of sins here is long."

Avery looked up and grinned. "I can see you and I really need to go out for a drink together. We'll have lots to talk about." She held out her hand. "I'm Avery."

"Valentina. Is that a rat?"

"Yes." That was probably it for the friendship. Too bad. She eyed the other woman as she waited for the inevitable reaction but the agent stunned her.

"Cool. Is she trained as a drug-sniffing rat?"

Surprised by Valentina's reaction and knowledge of the use of rats in police work, Avery nodded in delight. "Yup."

"Then, if you're through with the coffeehouse chat and the blood sisterhood, maybe we could focus on the case?" Cole asked.

"Ouch," Big A said.

The two women stared at him; Valentina raised an eyebrow in disbelief.

Big A closed his eyes and rubbed the root of his nose.

"That was a little harsh. I'm sorry," Cole said.

"You put your foot in your mouth again?" said Valentina, who seemingly had no inhibitions about confronting him. *Very sympathetic*, Avery thought.

"I'm sorry. My comment was inappropriate and out of line."

With a majestic nod, she accepted the apology. Big A looked at her.

So that's how it is, Avery thought, tucking this info into the recesses of her brain for later use.

After the room fell silent, she used the moment to bring the conversation back up to a professional level. Avery grabbed the meager documents she'd received from her supervisor and cleared her throat. "The FBI has been assigned a case by local authorities. Namely, that of a possible serial killer. All the victims are male, of different origins, and have turned up in a variety of places. Stabbed over twenty times, at least. In total, there are already five dead. That is, five that we know and assume are related. Because the incidents happened in different counties, it took a while to make a connection."

"Now it also makes sense that the FBI got involved but the question still remains, what are you doing here?" Cole asked.

"Are there parallels between the dead?" Valentina asked.

"All the bodies have one thing in common: the coroner's office found a large amount of drugs in their blood. Monsanto drugs. Or at least drugs that the DEA suspects came from Monsanto's kitchen," she said.

Cole slumped back in his chair. "Shit. No wonder you'd like to be on the East Coast."

Big A shook his head anxiously and whistled softly through his teeth.

Valentina looked from one to the other. "Did I miss something?"

"I'm lost, too," Big A grumbled.

"I was working undercover and had successfully infiltrated the Monsanto family when a couple of overzealous FBI investigators thought a raid was in order," Avery said.

"Overzealous is a strong word," Cole objected.

Avery turned to him, eyes flashing angrily. "The raid was premature. The evidence was completely insufficient. You know that very well. Otherwise the entire Monsanto clan wouldn't still be at large. The only one who has permanently disappeared behind bars is Maria."

"Be happy." Big A nodded toward her.

She nodded back in Big A's direction. "Of course I'm glad. I hope she stays there for a while, too."

"I assume Maria was your alias?" Valentina concluded. "You had to give up your position within the family and now you've been entrusted with a case that brings you close to these people again." She looked at the others in wonder. "I didn't know we supported kamikaze police work? I mean, even if she stays in the background, the chances of someone recognizing her are still very high."

"*She's* sitting right here. You're welcome to discuss your concerns with me directly." While Avery was reluctant to put the other agent, who was basically very sympathetic to her, in her place, she'd been around long enough to know how the system worked. Either she proved that her voice carried weight and she was a serious addition to the team, or she was doomed. Normally she had that problem with men, but Big A had been surprisingly affable.

Cole, on the other hand, was a different story but they would sort that out later. After duty.

"*OOPS.* Sorry," Valentina said. "Force of habit. Didn't mean anything by it. Don't worry, I'll get used to your presence in a minute."

Avery nodded and accepted the apology. She hadn't taken it personally. She had stopped doing that a long time ago. As she stroked a hand over a snoozing Miss Marple on her shoulder, she addressed Valentina. "My instructions are clear. I am to remain more or less invisible. The legwork will fall on you. I work from the background and provide you with the necessary information on the lives of Monsanto family members. In addition, I've been entrusted with the task of using my qualifications as a profiler to paint as accurate a picture of the killer as possible."

"Sure. Monsanto drugs don't prove that one of the family members is going Jack-the-Ripper."

Big A whistled through his teeth. "Put it that way, I'm not even sure what good it does for us to know where the drugs are coming from. It's not like they only have two customers."

Avery grimaced. "That's the way it is, unfortunately. Still, it's the only concrete lead we have at the moment."

"Is it the only link between the victims?" asked Cole.

"Thankfully, no," Avery said. She lowered her hand, which had still been petting the rat, and reached for the crime scene photos in her folder. With a fluid flick of her wrist, she dropped them side by side on the large conference table. "I would prefer if you say out loud everything you notice about the pictures, no matter how trivial it may seem, so that I can record it here on the flip chart. Your view is fresh and unbiased and will help me see things I may not have noticed."

Cole watched her. The mix of elegance, arrogance, and professionalism were very attractive. He'd only seen her at work once, back when his sister Tyler had been threatened and kidnapped by a stalker. The profile she'd created had been frighteningly accurate. She gave him a scrutinizing look and he hurried to put on his best poker face. After all, there was no way she was going to catch him studying her rear end while she worked.

Avery felt a prickle on the back of her neck as she leaned forward to study a detail in the photo Valentina picked. *Is Cole looking at my butt? Now?* She peered over at him and found her suspicions confirmed. She suppressed her grin. *At least I have the answer to whether or not he still finds me attractive.* That didn't seem to have been his problem but what was? *Don't think about that now. It can wait until after my shift ends. We have a case to solve here.*

CHAPTER FOUR

"Of all the people on this planet, you're stuck working with Cole?" Tyler chuckled on the other end of the line.

"He's one lucky guy, isn't he?" Avery asked, the sarcasm unmistakable.

"Well, I don't know," Taylor said. "Looking at the intimate embrace in the photo, it could be quite a...hot time in California. Thank God Pat's coming with us, or I wouldn't be able to stand next to you two."

"Forget it. He stood me up that night, remember?" She asked. "And what photo?"

"Well, the one on the Facebook page," Tyler said.

"Whose Facebook page? Cole's?"

"No. Of course not Cole's! The Diner Sisters' page," Tyler said as if it were the most natural thing in the world.

"Again, slow down so I can take notes," Avery said. "The Diner Sisters have a Facebook page? That's horrible."

Tyler laughed. "We all agree with you about that but everyone still checks in daily to see what the news is."

"It's like an accident," Avery said. "Everyone stops and stares. I have to admit, I wouldn't have thought they had that much computer knowledge."

"Aileen, the pair's niece, who's been living with them for a few months and helps them out in the kitchen, apparently gave them an introductory course to the world of the Internet with the best of intentions. The two were immediately in their element as they realized the potential of social media."

"Lordy!" Avery shook her head.

"You can say that again. After all, the betting pool is thriving like never before. Your name is on the list, by the way."

"You don't say." She didn't dare ask in what context.

As they continued to talk, Avery searched for the Facebook page on her tablet. Sure enough, posts about everyday life in Independence and gossip about its residents filled the pages.

"Did you know the Diner Sisters are fascinated with our firefighters?" she asked.

"I know! They've also shown up at Pat's studio during workouts and tried to take pictures," she laughed. "Under the guise of going to yoga class, of course."

"Did Pat kick her out?"

"That was me."

"Respect. Can't have been easy."

Tyler snorted. "You can say that again."

"What did you blackmail them with?"

"Oh, it may be that I threatened to commission Paige to write an ambiguous article about the interesting ménage-à-trois between them and your grandfather."

"You can't be serious!" Avery was shocked.

"Yeah, what was I supposed to do?" Tyler asked. "Let them photograph my husband in nothing but his track pants?"

"Uh, yeah, if you ask me that way." She was indeed of such an opinion and knew her grandfather flirted with the Diner Sisters unabashedly. That was just the way he was but to drag his name through the mud because of that...

"Calm down. They didn't want that, after all. I had expected as much. Of course, I wouldn't have carried out my threat. Paige wouldn't do that at all. She still lives here. While we're gone, she'll be living in my old apartment above the police station. Professionally, she's mostly doing marketing for Kat's *Safe Haven* Animal Shelter these days."

"Oh. *PHEW*. I'm so glad," Tyler said. "I would have been sorry to have to terminate our friendship. Tell me, where's the picture of me and Cole? I can't find it with all the sexy firefighters and stories about the latest developments."

"Keep scrolling down. It's been two weeks already."

"That's right. Now I remember who took the photos."

"Who? Because I would be interested in that, too. I already suspected they had their sources. Just photos from the diner don't give much away, after all."

"The two girls. Leslie and Shauna. That's her name, right, Shauna? Nate's little girl?"

"Yes, that's Shauna. I thought they took pictures at the christening on behalf of Jaz?"

"That's what they told me, too. I suspect that part of the story is true, too. It's just that they were also on the road for the Diner Sisters."

"That's pretty mean, sending innocent kids out. You can't say no to them."

Finally, she found the picture. Speechless, she stared at it. She and Cole really made an intimate picture. With the barn decorated with flowers in the background, they almost looked like a bride and groom. A somewhat unconventionally dressed one, perhaps, but the chemistry between them was so clear it made up for the lack of wedding attire.

"Did you find it?"

Avery suddenly had a lump in her throat. She cleared her throat. "Yes. Let me guess. The bet on me and Cole's about our wedding date?"

"Right. Why do you think that?" Tyler asked.

"Look at the picture again." Avery swallowed. *I wonder if Cole has seen this. Probably not. If he did, he'd have run screaming to Alaska by now.* Strangely, she didn't feel her usual familiar flight reflex. The photo touched a place inside her she hadn't known existed.

"You're right. Now that you mention it? It might be a picture from a wedding. Just before leaving for the honeymoon or something." Tyler chuckled.

"Well, I hope I choose something more comfortable for my honeymoon. Flip-flops or something," Avery lightened the mood a bit. "After all, thanks to Facebook, I can keep up with what's going on with you guys when I'm away."

"True. It's quite good for that," she said. "It doesn't bother me much, to be honest."

"Of course it doesn't. After all, you're taking off to California in a few days. Then they can't write about you," she teased her friend.

"Well, I don't know about that. You're in California, too, and they still managed to write about you. Check out the status update."

Avery scrolled up and stared in bewilderment at the latest news story. Under another picture of her and Cole standing side by side inside the barn, holding hands, it read, "Is our star investigative team finally coming together for good? Confidential sources have told us the two agents have been working together on a case in sunny California as of late. We're keeping our fingers crossed for them on their latest case. Bets regarding the case are now being taken."

"It's kind of creepy." Avery sighed.

"Very much so. However, the explanation of how they know so much is simple. I'll bet Cole was on the phone with Sam or Jake while they were in the diner."

"Then it's probably Sam. Jake's not doing much right now other than working or spending time with his family."

"I would, too, if I were him," she said, "and with two such great women waiting for me."

"That's right. I'm really not a fan of babies. Never have been but I have to admit Cammie is adorable." Avery sat up straight and spotted Miss Marple on the kitchen counter. The rat was just trying to get her supper, as her owner was apparently too busy to concentrate on her urgent needs. "I have to feed Miss Marple. Why don't you call me when you leave Independence? Then I'll know when to expect you."

"Can do but I'd better keep you posted daily. Pat doesn't have to start work for another whole week. We plan on taking our time getting out there. We'll definitely stop at a national park or two."

"Good to know. Have fun then!"

"We certainly will. And…"
"Yeah, what?"
"You have fun with Cole, too."
"Oh, you!"

After Avery hung up, she sat for a long time staring at the photo. Cole and her. Thoughts swirled as she recounted encounters she thought long forgotten. She loved how they both saw life as a challenge. She remembered the races through the woods together. How much fun was that? And how unexpectedly it hit her when she fell suddenly in love with him during that last summer together. For a short while, everything was perfect. She sighed wistfully as she relived that time. They had been so close. And, unfortunately, so similar. Too similar, in the end, most likely.

When the question of what their future together might look like came up, it became clear they were both too stubborn to deviate even a millimeter from their lives. After two days of heated arguments, she called him and asked to meet.

Cole had arrived at Avery's favorite place, a rock far up in the mountains, from where one could see the whole plateau.

She explained to him why they could no longer be together. The talk was the most difficult thing she'd ever done in her life.

Fortunately, he understood the necessity. He didn't want to lose her friendship any more than she had wanted to lose his. He surprised her then: after they had formally shaken hands and sworn eternal friendship, he took her in his arms and made her an irresistible offer. To make love once more. To seal their friendship. She knew all her friends would have found that impossible but since the decision to break up with him had been a purely rational one and had had absolutely nothing to do with the very strong attraction that existed between them, she was on fire for his proposal. In the truest sense of the word. The fact that they had not caused a forest fire that afternoon still amazed her.

That was the beginning of their being "friends with benefits." An ideal solution for both, it seemed, even though she wasn't so sure how healthy it was in the long run. If she was honest, the chance of getting over him and maybe meeting someone new amounted to less than nothing.

A clang jolted her out of her daydream. Miss Marple had managed to knock the can of special rat food off the counter. In the process, the lid had come off. She sat on the floor amid the various grains, grinning cheekily while munching her food.

Amused at her inventive companion, Avery shook her head and went to the closet to get a shovel and broom. She might as well let Miss Marple eat for another five minutes before she cleaned up the mess. At least the question of dinner, as far as Miss Marple was concerned, was settled.

Noticing her own growling stomach, she opened the refrigerator door. Half a jar of pickles, a couple of eggs, and a six-pack of beer. Not exactly enticing.

She closed the door and went to the window to let in some fresh air. The memory of old times with Cole had made her restless.

She missed her childhood home's clear air, imposing mountain tops, trees...

Avery inhaled the salty breeze that blew from the Pacific—very different from the mountains and endless trees of Colorado. *I might as well take advantage of what's here.* A walk along the harbor would do her good. She could buy something to eat, too.

I might as well tell the Monsanto family in person that I'm here too, if I'm stupid enough to stroll right through their territory. Resolutely, she banished the fear. She would not let them dictate where she could and could not stay.

After Miss Marple finished eating and she maneuvered most of the scattered food back into the storage can, Avery slipped on her biker boots. Unlike the Rockies, California was pleasantly warm, even in November.

The wind by the ocean could become quite drafty at times, so she put on her windproof vest, which also made it easier for her to take Miss Marple along. The little one definitely had to stay out of sight at the harbor. The rat was the most precarious part of her former cover; Miss Marple would be an easy giveaway.

Miss Marple safely tucked into her jacket, she sheathed the knife inside her boot. No need to get careless. One last time, she went through her belongings. Miss Marple was there. Money, sunglasses, keys, knife, and lip balm. *Everything a woman needs to go out for the evening.* She opened the door briskly and raised both eyebrows in surprise.

"You!" It came out sounding more like an accusation than a question.

Judging from Cole's irritated expression, he'd perceived it that way. "Yeah. Last time I checked, it was still me. Mind if I come in?"

"Uh, if you want to be clear, yes, I do mind. As you can see, I was just about to leave."

"Where to?"

"Not that it's any of your business, but I was on my way to the port." She inched her way toward the front door.

"To the port? Do you have any suicidal tendencies I don't know about?" He gave her his half-cocked grin.

"Still so dramatic, *TSK, TSK*. You should try yoga sometime. Center yourself. Ask Jaz for a free intro lesson." She activated the alarm and closed the door behind her.

"You already know that sometimes you get on my last nerve."

She snorted. "That's easy for you to say. What do you call what you're doing? Standing outside my door uninvited and trying to tell me where I can and can't go? Not exactly in the most appropriate behavior. Next time? Try to be a little more diplomatic."

Avery gritted her teeth to break the stream of biting words trying to escape. With memories so raw, it was difficult. Apparently, nothing had changed. After ten successful years with the DEA, he still felt he had to protect her. What did he think? She wasn't strong enough? Not smart enough? Just a pretty face? Avery felt like punching him in the nose so he could feel firsthand how well she knew how to fight, but she stared over his shoulder at a point on the horizon to distract herself.

Cole ran a hand over his face and looked contrite. After a deep breath, he said, "I'm sorry. I was surprised by your answer. Don't you think the risk of being recognized is extraordinarily high at the port? And before you rip my head off, I know very well that you can take care of yourself. It's just..." He fell silent.

Surprised he'd grasped so quickly why she was upset, she turned her attention to him. "It's just...what?" She really wanted an answer, especially considering they'd be forced to work together over the next few weeks. Because his doing so also interested her privately was beside the point. At least that's what she told herself.

"I...care about you." He shrugged, averting his eyes. "I did then. Still do. Even though I know you've got it all figured out. But you and I? We both know things don't always go according to plan in our work." He looked her straight in the eye. "If the roles were reversed, would you want me to recklessly put myself in danger?"

Not knowing for a moment how to answer, she decided on an attack tactic. She raised an eyebrow. "Reckless? Really now? Is that your idea of diplomacy?"

Frustrated, he shoved his hands into his pants pockets. "All right. Not reckless. Not the right word but you have to admit it does pose a bit of a risk. For some reason, your boss sent you to us as a profiler. I suspect he hoped it would keep you behind a desk."

She crossed her arms and shrugged. "The thought crossed my mind, too. On the other hand, the Monsanto brothers don't expect to see me. Especially not the way I look and move right now. I, on the other hand, know exactly who they are and what they look like."

He nodded. "So, what would you advise me to do?"

"Advise you?"

"If I were in your position."

"Oh, that." She hoped to avoid that part of the question. "I wouldn't stop you."

"Really?"

"Yes," she said, putting up a finger. "But I would insist that you at least take reinforcements with you."

Cole reached for her hand and kissed her knuckles. "Then it's all the better that I unexpectedly showed up on your doorstep. A happy coincidence, so to speak."

Of course, she saw the sparkle in his eyes. It was unmistakable but she supposed he deserved to be a little happy about her admission. She nodded hesitantly. She didn't have to show she was happy to see him. "Well then," she said, "I hope you're in the mood for a simple meal like fish and chips."

"You know me," he said with a mischievous wink. "I'm always up for a quick, greasy meal out of a paper bag."

Hard to believe he's in that great of shape if he eats that way regularly. She pictured his well-built chest and ripped abs. *It's a good problem to have, though, isn't it? At least he cares about me a little. Maybe he still has deeper feelings for me, too.* She gave him a quick sideways glance but no. That could not be. Could it?

Nevertheless, her heart beat a little faster as they made their way to the harbor.

CHAPTER FIVE

THE NEXT DAY, Avery distributed the document copies to the agents as soon as they entered the meeting room of the San Diego DEA field office.

Big A groaned and propped his head in both hands. "I can't take pictures of dead people on an empty stomach. Do we have time for some coffee?"

She glared at him. "Sure, so long as you treat everyone to coffee. I'll have mine black with two spoons of sugar." She glanced around the room. "Anybody else need coffee?"

Valentina smiled like a cat that had just been promised a bowl of milk. "I'd like a large latte, but with soy milk and hazelnut creamer, no sugar. And something sweet to eat."

Big A rolled his eyes and reached for a piece of paper to take orders.

Cole tried to stifle a laugh. "Regular coffee for me, black."

"Finally, a simple order. Your wife is a tough boss."

Avery pricked up her ears and looked at Cole. How would he react to Big A's statement?

"That's what you get for whining about needing coffee," Cole said.

Exciting. She'd expected him to be upset about "your wife". Instead, he'd backed her up. *Wow. Guess I could get used to someone having my back. Now, back to the meeting.*

She cleared her throat. "While Big A takes care of coffee, let's go over the facts again." She turned to the flip chart. "We have five victims. All are male, under twenty-years-old, rather slight in build, three of them white, one African American, and one Latino. You'll find the details of their respective lives inside the reports. We'll take turns going through the files. When everyone's had a chance to look it all over, we'll compare notes. For the first pass, this shouldn't take more than half an hour."

"And if we don't find anything in such a short time?" Valentina asked. "In my experience, it can easily take days studying files."

"Well, in my experience, if there's nothing notable right away, the most important evidence just isn't there. It's better to question the witnesses or family members again. After all, the words in the report are already shaped by the bias of the officer on duty. That doesn't mean it's wrong but at that time, the officers didn't know this was a serial killer. Knowing that, different questions may arise."

"Makes sense." Valentina took the files and sat with them by the window.

Avery handed Cole his files. When he picked them up, she didn't let go right away. He looked at her, perplexed.

"Thank you," she said and let them go.

"Does Big A good to be on coffee duty, too," he said as he took the files. His eyes never left hers.

She allowed herself to sink into his blue eyes for another second before averting her gaze and plopping down on the nearest chair. Miss Marple sat on her knee, watching the proceedings.

Cole watched Avery and Miss Marple. *I'm jealous. Those two make a great couple. How am I ever going to compete?* Cole didn't quite know what to make of the rat. *Really cute, actually, when she isn't nibbling at me with her sharp teeth. Or stealing my food, like she did yesterday with my fries. I was too distracted by Miss Marple's keeper to notice. Don't want to let her nip me again like she did at the baptism.*

"How did it only take you fifteen minutes?" Avery asked Big A, who'd returned with the coffee and munchies.

"Getting coffee is my superpower," Big A said. "Well, one of them."

"I'll give you that." Avery laughed, as did he. The others didn't hesitate to grab their stuff.

Minutes later, only empty paper cups and a pile of powdered sugar remained.

Avery wiped her hands on a paper napkin and handed Big A his files. "Here. We're going to be looking for commonalities, salient features...things like that for the next few minutes, but I'm sure you're already aware."

"*MMMH*. Sure. Thanks."

Avery turned back to her papers. Immediately, she was struck by a recurrence she bet was probably more than just a coincidence. Most of the victims wouldn't ordinarily be missed.

Before Avery had a chance, Valentina spoke up. "I can't shake the suspicion that all these boys were hustlers. Prostitutes."

"She's right," Big A said.

"What makes you think so?" Avery asked. It matched her observation that no one missed the victims, but she was still surprised how they came to this conclusion.

"The location. All the murders happened in the immediate vicinity of relevant bars," Cole said.

"Really?" Avery asked. "If true, that's valuable information." Avery nodded. "That's why I really appreciate your knowledge. I only know the area around the harbor and downtown San Diego." She laughed. "Before I went undercover, I'd only ever been to California as a tourist."

"And yet you've never visited a gay bar? Unbelievable," Big A teased.

"Somehow, I missed out. Too busy with work. Go figure." Amused, she winked at him. She credited him for taking the job of fetching coffee in stride.

She turned back to her notes. The cogs in her profiler brain were rattling. With this new piece of the puzzle, she suddenly had a first idea about the psychological background. She looked around the room. "Does anyone else have anything?"

Cole chimed in. "My guess is the perpetrator brought the drugs with him because they have the same chemical composition."

Avery drummed her fingers on the table. "If only we knew if the perpetrator was just buying his stuff from the same place every time or if there was actually a direct connection to the Monsanto family."

"Impossible to say at this point," Valentia said.

"Unfortunately, I agree with Valentina's assessment," Avery said. "Well, then we'll have no choice but to re-interview all the witnesses and hope we come across a new lead."

"Good idea," Cole said. "While you're working on the psychological profile, we'll take care of that."

She opened her mouth to protest, but as soon as Avery read the challenge and warning in Cole's gaze, she shut it again. *Great. One step forward, two steps back. Didn't we work this out yesterday?* She swallowed hard and knew she had to deflect. She said, "Big A, you're escorting Valentina."

The big man grinned broadly and rubbed his hands together in delight. "About time I got rid of that ugly troll." He stood up and gallantly offered her his arm. "Princess? Shall we?"

Valentina laughed. "You're irresistible!" She got up and packed her things.

"Are you coming, too?" Big A asked Cole.

"Go ahead and start with the first two bodies.. I'll take care of the other three."

"Uh-huh."

"Now get out," Cole growled.

Avery had to stifle a grin. It served him right if his partner made fun of him.

As soon as the others had left, she crossed her arms and stared at him darkly.

"I know what you're going to say," Cole said. "But there's no point in both of us putting ourselves in danger."

"No. Of course not. It's much better if only the strong man does it." Her voice dripped with sarcasm. "Chalk another one up for the patriarchy," she said.

"Uh..." Cole said.

While he processed what she said, Avery stowed Miss Marple in her bag and slipped her service weapon into her waistband. She hurried to the door. "Are you coming?"

Confused, asked, "Where to?"

"To the witness interviews for cases three, four and five."

Perplexed, he looked after her and then, when his brain finally turned back on, hurried to catch up with her. "Okay."

"So, now you want to come, after all?"

"Yes."

"So you no longer think only one of us should go?"

"*OUCH!*"

She gave him a sidelong glance. Cole had his teeth clenched so tightly that the muscles on his jaw stood out. "You're right."

"Are you okay? A woman being right is going to kill you?" she asked, trying to stifle a laugh. She failed miserably.

"All right, all right. You've got me. Can we be friends again?" he said as the left corner of his mouth twitched.

"Sure," she said. "So long as you drive to make up for your idiocy." She tossed him the keys.

He caught it with one hand. "How kind of you."

"Not really. You know your way around here better than I do. It'd be great if we can get out of here quickly."

"Oh, now you suddenly expect us to leave in a hurry?"

"It's not a good look when you deliberately play dumb."

"Wait? What?"

She laughed. "Come on, you knuckle-dragger. Follow my lead."

They left the concrete and glass building and got into the car.

Arriving at the first address, they got out and looked around the typical apartment building. The run-down apartments had plaster peeling off the walls. The stairs sported large cracks. Garbage bags lay scattered around and filled the air with the stench of rotting food and God knew what else.

"Casey Peters," Avery read off her phone. "Eighteen years old. He supposedly lived here in apartment twenty-one."

"Well then, let's go."

They climbed the broken staircase until they reached the second level. The door still had the local police's warning tape. "Obviously, no one's shown any interest in the apartment yet. Otherwise, the owner would have long since asked for the lock to be opened," Cole said.

"True. Early bird gets the worm." Avery removed the seal with her knife and opened the door. "It's stuffy in here. Leave the door open," she told Cole, opening a window on the other side of the room.

Cole flipped on the light switch. The apartment was spare, with the main furniture centering around a worn sofa with stains of undefinable origin. Dirty dishes were piled in the sink. The small garbage can overflowed.

A second door led to the bedroom. A tattered bedspread lay on the floor. Various pieces of clothing hung over the edge of the bed. A rickety nightstand stood on the right side of the bed. "We'll have to look at the evidence at the police station," Cole said.

Avery nodded. "True but I'm not too interested in that stuff. In order to profile the perpetrator successfully, I need to find out as much as I can about the victims. We already know they were using hard drugs."

"Blood tests confirmed that," Cole said.

"Evidence included syringes and a small amount of heroin," Avery added.

"Does the report say if any of the victims' fingerprints were found on these things?" Cole asked.

Avery stopped examining a movie collection and looked up at him. "I don't know. I'll have to check into it. Why? What are you thinking?"

Cole shrugged. "Just that drugs in the blood don't necessarily mean someone's an addict. We should still look closely at the autopsy report on the others, too."

"Do you think it was a setup? Maybe to make it seem like they were addicted to heroin?" she asked.

"Could be." He shrugged. "I'm suspicious when something's so obvious. Most users try to hide their addictions."

"I couldn't agree more. However, at this point, I don't see how their drug use is relevant. If the victims had died of an overdose, I would agree with you and would be skeptical, too. However, they were stabbed to death."

"True."

From the corner of her eye, she saw Cole wander into the bedroom. Stopping at the nightstand, he pulled out the drawer and rifled around. He pulled out an old notebook and started reading.

Avery continued her own search for a few minutes before returning her attention to Cole. "Find something interesting?"

Cole looked up. "Yes, as a matter of fact, I think so." He waved the notebook in the air. "This seems to be some kind of diary."

"Is there anything in it that will help us?"

"Maybe. He talks about how he met a rich man. Apparently he was hoping to find something like a sugar daddy. Looks like he got tired of working as a hustler."

"Can't blame him." Avery frowned. "Maybe his plans and his new lover's plans didn't match. However, that would speak more to a one-off relationship crime, and not a serial killer."

"Unless the perpetrator befriends each of his victims?"

"Possibly. Let's talk to the property manager. Maybe he knows something about the victim. A rich friend is bound to stand out in this neighborhood."

"Good. Let's go."

"Wait. Not so fast. I'll send Miss Marple out. Maybe she'll find something."

"Drugs you mean?"

"Could be."

She put Miss Marple on the ground and gave her the hand signal to search.

After a few minutes of the mouse scurrying around, she came back empty. The only place the rat sounded the alarm was where the drugs had been found in the first search, and on the living room table where the victim had presumably taken a shot. She clicked both times and gave Miss Marple a popcorn as a reward.

"Who would have thought that our third dead man was so organized? Usually people like him are much messier."

"Takes all types," she said. "I think our work is done here." She made for the front door. Cole followed and waited for her to walk out past him so he could reapply the crime scene seal.

"*PHEW*. The air out here isn't much better than the air inside," she said.

"Yeah. It's awful," he said. "By the way? What is Miss Marple actually trained to do?"

Avery stopped and looked back at the apartment. "Her strengths are narcotics, specifically cocaine and heroin, gunshot residue, and money. Why?"

"Did we have her look for money?"

She shook her head. "Yes. Miss Marple knows the signatures of these four smells. If she picks up a scent from any of them, she'll let you know."

"*HMM*. No money here. Don't you think that's strange?"

"Why? Do you always have money lying around?"

"Not much but probably ten, twenty dollars for emergencies, food, that sort of thing. Did he have any money on him when he was found dead?"

"Hold on. Let me download the reports for a minute. Then we can clear up any lingering questions right away." She slipped out her phone, opened her files.

"You do that. I'll go and find the janitor's door in the meantime."

"Great." Avery almost touched the wall, but refrained when she spotted the filth. *Disgusting, this neighborhood. Gonna wait in the car for him.*

"Can I help you?" An unkempt man in an undershirt, sweatpants, and bathing slippers opened the door when Cole rang the bell. A cigarette butt hung in the corner of his mouth.

Cole showed his badge. "Agent Carter. FBI. I have a few questions about your tenant from number twenty-one."

"I've already told the police everything I know," he said sullenly, making a move to close the door.

He put his foot in the gap. Thank goodness he wore his sturdy biker boots; Avery wore the same ones. Almost made him smile, but he caught himself. "I know you've already spoken to the police but there are still a few loose ends. It won't take long. I promise."

Cole's politeness seemed to take the wind out of the other man's sails. He lost some of his belligerent attitude and seemed to slump. "I suppose that's all right. Fire away," he said, then cackled as if he'd just said something hilarious. When Cole didn't respond, he stopped as suddenly as he started.

"Have you noticed if your tenant had any new friends lately?"

"*HA*, I suppose you think I don't know what that creep was doing? A queer did that!"

Cole gritted his teeth and ignored the homophobic slurs. He was here to find out more about the victim, not preach tolerance, as much as he wished he could.

The man went on. "Once, not long before he died, he even brought one here but I told him right away that I wouldn't tolerate it on the property."

"And how did he take that?"

"Came at me all upset. Called me names. Said he wouldn't be here much longer, anyway. Looks like he was right." He broke into his annoying laugh. "Guess he didn't mean it like that."

"Interesting. Where was he going?"

"Well, moving in with his *lover*," he said, making air quotes to express how he felt about it.

"Who was that guy? The friend?" asked Cole, struggling to keep a neutral expression.

"Well, a queer." The janitor looked at him as if he was slow on the uptake.

Cole massaged the root of his nose. "If we disregard his sexual orientation for a moment, can you think of anything else? Age, appearance? Were his clothes new? Did he drive a car? Things like that."

Perplexed, as if this information were completely beside the point, the man scratched his head and thought. "Now that you mention it, he dressed like he was rich. Gel in his hair, long coat, shiny shoes."

After all, his dislike extended not only to gays, but consistently to anything even remotely outside his worldview, Cole thought.

The janitor didn't notice Cole's increasingly bad mood and continued with his narrative. "He drove a big car. A Mercedes or something. Definitely not an American car."

Cole was sure that was considered a mortal sin in his world. "So what?"

"Yes, indeed. *So what!*" He had visibly reached the end of his patience. "The man had money, drove a fat sled, and slept with his little friend. End of story. Probably killed him afterward. Are we done now that I've solved the case for you?"

"Not quite. You wouldn't happen to have a name?"

"No!" With his last word, he managed to slam the door shut.

Cole shook his head. Oh well. At least he knew a few more details about his victim.

"Troublesome witness?" asked Avery as he joined her in the car and she saw the look on his face.

"Let's put it this way: this guy is not going to win the Solidarity Award this year, unfortunately."

Avery laughed softly. "That's usually the case with the people we deal with."

"I know but sometimes I get so tired of it." He rubbed the back of his neck.

"I know the feeling. I'm tired of drugs being sold to kids and firearms getting sold to the wrong people.

Human trafficking. If we have to come in contact with that scum to help rid the world of it, even just a little bit, then so be it."

"It's just so tedious." He closed his eyes for a moment. "In a perfect situation, I'd just like to do raids. Get in with the team, save the world, and get out."

Avery snorted. "I don't want to ruin your rose-colored dream but you didn't exactly save the world during your last raid. On the contrary. Now they're even more on guard and my entire cover is likely about to be blown. At the very least, it's no longer useful."

"Okay, okay but failures are to be expected." He let out a resigned sigh.

"True but you can eliminate those pretty well by doing thorough preliminary work. That's the point that excites me much more about my work. The blind obedience that's required."

The corners of his mouth twitched. "What?"

"Honestly, I've always wondered about that. That you chose a job where you have to be told what to do, how to do it, where to do it, and when to do it. You've never been good at taking orders."

She punched him as hard as she could in his shoulder.

"Hey! Ouch!"

"Serves you right." Satisfied, she watched him rub his shoulder where she had punched him. She couldn't help but smirk. "Maybe we'll think of something to change the system but for now? We have a case to solve."

CHAPTER SIX

"Look, Pat, there's the Pacific Ocean up ahead!" Tyler leaned forward in her seat. They'd rented Nelly, the same RV Kat had rented back when she'd first moved to Independence. The vehicle was getting a bit long in the tooth, with all the miles it had on its hump, *er*, wheels, but it had held up bravely during their road trip to California.

Ranger, wanting to know what the fuss was about, stood on his hind legs and put his front paws on the dashboard.

Tyler put her arm around the dog's neck and pointed with the other to the infinite, turquoise-blue glittering surface. Small whitecaps shimmered across the water. "I'm really a mountain person," she said. "But I could get used to the view here."

She caught affectionate looks from the side. "I can understand that." Pat had moved to Independence from Seattle a year before.

"Do you ever miss it here?" she asked.

He shrugged. "Sometimes. But the Rockies are equal as far as nature goes. That being said? The sound of the surf and the salty air are hard to top. Have you been to the ocean before?"

"Yes, of course. In my star ballerina days." Realizing those days were gone for good, she felt a little wistful.

Pat put out his hand. Gratefully, she squeezed it. Supported and comforted, it was easy for her to shake off her melancholy mood. She said, "We've only ever been to the East Coast. I'm seeing the Pacific for the first time today."

"Then we definitely need to take the time to drive up to San Francisco. Does Fisherman's Wharf mean anything to you?" Pat asked.

"I think Kat mentioned it once. Isn't that where the seals live?" Tyler asked.

"Exactly. Hundreds of them. Although, I'm sure there are some here in San Diego. I'll have to look it up," Pat said.

Tyler looked at her watch. "How far is San Diego?"

"About twenty minutes. What are you thinking?"

"We're not meeting my brother for another two hours. Let's go to the beach. Or did you want to see our new place first thing?"

They'd rented a small cottage in Carlsbad, right on the beach. Both of them looked forward to jogging with Ranger before work.

"Good idea about a beach walk." He looked at the clock on the dashboard. "It's been three hours since our last break, too. Our house isn't going anywhere. The owner runs a pub in town. We can still get the key from there late at night, he assured me."

"Great." She leaned over to the German shepherd and cuddled him. "Watch out, Ranger. You'll be able to chase seagulls in a minute."

Pat laughed out loud. "As if this model student would even consider it." He put on his blinker and turned into a large parking lot. "There it is and here we are," he said.

In a blink, Tyler opened the door and let Ranger loose. He ran toward the shore and she hurried after him, laughing the entire time.

"So, what's the latest news from Independence?" Cole asked his sister Tyler as soon as she stepped in the door.

She and Pat had just arrived with Ranger, and greetings and hugs were exchanged.

Hearing the commotion, Avery emerged from the kitchen and gave him a playful shove, forcing him to brace himself against the wall. "Why don't you let them unpack first?" She turned to their guests. "How many hours have you been on the road today?"

Tyler glanced at Pat. "Seven or eight hours? I think there were six hours in the car and two during which we took a break. I really had to show Ranger the Pacific."

Pat laughed. "Ranger was pretty mellow when it came to the waves, though. He was more excited that Tyler was excited, I bet."

"He actually barked at me." Tyler looked like she couldn't believe it.

Miss Marple emerged from Avery's oversized sweater and perched on her shoulder.

Tyler took a step toward them and held out her hand for the rat to sniff. Miss Marple's little ears turned in her direction. Her whiskers quivered with interest. "Hello, beautiful. Found anything exciting today?"

"Unfortunately, no," Cole sighed. "But about that later. Avery and I just got home."

"The first few days in an older investigation are always tedious," Avery added. "A lot of running around and talking to uncooperative witnesses."

Pat, who had been quiet until then, raised an eyebrow mockingly. "Just the two of you together all day? That sounds really cuddly."

Tyler gave her companion a dirty look.

"What?" Pat asked. "I need to know what to bet on tonight, don't I?"

"Listening to these two makes you wonder why women are always the ones accused of being the big gossips. Guys are much worse."

Tyler nodded. "True, isn't it?"

"How are you going to bet tonight? The diner isn't around the corner like it was back home in Independence," Avery said.

Tyler winced.

"As of late, you can do that online," Cole enlightened her.

Avery's eyes widened in disbelief when she heard that. "Really? Wow."

"Sure. They even have the diner all over social media. The Diner Sisters put it up," Pat explained.

"Well, if they don't get in trouble," Tyler said.

Pat frowned. "What would they get in trouble for?"

Cole looked to the side, away from Avery. She gave him a nasty glare. "You could help me here, too. After all, you know perfectly well that there are legal regulations against gambling on the Internet."

He remained silent, knowing full well she was right. *ARGH. Men.* She took Miss Marple off her shoulder and placed her in the crook of her arm. Placed that way, she tickled her belly.

"Food?" Tyler changed the subject.

Avery was only too happy to oblige and led them into the kitchen. *Let the two chatterboxes continue discussing the betting parlor.* "Sure. We did some extra shopping beforehand. Salad, potatoes, and steaks. I hope you don't mind if we barbecue."

"You can hear crickets in November," Tyler sighed. "Just great. Maybe I could spend the winter months here and the summer in Colorado."

Avery, her head stuck in the refrigerator, laughed out loud. She stood up with the food and put it on the counter. "That's a great idea because I can never decide where I like better."

She put the potatoes in the oven and prepared the salad.

Tyler looked around the apartment. "This is Cole's place, right?"

"Yeah. Why?"

Tyler spun around once and pointed to their surroundings with open palms. "It's just so...empty."

"I don't know. It's best to ask him yourself about that. Contrary to popular belief, we don't live together, nor am I pregnant, and nor are we making marriage plans."

"Oh, what a shame. And I was beginning to think I was the star of the day when I called home tonight with exciting inside information," Tyler said.

"I'd like to think so. I honestly avoided looking at their page again. My two minutes of fame were enough."

"You wait and see. There's bound to be more," Tyler teased.

"Don't they have anything better to do? No better topics to worry about?"

"*HMM*, no, things are pretty quiet right now." Tyler swiped a few cucumber slices from the large salad bowl. "*UMM*, yeah, maybe. Now that I think about it. Paige seems to have settled in pretty well. After Paula so generously shared about what an important role she played in setting up Leslie's college fund, the other Independence residents have warmed up to her a bit."

"I'm happy for them. Independence is great. As long as you have the people on your side. Otherwise, they'll leave you starving by the side of the road without a second look." Avery shuddered.

Tyler eyed her. "Was that the reason you ran off head over heels?"

Avery's gaze wandered through the open door into the living room, where the two men were still engrossed in conversation.

"In part," she said.

Tyler seemed to sense that. At least she didn't pry. "I thought it was all totally exciting at the time. I was five years younger than you guys, and I loved following the drama."

Avery glanced at her out of the corner of her eye. "Are you making fun of us?"

"No, no. I'm completely serious. Just try to look at it from my perspective. I was thirteen, the spoiled brat. My big brother could be really annoying at times. Watching you drive him crazy was very amusing. Tell me," she asked after a pause, "the pine nuts, were you going to spread them over the salad or are they meant as a snack for your rat?"

"Oh!" Avery turned and plucked Miss Marple from the tabletop. Resolutely, she placed her in Tyler's arms. Ranger, who had followed them into the kitchen, looked at the rodent with interest. "Well, you two. Make up."

The two men came into the kitchen. Cole got the meat out of the refrigerator and said, "We'll fire up the grill, okay? Does that work for the timeline?"

"Sure. I'm almost done here."

Pat stood by Tyler and stroked Miss Marple's spotted fur. "Babysitting duties?"

"It sure looks like it, doesn't it?" Pat said. "I've been wondering all along if this is a downgrade or an upgrade from my dog ownership duties."

He grinned. "An upgrade, definitely. Rats are a lot more complicated than dogs."

"*HMM*. Still not quite convinced." She gave Avery a questioning look.

"Definitely an improvement," Avery said.

"*HA*," Pat said. "You're just afraid that if you say something wrong now, you'll lose your new rat guardian."

"Sure." Avery grinned.

Loaded with the barbecue and a cooler filled with cold beer, the men disappeared through the large glass doors that led out onto the balcony. Ranger, who was not entirely comfortable with Miss Marple, slipped out behind them.

"So, back to Independence," Avery said. "Is that where Paige wants to stay? I mean, originally she ended up there more by accident than anything else."

"I think she feels like she needs to do some more penance," Tyler said. "In any case, she's now helping Kat with PR for the *Safe Haven*."

"That's good," Avery said.

Tyler nodded. "I'm sure Kat can use all the help she can get. She would prefer going out with the dogs instead of sitting at a computer."

"Right." Avery frowned. "Now that you've told me what Paige is up to, I hardly think she's going to make that a topic of conversation."

"Except that Miss Minnie got it into her head to get her and Ace together," Tyler said.

"Ace," Avery reflected. "Is that the fire chief?"

"Right. I think you saw him once briefly back during that scary stalker situation. He's only lived in Independence for a couple of years."

"A stranger. How exciting," Avery joked. "I wonder how long it will be before he runs away."

Tyler nodded again. "Miss Minnie claims to have inside information."

"She knows how to boost her betting pool, too." Avery snorted.

"Probably."

"*HMM*. Okay, what else? So far, it doesn't sound like Paige is the right candidate to get in the way of me and Cole."

"Aileen is one to look out for, too. In fact, they would definitely be more exciting than you and Cole. You guys are almost old hats."

"Whatever. Who's Aileen?" Avery poured the dressing over the salad and wondered how she and Cole could be an old hat when nothing had even started yet. She bristled at the suggestion. *Do I want something to start? Or should I say...continue?*

"Aileen is a distant relative of the Diner Sisters. They found out she's their niece."

"And what is she doing in Independence?"

"Until recently, she helped Miss Daisy in the kitchen. And not just peeling potatoes, but really cooking up a storm. She graduated from a prestigious culinary school, spent several semesters in Paris and..."

"Does the food at the diner taste the same, though?"

"*MMMH*, heavenly!" Tyler said, closing her eyes, her grin stretching across her face.

"Well, that's great. I'm sure the Diner Sisters are happy to have backups, too."

Tyler shifted. "Did you hear? There's going to be a coffee shop in Independence soon. Kind of like a Starbucks, without the chain, of course, and with more style."

Avery glanced at Tyler. "Am I correct in assuming that Aileen is behind this? In that case, I imagine it'll cause some turmoil."

"It does. The Diner Sisters, in particular, are beside themselves that Aileen not only stopped working for them after they'd just gotten used to her, but now wants to compete with them, too."

"Oh, it'll do them good. After nearly three decades of being the only game in town when it goes to local restaurants, it's about time."

"I think it's great, even though I don't really get anything out of it because I'm stuck here in California." Avery sighed.

"Don't you like it here?" Tyler asked.

"Yeah, I do. It's more a general dissatisfaction with the job in general. It's going to be okay but enough whining.

What about you? Have you started something at the local school yet?" Avery asked.

"Yes, I actually have," Tyler said. "I have an interview with the school district superintendent and someone from Social Services next week."

"That's great!"

Tyler rocked back and forth in her chair as if she almost couldn't sit still. "I know. I'm excited. They really liked my concept. Now it just has to prove itself in practice but in a pinch, I know who to call when the youngsters get on my case. The FBI never fails to have an imposing effect." She grinned.

"I can imagine so," Avery said. "Will you help me carry these things outside?"

"Sure."

They went to the counter. "Here, will you take the salad out with you?" Avery asked. "I'll bring the potatoes."

She opened the oven. The scent of rosemary, thyme, and warm olive oil filled the room. With the help of two oven mitts, she pulled out the tray and tipped the potatoes into a prepared bowl. "Soon we feast!"

"Perfect timing," Cole said as they stepped outside, heavily burdened. He stood at the grill checking the cuts of meat. Satisfied, he grabbed the steaks with the grill tongs and placed them on a large plate.

A few minutes later, everyone was eating. Tyler and Pat were happy to finally eat something that didn't come from a highway rest stop. Cole and Avery were likewise glad for something home-cooked. For both of them, the donuts had been the last thing they ate that morning.

From the balcony, a small section of the sea could be seen between several houses. Every now and then a seagull would stray into the sky above them and let out a hoarse cry. Miss Marple, who had made herself comfortable on Avery's lap, always disappeared into the fanny pack of her sweatshirt on these occasions.

"I think you need to explain to her that seagulls are not related to birds of prey," Cole said.

"Says the man who still flinches when the rat comes near him," Avery teased. "Didn't I tell you that? She doesn't have any lions in her family tree either."

Tyler chuckled, clearly amused that Avery was teasing him.

"For good reason," Cole defended himself. "She bit me again today."

"Only because you still had powdered sugar on your fingers."

"Of course. Then everything's fine." Seeking help, he turned first to his sister. When he saw that she was laughing almost to tears, typical of his sister, his eyes drifted to Pat. Maybe some male solidarity? Alas, no. The corners of his mouth twitched suspiciously, too. He rolled his eyes, wondering why he had thought it was a good idea to invite these people. Then he spotted the amused twinkle in Avery's eyes, and it came back to him. To see that look in her eyes, he would endure many other things than being teased a little by his friends.

It was time they solved this case. Urgently. Otherwise he could not guarantee anything, employee guidelines or not.

On the other hand, it wasn't bad if the solution had to wait a little longer. This way he could at least spend some time with her without her slipping away again.

"Even though I almost don't have the heart to say it, this meat is totally delicious," Tyler said, changing the subject.

Avery glared at her.

Her friend gestured with the silverware as she struggled to swallow the bite.

"Normally, our family has an unwritten law of only eating meat from Paula's cows."

"Sounds macabre, but somehow it also makes sense. At least you know how they were raised."

"Exactly. And it's not like I know all two hundred of them by name."

Cole joined in the conversation and began quizzing Tyler on how the rest of the family was doing.

Avery leaned back in her chair and sipped her beer. It had grown dark. Cole set up a candle that cast a warm glow over the table.

She noticed earlier that the rest of the apartment was very sterile, almost cold, without a personal touch. Avery thought that was odd. Hadn't he stopped going undercover a while ago? He wouldn't have to move every few months, so what was going on? She decided to ask him about it when she got a chance.

If she was honest, she hoped her undercover stint as a goth streetwalker had been her last, too. She was tired of the constant moves.

While the others laughed at an anecdote Tyler told, apparently Leslie had fallen in love for the first time and was keeping Paula quite busy watching after all three of them.

Pat had her arm around Tyler and played with a lock of her blonde hair. Ranger rested at Tyler's feet and snoozed. Occasionally, one of his ears turned in a different direction when he heard something.

Cole laughed. It was a carefree, relaxed laugh. It was clearly good for him to spend time with at least one of his many siblings. *I wonder what it was like to be part of such a large, usually good-humored family.* Longing for belonging filled Avery. *I'm going to call my grandfather tomorrow. Last time, we didn't have enough time to really talk. I might not have such a big family, but my grandfather is the best in the world.*

The candlelight made the muscles under his tee-shirt stand out even more as Cole leaned back in his chair. As if she needed a reminder of his great physique. She averted her eyes. He'd made it abundantly clear last time he didn't want to continue their on/off relationship, or whatever they were going to call it.

She'd just have to admire him from afar. Again. She glanced at the clock. Ten already. The perfect time to feign tiredness and go home. Suddenly, she had to yawn. She didn't have to pretend. She was actually dog-tired and ready to call it a day.

CHAPTER SEVEN

ALBERTO STEPPED INTO the living room. His brother Tony reclined on the dark leather sofa, a drink in his hand. His hair was combed back and the scent of expensive aftershave lingered in the air.

The veins in his temples pulsed. He forced his face into a neutral expression. As he poured himself a bourbon at the generous liquor cabinet, he asked, "Is everything ready for the merchandise coming tomorrow?"

Tony looked annoyed. "Yes. Everything is prepared. Just like you ordered."

Alberto raised his eyebrow. "I hope so. One of us has to keep the business running smoothly, after all. Your specialty is spending money, it seems." Lurking, he eyed his brother, ready for his reaction. He was itching to show Tony once and for all who was in charge. Preferably with his fists. Maybe then he would finally come to his senses.

"You might want to try that sometime," Tony said, keeping his cool. "Enjoy your life a little. What's the point of raking in money if you're just going to keep it in the safe?" He pulled a plastic baggie from his breast pocket. With great fuss, he sprinkled the powder onto a silver tray lying on the table in front of him.

Alberto raised an eyebrow. "Big plans tonight?" He wanted to see his brother's reaction. It wasn't like he needed to know. He'd find out soon enough. He knew his attention to detail was the reason he was successful at what he did. "Trust no one but yourself" proved to be a valuable motto.

Tony leaned down, straw coupled between his thumb and forefinger.

Alberto looked away; he couldn't bear to see his brother partake. He hated even just listening to the sound.

"You know me, brother," Tony said, his voice sounding plugged up. "One conquest at a time. Never let anything go to waste. Life's too short for that. Mindi's waiting for me."

Alberto pictured the vapid, silicone-laden girl with the attention and lips of a goldfish who'd been accompanying his brother. He boiled up. The urge to wring his brother's neck and get rid of the problem he posed once and for all grew by the minute. He forced himself to relax his fists and limited himself to a verbal blow. "I know all too well how you spend your valuable time."

He swore he saw fear flash in Tony's eyes; Alberto knew all his secrets. Tony squirmed on the sofa. "Have your efforts to find Maria turned up anything?" he asked, almost stuttering.

Alberto waved his hand. "She's in juvenile hall. That settles that issue."

"Really?" Tony asked.

"Really," Alberto said.

Alberto had made a big drama out of it when Maria couldn't be found the day after the raid. Tony hadn't understood what the fuss was about. Alberto had voiced his suspicions about a girl who lived on the street and spent most of her time talking to her rat was in cahoots with the cops. But to Tony, that seemed very unlikely.

Tony liked the girl. Through her, he could live vicariously. That was much safer for him. Moreover, she had unknowingly provided him with an alibi several times. When she hadn't shown up after a week, he resigned himself that she wasn't coming back. Life on the streets was hard; it hadn't surprised him that it had gotten to her. Too bad, because it wasn't unnecessary. He'd offered her many times to live with them but she had always disappeared for hours or days at a time.

"So, she wasn't a snitch after all?" Tony asked.

"For the second time, and from the looks of it, no."

Alberto pointed his index finger at Tony. "But you didn't know that when you brought her into the family. Let that be a lesson to you in who you associate with." Abruptly, he turned and left the room.

Completely exhausted from the verbal sparring, Tony fell back into the blood-red velvet cushions. That had been close. Or did Alberto actually know? That thought turned the blood in his veins to ice. He shook his head. *No. That couldn't be.* Otherwise he would have felt the wrath of his brother long ago. Or he would be dead, blood ties or not.

He allowed himself to relax. His brother always thought he was so smart.

With a smile on his face, Tony toasted himself in the large ornate mirror that hung above the fireplace. "I'm just worrying unnecessarily. Life is great. A few hours of partying in the right places and with the right people, and the rest of the night will be mine." He laughed and eyed the powder on the table, ready for a second hit.

Avery paced back and forth in front of the board as she pointed out her preliminary offender profile to the rest of the squad. "As we can see from the repeated testimonies, all of our victims have had a *benefactor* recently." She used air quotes to highlight the term "benefactor" so they'd read between the lines. "In addition, we know that all five had enough heroin in their blood to score an elephant when they died."

Valentina looked up from her phone. "I just got answers from the coroner's office. Apparently, three of the dead were not regular consumers."

"Missing puncture marks?" asked Cole.

She nodded and gave the names of the victims involved.

Avery noted the names on the whiteboard. She looked to see if any of the others had anything else to contribute.

Big A cleared his throat. "Forensics confirms there were no foreign fingerprints anywhere," he said, "which is pretty strange, since in at least four cases we know about, our perpetrator visited multiple times."

"Thorough work," Cole said.

Avery processed the new info while she studied the board of photos and clues. "That basically fits with everything we've known. While the acts obviously reveal a high degree of rage—no one stabs a person thirty times if it isn't personal—the surrounding circumstances reveal a very level-headed approach. These are calculated murders perpetrated by a person who is ice-cold."

"Great," grumbled Big A. "Another perfectly logical maniac."

"I don't like it either," Cole agreed. "With killers who are insane, they make more mistakes."

"It doesn't get better," Avery interrupted. "According to my profile, the perpetrator is between thirty and forty years old, strongly principled, probably successful in his profession, and not used to losing. He's probably homosexual, given that the victims were all male hustlers, and very likely not at peace with himself about his own homosexuality."

"And how do the drugs and the lack of money fit in?" asked Valentina, her eyes steely and dark. Big A beamed when she spoke, Avery noticed, and it wasn't just because she was a brilliant collaborator. She picked up some serious vibes.

Cole had noticed it, too, she knew. She overhead him teasing his partner about it relentlessly. Big A had put up with it good-naturedly for a while, until Cole had overdone it. Then the big man eyed him with a raised eyebrow and asked, "Seriously now, buddy? Are you sure you want to pursue this?"

Cole grinned and said cheekily, "Of course I do. Why not?"

Big A had turned and shot a pointed look in Avery's direction, whereupon Cole quickly changed the subject.

His partner had grinned knowingly.

Cole couldn't help himself as Avery paced the room, showing off her long legs, working with them to profile the perpetrator; she intrigued him. The outward package was worth a second—or even third—look itself. That she was a good friend, compassionate, loyal, and up for any mischief between them, Cole had also known for years.

Seeing her in action, witnessing how her sharp mind worked, recognizing the methodology and how she processed reluctant witnesses, pushed his feelings for her up a whole new level. When he thought about how there'd been a time when he tried to convince her the job was not for her, he felt ashamed.

How arrogant had he been? He was lucky she didn't hold a grudge. Or maybe she did? He squirmed in his seat. At some point in the near future, he was probably due for an apology. If he hoped to end up in her bed afterward—well, he was only a man.

He snapped out of his daydream when he realized everyone was staring at him, expecting an answer. "Sorry, I missed the question. What?"

Amused, Avery raised an eyebrow, and he realized he was getting hot. Embarrassed, he scratched the back of his neck. *Could she read minds, too?*

"The money."

Avery had searched all the crime scenes with Miss Marple. At the last one, they had finally found something. Ten thousand dollars in fresh bills. They had all hoped that the bills would help them.

Again all business-like, Cole said, "No luck there, I'm afraid. In our case, the money's notes were not registered. Unfortunately, they weren't counterfeit, either. I'm still waiting to hear back from the various banks. If someone withdrew ten thousand dollars around the time of the murder, we'll know more."

Valentina made a doubtful face. "On the other hand, the murderer could have made several smaller withdrawals at different times so it would be harder to trace."

"Right. Since larger amounts would be audited."

The others groaned. "That's going to be a ton of transactions to review," Valentina said.

"Don't worry," Avery said. "I bribed the finance guys. They're helping us comb through the list."

"Bribed? How?" demanded Cole.

Avery just stared at him.

"I mean...with like Starbucks gift cards?" he asked, trying to diffuse his awkward question.

"No," she said. "Nothing so shallow. But a magician never reveals their secrets, do they?"

He ducked his head and said, "I was just curious. Sorry if that came out wrong. Usually they're incredibly stubborn and so overworked that it's almost impossible to get a favor from them."

"Fine. I'll dish. Homemade caramel sauce and a basket of apples worked beautifully," she said. "With a recipe I got from my friends, the Diner Sisters in Independence. Maybe you've heard of them?"

"I'll have to remember that trick," Valentina said. "Not that I can make caramel sauce."

Avery gestured with a bag of sunflower seeds, which she fed to Miss Marple, who sat on her table. "A bag of nuts is more my thing. Or chips." At the word chips, the rat visibly perked up.

"That's amazing," Valentina said.

She tilted her head and looked expectantly at Valentina. Such praise always meant treats, after all.

"Just ignore them," Avery instructed her, knowing full well how persuasive Miss Marple could be.

"Not much of a cook?" Big A asked Valentina, amused.

She shook her head. "No, but give me a knife and I'll hit any spot when I throw it. Just don't expect me to use it for cooking."

Impressed, Avery looked at Valentina with a newfound respect.

Big A was also impressed. "Then I guess I'll have to cook you some dinner in the near future," he said with an ambiguous wink.

Valentina blushed.

"As entertaining as I find all this, we still have a case to solve," Avery said and rapped her knuckle on the nearest tabletop. "Back on topic. We've now covered age, gender, education level, tracks, and the drugs. Does anyone have anything else to contribute?"

"The drug thing—the Monsanto family connection— does that mean anything?" Valentina asked.

"My gut tells me yes. However, I have no idea in what regard that might be." Avery ran a hand through her hair. "It's not like the DEA has enough evidence to take to the DA."

"Unless you suspect one of the Monsanto family of being the killer, I don't see what relevance it should have to where the drugs came from." Big A leaned back in his chair and crossed his arms in front of his chest.

Avery bit her lower lip. "You're right. That's bull-stuffing. The brothers don't dwell on something as ridiculous and as petty as murder, do they? They've got much bigger deals going on. I just can't shake the feeling that we're missing something."

Cole sat up straighter. "What the DEA can or can't prove to make the case stand up in court doesn't interest me. How sure are you that the Monsanto family is behind this?"

"One hundred percent. Unfortunately, everything is based on circumstantial evidence," she said. "Too little there to accomplish anything."

Cole let out a wolfish grin. "But enough to invite them in for a chat?"

"*HMM*, yeah. It doesn't take much for that." She ducked her head. "My boss won't like it. We're supposed to handle the Monsanto family with kid gloves. That's why they weren't at all pleased with your raid. Which, unfortunately, was also unsuccessful."

"So what?" Cole said. "The way I see it, we have five homicides to solve. If we don't move soon, probably a sixth."

"Without wanting to seem irreverent," Avery said. "A sixth murder is probably one of the only things that would help us at this point."

CHAPTER EIGHT

"At least we didn't have to wait too long for the next clue," Cole said. "It hasn't even been twenty-four hours since our meeting...and your prediction there'd be another body being pulled out of the harbor."

Avery didn't even feel awake. "It's nippy, even for dawn in San Diego." The damp morning air crept into her clothes. She hunched her shoulders to keep warm. Maybe it was just because she hadn't slept enough. She rubbed the sleep from her eyes. "I don't even want to know what I look like. Five in the morning is definitely too early for makeup."

The thought of mascara made her shudder. She gave Cole a sideways glance. It was a given that he looked incredibly sexy. The stubble made him seem more dangerous—tougher, somehow.

Aside from the inconvenient fact Cole was off-limits to her while being a teammate, she really liked working with him. She was discovering facets about him she hadn't seen before, and the more she recognized, the more she liked. Whether that was a good thing or not remained to be seen.

She pulled her black sweatshirt tighter around as she stopped in front of the body. "Too bad the perp didn't leave him where he killed him, as has been the methodology up until now. That would have helped us out."

"Then this throws the perp profile off," Cole said.

"Believe me, I wouldn't care if we could get to the bottom of who did this if it means the profile wasn't right."

She was so frustrated that she was tempted to kick the corpse, even though she knew doing so wouldn't help. The pathologist present wouldn't approve, either.

Avery pulled herself together and let her eyes wander over the pier.

"I'll be right back," she said to Cole.

"Of course," he said, giving her shoulder an encouraging squeeze.

She nodded and tried to classify the various ships. *Mostly cargo ships. Only at the outer end are a few private ships visible. Big motorboats and elegant sailing yachts.* Her gaze fell on a silver-gray yacht. She squinted. Was the boat called *Magdalena*? A memory stirred. She had heard the name from the Monsanto brothers, she was sure, but couldn't remember in what context. Did it even matter? Probably not, she realized. After all, "Magdalena" was a common Italian name.

Cole approached her. "Don't want to interrupt, but..." He held out a steaming coffee. "Got you something."

Without asking where he'd found coffee at such an early hour, she greedily reached for it and took a big gulp. "*AHH*. Better. Thanks. You know my early morning mood is in direct proportion to the caffeine I ingest."

The right corner of Cole's mouth lifted into a half-smile. Involuntarily, she returned it. Finally, she set the coffee down and handed the cup back to him. "That was exactly what I needed."

"You're welcome."

They walked back toward the pathologist, who knelt near the body doing her work.

Once there, Avery spoke up. "Can you tell us more about the dead man yet?"

"You'd think with all the TV shows these days, people would know better," the pathologist said.

"Apparently not a morning person, either," Avery said. "I can understand that all too well." She crouched down next to the pathologist and said, "I'm sorry. Of course, I know most tests can't be done until you get to the lab. I just thought that, thanks to your wealth of experience, you might have already come to one or two conclusions."

The pathologist's expression softened. She wiped a strand from her face with the back of her gloved hand. "He was stabbed. Like the others. Whether he had drugs in his blood as well, I can't tell until the tests are done. If you contact the Coast Guard, I'm sure they can tell you roughly where he was thrown in." She shrugged. "Otherwise, you guys are on your own. I doubt this guy has any more clues in store."

"No perp signature on the belly?" quipped Cole.

The pathologist grinned. "Other than the knife wounds, no signature, I'm afraid. Maybe you'll ask the fish. They might know more."

She closed the body bag and waved two officers over to take the body away.

In the car, Avery lowered her head to the neck rest. "I suppose there's no point in searching the harbor for evidence."

Cole shook his head. "Unfortunately, no. First of all, the harbor is so full of garbage we wouldn't have a clue what we were looking for."

"So basically we're still not a step ahead?"

"Maybe not. After all, this murder is fresh and not several weeks old like the others. Who knows what else awaits us today."

"You're right. Let's go have breakfast. We can call the others. Tell them to come, too."

Cole glanced at the clock. It was only six-thirty. "At this hour?"

She smiled mischievously. "The early bird catches the worm. Or why should we be the only ones racking our brains at this inhumane hour?" she asked.

"You do realize I'm not completely comfortable with you when you start throwing around proverbs?"

"Come on. Chop, chop, I'm hungry."

"Yes, ma'am."

Instead of taking offense at the salutation, she laughed. "That's right."

Half an hour later, Big A and Valentina trundled into the diner. While the two complained loudly, Avery studied the restaurant. *Reminds me a little bit of the diner in Independence, but that's probably due to the aroma of fried bacon, eggs, and coffee more than anything else.*

The service was friendly and efficient, but quite business-like. Made sense in a city like San Diego, after all, but a wave of nostalgia for Independence filled her. *I'm going to call Tyler later today and maybe we can talk. Get the gossip.*

Avery checked to see if anyone was watching. Believing no one was, she sat Miss Marple on her lap. A rat was not a welcome guest, trained or not, in restaurants. *Completely incomprehensible with these cute little animals, but it is what it is.*

Cole sat next to her on the bench and noticed. He put his crumpled jacket on his lap so the little helper was hidden better. "Hopefully no one sees," he said. "We don't want her discovered."

Surprised by his thoughtfulness, she thanked him.

"No problem," he said. "As long as she stays away from my breakfast." He laughed a little. She did, too. "Funny. Not funny."

Avery pulled her head in a little. "Can't promise that. Miss Marple's not very amenable to bartering of that sort." She gave the rat a pat on the head and looked at the group. "I'd like all four of us to go to the dead man's apartment."

"Do we know who it is yet?" Big A asked.

"Not yet. But I don't think it will take too long. As soon as we know approximately where he was dumped into the sea, we'll search the area for relevant establishments. There's no reason to believe there was anything different about this victim than the others."

Big A and the others nodded in agreement.

Cole's phone rang. After a brief conversation, he turned to the others. "That was the local police. Apparently there's a young man missing."

The others glanced at each other.

"A hustler?" Avery asked.

"It's not clear yet. His life partner reported him missing."

"A possible suspect?"

Avery shook her head. "I don't want to rule anything out too soon but I don't believe that'd be the case."

"Do you trust your profile that much?" Cole asked.

"Actually, yes," Avery said, indignant. "Unless we find a connection to all the other victims, we can take that into account. But at this point? I think the poor man just has the misfortune of being friends with the dead man."

"If the media had reported it," Cole said, "the chance could be high that we'd be dealing with a copycat offender."

Big A chimed in. "Yes, in that respect, it's beneficial to us to know that the victims are people who are not noticed to be missing, so to speak. Sad, but true."

Avery wiped her mouth and fingers with a napkin before reaching into her pocket and pulling out a few bills. "Breakfast is on me."

"In that case, feel free to call me in early again," Big A said. "Thank you."

Avery waved off the expressions of gratitude from Valentina and the others. She couldn't wait to start the day.

Miss Marple, sensing her impatience, hurried to climb first onto her shoulder and then into her sweater. *At least this little one will never get lost. Love her never-ending energy.*

An hour later, the four of them stopped in front of the nondescript building where the latest victim had lived.

Avery peered out. It wasn't quite as run-down as a few of the other apartments she had seen during the course of the investigation but it was also a poorer, yet reasonably well-maintained, neighborhood.

She reached for her phone and checked her texts. "The victim's life partner is waiting for us at the local police station. After we have a look around here, Cole and I will go and interrogate him." She looked up from her smartphone and nodded toward Big A and Valentina. "You two talk to the neighbors while Cole and I check out the building. Whoever finishes first, come find and join the others. All right?"

The two nodded and got out of the car. "Got it," Valentina said.

Avery checked to make sure her gun was loaded and the safety was on and slipped it into the back of her waistband holster.

Cole did the same.

She looked at him. "Is it just me or does the situation here feel strange?"

He sighed. "I'm glad you said so. I feel the same way. Let's be careful. Okay?"

Avery bit her lip. "As always," she said. *That makes two of us feeling uneasy.* On impulse, she pulled Miss Marple out of her sweater and stowed her in the small box on the back seat. "So, my girl, I need you to wait here. When the coast is clear, I'll come get you." She didn't want to have to be considerate of her companion in case of any scuffle. That would distract her. And distraction could be deadly in her line of work.

No sooner had she finished that thought and gotten Miss Marple to safety than a shot rang out.

"Whoah," Cole said, jumping out of the car.

Avery followed on his heels. He'd already turned the corner in front of her when she heard him swear. *What's going on now? I Hope it's a false alarm.* The thought that one of the team might be hurt filled her with dread.

The next moment, someone ran into her and pushed her aside.

Before her head crashed against the stone wall, she saw dark eyes in the shadow of a hat's brim. The eyes widened as he looked her in the face. She struggled to memorize the details but to no avail.

A cloth covered the lower half of his face. In a feeble attempt to grab it, she pushed herself off the wall with her elbow. The movement turned out to be too much for her and she blacked out.

Cole's heart nearly stopped when he saw Avery slammed head-first into the wall. The man had appeared out of nowhere from a dark corner and pushed him too aside as he ran. Cole lost precious seconds before catching himself and turning to face her.

Unfortunately, it had been too late to warn her.

Her collision with the wall had almost no effect at first, it appeared.

As if spellbound, she stared after the fleeing man.

At the last moment, her legs gave way. Cole caught her before she hit the pavement. Torn between the need to look after her and to pursue the culprit, he remained rooted to the spot. Finally he realized the fugitive was too far away to catch.

"Shoot, shoot, shoot," he cursed as he carefully placed Avery on the ground.

Gently, he felt her pulse. It was beating strongly and regularly. Relieved, he let out the breath he had been holding.

Avery, already regaining consciousness, swatted his hand as though it were an insect. It banged him in the eye, leaving a red mark around the rim.

"Hey, ouch," he said, flinching. "You seem to be alright."

She squinted and blinked as she recovered from the hit.

"How are you feeling?" he asked.

"Like my head's through the wall?"

"That's nothing new for you." He grinned.

She asked, "What happened to your eye?"

"You happened," he said.

Her eyes widened. "Me? I did that? How?" She frowned.

"Don't worry. It's nothing. You just surprised me when you suddenly grabbed my hand."

"Shouldn't have been near my neck. You should know better. And besides? I know better places where it could be used."

"Uh-oh," he said. "You definitely hit your head hard if you're flirting with me like that. I'll call an ambulance."

"No. No ambulance," she fought back, panic in her voice. "Anything but that. I promise to behave myself." They both laughed.

"Wait? The gunshot! Are Big A and Valentia okay?" She tried to sit up, but let out a groan and slumped against the wall.

Cole shook his head. "I'm sorry, but in your condition, you're not going to be able to avoid at least getting checked out by a doctor. I'm calling it in." He dialed dispatch.

When he finished the call, he knelt down beside her. "Can you wait here? You're right. I need to find out how the others are doing."

Avery turned her head away and nodded. Cole wanted to say something else—something a lover or partner would say—but decided otherwise. "See you in a bit."

"Take care," Avery said. She closed her eyes and tried to make sense of the snatches of images swirling around in her head. Had she actually recognized the attacker? Or was it just her vivid imagination combined with the blow to the head? Damn. She didn't have time for a concussion.

The ambulance came through the intersection with blue lights flashing. Behind her, she heard Big A swearing heartily while someone else, probably Valentina, scolded him. Despite the buffalo stampede in her head, she had to smile. Valentina really had a temper. Just the thing to keep someone like Big A in check.

Slowly, so as not to trigger another wave of pain, she turned her head toward her team. Cole and Valentina were supporting a limping Big A. His leg was covered in blood, but that didn't stop him from ranting.

"You know, Big A, when I wished for more blood this morning, I didn't mean for you to get shot," Avery called out.

Big A gave her a scowl, then noticed her sitting against the wall. "You're one to talk. Look at you!"

Despite her headache, Avery shook her head and closed her eyes. "Is it that obvious?"

He grinned. "No, it wasn't. Not until now."

"You're not entirely wrong."

"By the way? If it's any consolation? We all took some pretty big hits here."

Her eyes widened. She pointed to his bleeding leg. "What happened? We heard a shot. And you're still standing?"

Big A grimaced. "I think we should interview the neighbors. Makes sense to start with the ones who live next door. Turns out the neighbors weren't home. The victim's door was open a little. We were just about to enter and announce ourselves when someone shot through the door."

"Bad?" Avery asked.

"Nope. Just a graze. Bleeds like a pig."

Avery could see, however, that his face had taken on an uncharacteristic shade of gray. Sure. No big deal. Just a scratch. *Men.* She patted the ground beside her. "Come. Sit down."

"I'd rather not. Don't know if I'll be able to get back up."

"Makes sense," she said. "We really need to search the apartment. Is forensics on the way?" It bugged her that she couldn't get into the apartment right away. Miss Marple was still waiting in the car, too. The case was picking up speed and she couldn't think straight or move freely.

Big A said, "I think so. Valentina was going to take care of it."

"I'm relieved you've organized everything, Valentina." She closed her eyes again. "You're a great team member."

"Thanks," Valentina said. "But save your strength. You're going to need it."

Meanwhile, Cole waved the ambulance closer. Once it stopped, two paramedics jumped out, retrieved a stretcher from the back, and approached.

The two paramedics set about hoisting Avery onto the stretcher. She would have liked to protest against being transported like a forest full of monkeys but knew it'd be futile, so she kept her mouth shut. Big A limped toward the ambulance and sat on the back bumper.

Cole gave her hand a quick squeeze. "Valentina and I will continue here. Later, I'll stop by the hospital and take you home. If they want to keep you overnight, let me know. I'll bring you some things."

She nodded. "Thank you. Will you take care of Miss Marple? You'll find oatmeal and other seeds for her in the glove compartment."

"Will do," he said. "She'll be in no better hands." He turned to Valentina. "Come on. Let's go because I'm burning to know what's so important in this apartment that someone would start shooting at two FBI officers in broad daylight."

Across the street, well hidden behind two trees, the perpetrator watched as the two officers made their way to the apartment. Two out of four were taken care of. Good, but not good enough. He had no idea how the FBI could have gotten on the scene so quickly. With the others, it had taken weeks for the police to show up. Knowing they had sent the FBI right away could only mean they had made a connection between the victims. He'd have to be even more careful. That didn't pose a problem; he loved challenges. He just hoped he hadn't spoiled everything in his haste.

He knocked the dust off his gloves and stowed them, along with the cloth, in his small backpack. All in all, he'd been lucky. The look from the female officer he'd pushed into the wall haunted him. It was as though she recognized him but that was impossible. *Or was it?* He shook off the strange feeling and cautiously retreated back into the safety of a nearby alley.

CHAPTER NINE

Avery's patience had been sorely tested over the past twenty-four hours. Unlike Big A, who had been sent home with a bandage around his calf and a tube of antiseptic ointment, she had to spend the night in the hospital for monitoring, even though she'd passed all the tests. And all because Cole, the tattletale, had revealed to the paramedics that she had briefly fainted.

"Do you have someone to watch over you? Wake you up every hour and ask you questions?" the young doctor, who looked like he was graduating from high school, had asked.

"Of course," she bluffed. He wordlessly handed her the phone, which was on the table with her other personal belongings. Unfortunately, she hadn't reached Tyler. There was no way she was going to get her boss involved. That left Cole. Whom she also didn't want to call, for reasons she preferred not to think of too closely. Defiantly, she had put the phone back on the table.

"Then everything is settled," the doctor had answered cheerfully and left. The only thing she had to give him credit for was that he hadn't grinned.

At least she had been given medication that reduced her pain to a tolerable throbbing and made her sleepy. Otherwise, there would have been, at best, an unfortunate, untimely demise of the sadistic nurse who had dutifully woken her at regular intervals and asked idiotic questions.

The worst part was not being able to fall back asleep quickly. She'd wished Cole were there. Well, not really but a little bit. Sort of. The feeling of missing someone was quite unfamiliar. She was used to managing her life on her own. No wonder she was in a bad mood when she wasn't clear about her own feelings. She liked to have order in her life. Not the emotional chaos she struggled with.

"Finally!" Avery said, pushing herself off the bench outside the hospital lobby where she waited for Cole. She opened his passenger side door and slumped into the seat. "Well, that took forever. I was beginning to think you guys were going to solve this case without me."

"I wish," Cole grumbled.

Avery narrowed her eyes to slits. "What spoiled your day? Since you didn't get hit in the head or shot in the leg, I hope you have a good reason." She crossed her arms in front of her chest aggressively. After the doctor had confirmed that she was free to go, she had been sitting on pins and needles, eager to finally rejoin the team and tackle the case. With a fresh lead, she was sure she would finally find something that would lead them closer to the culprit.

"You sound like an irritable bear," he said. "Do you know that?"

She spared a reply and continued to scowl at him.

He rolled his eyes and reached into the center console where two mugs of steaming coffee waited. "Here." He handed her one.

Murmuring a thank you, she took it.

"I actually thought you needed a little rest, a break after all the excitement," Cole said, "but I can see you're determined to be right back at it."

She shrugged as if it were a matter of course. "Good, then let's go to the office. The others should already be there."

That was impressive, Avery thought, *how well he knows my different moods and also reacts to them accordingly.* She eyed him from the side. He obviously hadn't shaved. Dark stubble adorned his angular cheeks. For some reason, the fact that he had gone straight to her instead of taking the time to shave appeased her. She put her hand on his arm. "I'm sorry I was so rude."

He smiled. "I'm just glad I got coffee." He looked at her for reassurance.

She boxed him amicably in the thigh. "Have you found out anything yet?"

"Unfortunately, not as much as I had hoped. I'd like to return to the scene of the crime today, if you feel up to it. Maybe Miss Marple will find something we missed."

"Where is she anyway?" she asked.

"Valentina took her to her house. Because they both seem to get along well, I thought it was a good idea."

Avery chewed on her lower lip. "Let me guess. She stole your sandwich again?"

Cole snorted sheepishly, suddenly focused on the traffic. "Sure," he grumbled. "Of course she stole mine. Much to Valentina's amusement."

Convulsively trying not to laugh out loud, she changed the subject. "What have you found out? Geez, do I have to beat it out of you?"

"You'll hear it at the meeting," he defended himself.

"I'd like a quick summary, though. Now."

He said something that sounded suspiciously like "stubborn mule." Avery decided to ignore it. After she'd had her coffee, it was easier to remain composed. *Such a wonderful thing, coffee. Only chocolate is better, or maybe peanut butter.*

Belatedly, she realized that Cole had begun to list the previous day's findings. "Also confirmed he was homosexual, but we already knew that about his partner."

"Did he say anything about whether they were seeing other people as well?" Avery asked. "Or were they a monogamous couple? "

"First he insisted they were soul mates, meant for each other, blah blah. You know how it is—as soon as someone dies, they're given a halo."

"In each case, it makes finding the truth that much more difficult."

"Exactly. After I couldn't get anything else out of him, Big A tried his luck."

Surprised, she looked over at him. "Big A? I would have expected you'd have put Valentina on him."

He shook his head. "Not with this guy. He's got a serious problem with women. She offered him a drink and he looked at her like she was trying to poison him. That's why I let Big A try first. I assumed we could keep Valentina as a secret weapon up our sleeve and use her to scare him to death if needed."

"Okay. All right. Then what?" Avery asked.

"Big A played the new best friend, consoling him after his harsh treatment of the bad cop from earlier, until he tearfully confessed his friend had found a wealthy benefactor."

Avery whistled softly through her teeth. "So, it may be our old familiar killer."

"Exactly. Apparently his friend convinced him they'd be stupid to pass up a chance at easy money. Now, of course, he claims he was heartbroken, but I suspect he wouldn't have been averse to the money it would have brought in."

Disgusted, Avery frowned. "I'll never understand what people get into for money."

Cole shrugged. "Greed is a common motivator."

"Thank you. I know the statistics. I still don't have to understand." She rolled her eyes.

"You're right," he admitted. "I don't understand it, either."

"I'm glad," she said. "Do you know if any money has flowed yet?"

"He says no but we'd be justified to arrange a search of his house. After all, in a murder case, the lover is always the prime suspect."

There was a malicious glint in his eyes. Apparently, the witness had annoyed Cole quite a bit.

"You don't really suspect him, do you?" she asked, just to make sure they were working with the same assumption.

Cole leaned back in his seat and put on his blinker to turn toward the FBI office. "No, not really. Too much circumstantial evidence points to our serial killer for that but then, the judge who has to sign the search warrant doesn't know that."

"That would be good. Maybe Miss Marple will find something that will help us. Even if it's ultimately only to prove the connection between the cases."

After Cole parked the staff car in front of the building, he glanced at Avery. He had been worried about her. Yesterday's exertions had left obvious marks. A graze was emblazoned on her cheek. Her temple glistened a dark blue. Dark shadows lay under her eyes, and her skin showed an uncharacteristic pallor. If he had his way, she would stay home and take it easy. However, he knew exactly what she would think of such a suggestion. So, he didn't say anything. Just took it upon himself to take extra good care of her. If possible, without her noticing. He did not want to incur her wrath.

Alberto paced up and down his spacious office, along the panorama window, which covered the entire width of the room, but his attention was not focused on the hustle and bustle of the port. Nor did he have an eye for the bright blue sky or the dark blue waters of the Pacific. The encounter with the FBI agents was still sitting in his bones. He almost arrived too late. He hoped to have removed all incriminating traces. He couldn't be quite sure after being interrupted in the middle of it. He cursed the speedy work of the FBI. Something else gnawed at him—the look from the female agent he'd collided with.

While he was almost sure there was no way she could have recognized him but "almost sure" was not good enough. He'd stayed awake all night pondering how she could know him. That he didn't remember her also puzzled him. While he never paid much attention to his subordinates, he was pretty sure he would have remembered a woman with such exotic beauty.

Finally, he gave up and interrupted his pacing. Difficult situations required appropriate action. He didn't have connections that reached into the highest circles for nothing. It was time to put them to good use; he was taking an additional risk by doing so but he needed certainty the agent didn't pose a threat.

He reached for the phone.

Without giving his name, he said, "I need information."

After the meeting, which had been rather disappointing, Avery excused herself and slipped outside to the roof terrace for a moment to get some fresh air. Miss Marple, who had been looking forward in her typical rat fashion to being reunited, accompanied her.

While she hid a few bills among the plants arranged lovelessly on the terrace, Avery struggled with herself whether to tell the others about her suspicions. On the one hand, she was very much in favor of sharing any findings with the entire team. On the other hand, she was the outsider here. The outside expert. If she was wrong, her reputation as a profiler would be gone before she even started working as one. And she wanted nothing more than to finally leave the endless undercover investigations behind her.

She crouched down and retrieved Miss Marple from the depths of her sweater. Gently, she placed the rodent on the gravel-covered ground and gave her the command to search. With each correctly indicated find, she clicked her tin frog and brought her a few grains as a reward. Meanwhile, her thoughts turned in circles but she came to no conclusion. A headache raged behind her forehead. If what she thought she'd seen wasn't so frightening, the decision would be easier for her.

Cole watched as Avery patiently worked with Miss Marple. The delicate work between them always impressed him. Suddenly he hesitated to disturb her. She looked so pleased, except for the deep crease on her forehead. He didn't like it. He bet that was likely due to the headache she had after the collision.

Sure, she had a hard head but the accident would have knocked out a small elephant. When she apologized, he was sure she was hiding something. Looking at her now, he wasn't so sure. After all, he didn't know her nearly as well as he would have liked. It was an illusion to believe she was still the same person as she had been when he first met her ten years earlier. They'd drifted apart, except for the occasional encounter. Somehow he had to succeed in changing that but first they had a case to solve.

After Miss Marple located the last hiding place, Avery picked her up, sat the creature on her shoulder, and turned to Cole. She'd noticed him a few minutes earlier. Since he didn't seem to be in a hurry, she quietly finished her practice session with Miss Marple—especially since she had no interest in facing his critique. Knowing him, he'd seen something.

To her surprise, however, he didn't ask her a single question. He just held his hand out to her and said, "Come on, let's go inside. We'll assign the tasks to everyone."

Glad he didn't push her, she gratefully grabbed his hand and allowed herself to be pulled up. "Okay. Thanks. Miss Marple is in top form. If there's anything to find, she'll definitely track it down."

At that moment, her phone rang. It was Tyler. She waved Cole off and mouthed, "Have to take this." He hurried away.

Tyler launched in without so much as a hello or a breath. "Tell me, what kind of trouble are you in? And why am I practically the last to know about your injury? Miss Minnie called me this morning and accused me of sabotaging the bets currently in progress."

"Miss Minnie did what?" Before Tyler could elaborate, Avery continued, "How did she even know? Pretty scary when you're over a thousand miles away from the Diner Sisters and still not immune to their machinations. Besides, I've been trying to call you."

"Yeah, you better remember that. Big sister is watching you. All I can say is that we live in an age of monitoring and instant communication! But don't distract me from the most important issue: what was the point of trying to bust through the wall with your head? Was that an elaborate plan to get Cole to play nurse?"

She glanced cautiously at Cole, who was leaning against the roof railing across from her. He seemed completely enraptured by the puny plants growing on the railing.

"No, I'm afraid not," she said, somewhat belatedly.

"Did he at least visit you?"

"You could say that."

"He's standing right next to you, isn't he? That's why you're being so cryptic."

"Right."

"Let me have it then," Tyler demanded.

With an apologetic shrug, Avery held up the phone. "Cole. It's for you."

He hurried over and grabbed the phone. "Hello?"

"Yes, Cole. I already had a conference call with half of Independence this morning. Our mother, among others."

"Mom called?" he asked.

"What did you think Mr. Wilkinson was going to do when you called to tell him Avery was hurt?"

"I don't know. I just thought he should know." Cole sighed.

Tyler's voice softened. "That was the right thing to do. Only you forgot to mention if *you* were okay or not. All he knew was that you were obviously there. In his worry, he went straight to the diner and poured his heart out to the Diner Sisters. Mom just happened to be there."

"Oh." He pulled his own phone out of his pocket and opened Facebook. Sure enough. Speculation had been flying about what must have been happening in California. He shook his head as he read how the story had unfolded. The beginning was harmless. There, in a standard news tone, it simply read "Avery, in the line of duty as an agent, suffered a run-in with a suspect and sustained a head injury." *So far, so good.* But just three entries down the line, it had turned into a car chase in which she had fallen over a cliff. It stated that nothing was known about Avery's current state of health or his whereabouts. "Oh, great. No wonder Mom freaked out."

"Yeah, right. Mom was so upset that she actually told Dad."

"She what?"

His dad was a professor and engineer and lived in his own little world most of the time. Usually, that was just fine with his mom. That way she could do whatever she wanted on the farm. Only in emergencies would she involve him but then he usually overshot the mark.

"Well, sure. You know how she is when she thinks something happened to one of her kids."

"Yes, I know," he sighed. "An angry mother bear is dirt compared to her, but let's get serious. Let the Independence people mind their own business. Or write a script. *Ready for Hollywood.*"

Avery took the phone from his hand and studied the timeline. As she did so, her eyes grew larger and larger with astonishment.

"Dad is about to call the director of the FBI and give him gruff." Cole sighed.

"Great," Avery said. "Just what we need in the middle of a complicated investigation."

"Then I suggest you call home," he said. "A statement on Facebook wouldn't go amiss either so people can sleep peacefully again."

With a deep sigh, Cole turned back to the phone. "Tyler? I have to run. They're calling." He closed his eyes and rubbed the root of his nose.

"Got it. No problem," she said.

"Appreciate it." He hung up.

"That's crazy," Avery said.

Frustrated, Cole ran his hand through his hair. "I moved away from Independence for these very reasons. I couldn't take it anymore that everyone knew everything about everyone else, what they ate for breakfast yesterday. Who they were sleeping with. Or not. You?"

"Me, too. But being far away apparently doesn't work anymore."

"The wonders of modern communication." Disgusted, he stared at the phone in his hand. "I need to call my mother."

Avery held the phone out and answered her own. The fleeting contact on the back of her hand sent a shiver down her arm, reminding her that her last tryst with this man had been far too long ago. This stupid case. It was about time they solved it.

"I'll let the others know. By the way," she paused at the door, "I made a statement on Facebook that we are both good and well. That should appease the gossipers a bit."

He frowned. "Good, do you think we should post a photo in addition?"

Surprised, she looked at him. "A photograph? Why on earth would you do that?"

"You know how people are. We have conspiracy theorists, too."

"Fine," she said. "I'm not entirely convinced it's necessary, but whatever needs to happen."

Avery stood next to him and let him take a picture of the two of them.

He held it out for her to examine.

She grimaced. "I hope my grandfather doesn't get a stroke when he sees the scrape and the bump."

"He'll be glad you're alive and well," he said, uploading the picture.

Shaking her head, she left him on the roof terrace and went to join the others.

Cole looked after her as she disappeared into the building. Frustrated, he let his eyes wander over the surrounding skyscrapers and took a deep breath. He hated drama. Especially drama that revolved around his person. He was a social person but such perpetual gossip was driving him crazy. He didn't know why people couldn't just mind their own business and let him do his job. He really wanted to close the case as soon as possible.

His plan to convince Avery that a real relationship between them would be a good idea was completely stymied as long as they worked together. That's how well he knew her. And the rules of the FBI manual, which were probably roughly congruent with the DEA's rules of conduct, stated the same.

He opened his phone to call his mother. The photo of Avery and himself appeared on the screen and made him smile. Despite her bruises, she radiated an irrepressible charisma. When he had seen her fall to the ground the previous day, his heart had almost stopped. Losing her when he had just realized how lucky he was to have her in his life, even if only marginally, would kill him.

With a newfound determination, he thought rules were there to be broken. Especially in their line of work, every day could literally be the last.

CHAPTER TEN

On her way home, Avery stopped at the supermarket to get something to eat and buy some household items.

As she got out of her car, she felt a tingle on the back of her neck. Alarmed, she looked around. A black sedan was parked behind her.

A man sat inside. The windows were darkly tinted; she couldn't see his face very well. She was sure he was staring at her. Involuntarily, she grabbed the back waistband of her pants and made sure she had her pistol handy.

The man didn't take his eyes off her, nor did she take her eyes off him as she walked past the car toward the mall.

When she came out half an hour later, there was no sign of the man or the car. *Not sure if this is good or bad.* She bit her lower lip. Of course she was glad that he was gone. On the other hand, she liked to keep an eye on her enemies.

She was reluctant to inadvertently lead him to her home. *Sometimes I wish I had chosen a service dog instead of Miss Marple.*

Avery stowed the bags in the trunk, got in carefully, locked the doors, and drove home.

She looked in the rearview mirror but didn't spot anyone following. Fortunately. She still felt uneasy. *Should I call Cole?*

As soon as she finished the thought, she called herself out. *What's wrong with me? I've gotten along just fine with-*

out him for the last ten years. So why this urge to call him at every moment? Not like he's ever been within reach. "It's just that his butt is so scrumptious," she said. *Great. Now my subconscious is negotiating with my libido.*

Once inside, she left the bags in the kitchen on the sideboard, fed Miss Marple, put her in her spacious cage, and got in the shower. Surely she would feel better afterward. She ignored the voice that whispered a serving of Cole would surely make her feel *much better.*

Cole pulled into Avery's garage driveway and turned off the car. He didn't get out right away, but remained seated, considering for the umpteenth time whether he'd better turn back, because he had no idea whether she felt even remotely the same. That she still desired him, he did not question. He knew her well enough to correctly interpret the sudden sharp intake of breath at random touches during the day. Or how she sometimes got red earlobes when he made a remark that could be taken two ways. He tried to pull himself together but it was just too tempting to watch her get embarrassed. And how she would catch herself and lash out in retaliation on the spot.

While he was still having this internal debate, the front door opened and Avery stepped out. She was barefoot. Her hair shone blue-black in the glow of the light mounted next to the door. She had changed her jeans for yoga pants and her blouse for a loose-fitting tee-shirt. She looked young and beautiful. Just like she did ten years ago.

He got out and stopped next to the car, suddenly not sure if she even wanted him here. For a few seconds they stared at each other. Their eyes seemed huge in the darkness. There were a thousand reasons why he had better leave. *But I need to be near her, to touch her and be touched by her.* It was stronger than any reason.

When she took a step back to invite him into her home, he was relieved to take a breath. Slowly, he strode up the stairs to give her time to reconsider. Even though, of course, he hoped she wouldn't.

"Hey," he murmured, reaching for her hand. Their fingers intertwined.

"Hello," she said, snuggling against his chest as if she belonged there. He kissed her neck. She smelled of sage and oranges. Ever since he knew her, he associated those smells with her. Just holding her felt right. Her body fit him perfectly. She was the right size and had the right curves in all the right places. It was like they were custom made for each other.

When she was around, he desired her. That had started ten years ago, and it hadn't changed since then.

He lifted his head and moved back a little to see her better. Then he kissed her.

She met him halfway. The entire day, she'd found it increasingly difficult to ignore him, to see him only as a work colleague. The previous day's events had shaken her more than she wanted to admit. Was it really so important to keep her distance? She'd been lucky yesterday. The headache was almost gone, but how easily things could have taken a different outcome.

The desire to be with him, to be really together, not just working together, to see him, to touch him, to taste him, to convince herself daily that they were both still breathing, living, and loving one another. *Where did these strong feelings come from?*

His teeth nibbling demandingly on her lower lip, followed by the softer touch of his tongue, drove the muddled thoughts away.

Later, as she lay in his arms, her head resting on his muscular shoulder, listening to his deep breaths while he was already asleep, it occurred to her she hadn't shared her suspicions. Nor to the others. She wasn't sure she should.

The investigation revealed the body had been thrown overboard at sea. The incoming tide washed it into the harbor. So they were looking for someone who was in possession of, or who had access to, a boat. Which, in turn, fit her suspicions when she thought about the yacht she had seen yesterday. *Was that really just yesterday?*

She had looked it up. The *Magdalena was* indeed owned by All Saints Corporation, one of the many companies in the Monsanto family's vast corporate conglomerate. That was not information in the public domain. Thanks to her undercover work, she knew more about the family and its sprawling business operations than most. Of course, a body could be hauled away in a small boat with an outboard motor. Theoretically. Her intuition told her otherwise. The whole series of murders bore the signature of the Monsanto family.

A rustle made her smile. Miss Marple bustled up and down in her closet, which had been converted into a cage. Although her work often kept her awake during the day, she still reserved a few hours each night to recharge.

Often, the inside of Miss Marple's area looked very different in the morning than it had just a few hours earlier.

Avery slipped out of bed and stepped up to the cage. "Hey, little one. Fancy a midnight snack?"

Miss Marple came to the bars and stood on her hind legs. Avery stroked her furry belly. "You were great today," she said. The rat had found cash and traces of drugs.

She was pretty sure the dead guy's partner would be flipping out because he hadn't found the money before they did. Unfortunately, he'd been stuck at the police station at the time Avery and Big A were attacked. Too bad. He would have made an excellent suspect. Unfortunately, it was never so simple.

She reached for a bag of dried cranberries and fed some to Miss Marple. "If only you could just lead us to the culprit," she said. She packed the dried fruit away, stroked her friend's pink ear with her fingertip, and slipped back into bed with Cole, who wasn't supposed to be there.

Her lips twisted into a crooked smile and she fell asleep.

Two days later, she stood in the harbor staring at the *Magdalena.* She was sure she correctly recognized the attacker outside the apartment of the last dead man. Only she had no idea what it all meant. The Monsanto family was really dirty. She knew that, and it was nothing new. However, they specialized in big-ticket things, such as drugs, trafficking women, and art. None of it provable but also nothing to suggest that anyone in the family was moonlighting as a serial killer.

The reminder that Cole was the reason she couldn't get any more inside information angered her. It wasn't really Cole's fault. More like the FBI's, she knew. These days, it took little for her to get annoyed when his name came up. Or her seeing him. Their night together should have cleared the air between them. Instead, she missed him more than ever. Ridiculous, since she saw him every day at work. Apparently, he'd had enough of her complaining after yesterday and had scheduled her with Big A today. He was currently at the Port Authority interviewing employees. She had promised to follow right up, but she wanted to take another look at the *Magdalena* first. Not that it would do any good. The chance of getting a search warrant was about minus ten.

While she was sure that the key to the murders was to be found on the boat, she was still not clear how the bloody crimes fit in with the Mafia clan. The Monsanto family was known for their cold-bloodedness and ruthlessness, not crimes of passion. She turned the thought back and forth a few times.

If she was honest, she couldn't imagine Tony in the role of butcher. He was somehow too...*soft* for that. And

Alberto? She had to laugh. He didn't even know how to spell the word passion. On the other hand, family honor was above everything for him.

She chewed her lower lip as she tried to get a grip on the theories. *Not sure this is a train of thought I should dive too deeply into.*

Avery gave it up. She knew she'd find no more answers.

She turned to leave as a man appeared on the deck.

Tony's driver.

Shoot.

She couldn't let him see her. Sure, she looked completely different from the last time he'd seen her, but she wasn't going to take any chances.

She ducked her head.

Too late.

He spotted her. "Hey, you there. What are you doing here?"

She didn't wait to hear what else he had to say, and took off.

The soles of her biker boots slapped the asphalt. She cursed her preference for the heavy boots and wished she'd opted for her jogging shoes.

At the end of the pier, she glanced back.

The man seemed to have disappeared.

She slowed her steps a bit to avoid three seagulls fighting over a piece of bread. Concerned for Miss Marple, she reached under her jacket to check that the little girl was still safely tucked away in the inside pocket. She felt her and sighed, relieved. *Poor thing. What your owner puts you through.*

Everything was all right. Relieved, she pulled her hand out again.

She passed the flat, gray Port Authority building just as Big A came out. Without comment, she walked past him toward the parking lot. He looked a little puzzled, but then followed her and got into the car without comment.

It wasn't until they made it two blocks away that he asked, "Are you going to explain to me what that was all about?"

"A Monsanto family employee caught me staring at the yacht," Avery said.

"So what?" Big A asked. "Maybe you're just a fan of beautiful boats?"

"It was a co-worker who knew me very well in my *Maria* time."

"Shoot."

"Exactly. That's why I ran away before he had time to take a closer look at me. That might make him more suspicious. Did you find out anything?" She changed the subject.

"According to the entry at the harbor master's office, the *Magdalena* did indeed sail on the evening in question," Big A said.

"Crap." She gave him a sideways glance. "I don't suppose you took a picture of said entry?"

"I took a statement from the employee." He held up his cell phone.

"Good, that's better than nothing," Avery said. "But it won't do us any good in terms of a search warrant."

"Why not?"

"Because you can be sure that the entry will be gone within the next half hour."

"But I have the recording right here!"

"Oh, come on. Don't pretend to be stupid now. You know how it works. The employee just made a mistake, everyone is terribly sorry, blah, blah, blah."

He ran his hand over his face. "Right." He grinned. "I just don't want to believe it."

Avery nodded. "I can appreciate that. Frustrating, this case."

Tony felt the fever gripping him again. He had a date with his latest flame later in the evening. He couldn't wait. Unfortunately, first he had to go to one of those darn concerts his brother sponsored but after that, he was free. He straightened his tie. The bag at his feet contained everything he'd need afterward. If his brother only knew, he would have liked to throw it in his face but he knew that would not end well. Certain things in life were better kept to oneself.

Speaking of the devil? His brother stood in the doorway and scowled. Nothing new. He wondered why it still made him nervous.

"What is it now?" he asked, emphatically bored.

If it was even possible, Alberto's gaze darkened more. His eyes bored into his. "Maria, the little girl you had to bring on...she works for the DEA."

"Are you sure? What could she do? I thought child labor was illegal?" He was honestly confused.

"She's twenty-eight," his brother said.

"How do you know all this?"

"You don't need to know that but if you want to check, check the inmate list at the juvenile detention center. Here's the list." Roughly, he pressed the papers into his hand. "The other piece of paper has her current address on it. Take care of that problem."

Alberto left the room.

What? Maria a DEA agent? My little sweet Maria? But...how could that be? I picked her up off the street myself. Gave her a home. And it was all just a charade? Anger rose. At himself. Especially with the girl—no—the woman— who'd made such a fool of him. *Everything makes sense. She was so insistent on her independence. Constantly came and went as she pleased. I should take care of the problem, Alberto said. By God, I will. She will pay me back for her lies.* The thought made him slightly nauseous but he had other plans for the night. Time to put them into action.

"And you're really sure you recognized Tony as the attacker?" asked Cole for the third time.

Avery rolled her eyes. "Yeah, that's what I'm saying. As sure as I can be. In case you didn't notice, I had just smacked my head pretty good right before."

"Exactly," Cole said. He glanced at Big A, who just shrugged.

"Don't look at me. I didn't get a good look at that punk," Big A said. "I was bleeding like a stuck pig when he came storming out the door."

"And you, Valentina?" Cole asked.

Valentina shook her head. "Honestly, I was paying more attention to Big A than to the perpetrator."

Cole huffed. *That's exactly why agents who worked together were better off just being colleagues. Anything else simply interferes with the work.* He ignored the guilt that rose in him at such a train of thought.

"You don't have to look like that. He'd just been shot, after all," Avery said, noticing his expression.

Cole said, "Nah. Wasn't thinking about that. Was wondering if you're just fixated on the Monsantos?"

"If you think so, I might as well go home," she said. "Whether you believe me or not is up to you but to question my professionalism, that's not okay."

He winced. "Sorry. It's just, I don't see it. Why would any of them suddenly focus on murder? There's no money in it. Why target homosexuals. Is one of them gay?"

Avery sighed. "Right. I came to those conclusions, too. Honestly, my profiler brain hasn't come up with a viable explanation yet either. In my opinion, they're both straight but who knows for sure." She frowned. "Besides, I was under the impression that Tony couldn't stand the sight of blood."

"And there's a lot of blood in that kind of killing." Valentina's voice sounded more fascinated than repulsed.

"What about Alberto?" Big A asked.

"Alberto?" Avery shook his head. "I can't imagine that. Killing someone in cold blood because they're a nuisance, yes. Murders of passion, no."

"We don't know if they were planned or not," Valentina said.

"Well, I think so," Avery said. "Despite the great emotion evidenced by the chosen method of killing, it does seem to me that there was some very precise planning behind it. Otherwise, we would have had a lead by now."

"However, you have to consider that in addition to the family members, the whole crew has access to the boat," Cole indicated.

Avery stood up and dropped her files on the table. "You know what? I'm going to go back and interview the dead guy's lover. What was his name?" She looked around.

"Travis Bolt," Big A said.

"Oh, yeah. That's right. Travis Bolt. Maybe he'll come up with something else to confirm my theory about the Monsantos." She glanced at her watch. "We can call it a night for all I care. I'll just do this on the way home."

Cole stood up. "I'll go with you. You two can go ahead and take off. I'm sure we'll all be fresher after the weekend."

After everyone packed up their things, they headed to their cars.

Big A and Valentina watched the two drive away.

Finally, Valentina broke the silence and asked, "Are you going home now?"

Her partner hesitated. "Actually, I'd like to pay a visit to the Monsanto family. See what's going on there."

"Understand. The prospect of doing something more exciting than questioning witnesses sounds great," she said. "Let's get some coffee. And cinnamon buns. Observing always makes me hungry." She turned on her heel and headed back to the office building.

Big A grinned. *This girl is seriously fine. And sexy, but I better not think about that too much if I want to survive the next few hours in close proximity to her in the car.*

As they were walking, he glanced at her from the side. "You're not exactly squeamish."

She gave him an irritated look. "Squeamish? If I was, I probably wouldn't have survived the training with all the harassment from my colleagues."

"I didn't mean it that way," he said. "I just noticed that you don't mind blood, dead bodies, and so on. On the contrary."

She shrugged. "It's always been that way. I used to bring all the dead animals from the road into my living room, too." She rolled her eyes. "I'm sure you can imagine how that went over with my mother."

He laughed softly. Their eyes met and he swore he felt a connection, especially as she quickly averted her eyes.

"Fortunately, I carry a good amount of empathy in addition to my morbid fascination," she said, slipping right back into career speech. "Which is why I chose the FBI."

"I've never heard such an explanation for a career choice."

She winked. "I'm anything but normal. And that's a good thing."

"That's definitely good. More than just good, actually," he said.

Valentina nodded. "What were your motives for signing up?"

She sounded genuinely interested. For a moment, Big A was tempted to tell her all the reasons but decided to go for the public-spirited option. Even though he felt he could trust her, he had only known her for a few weeks. "Well, the usual stuff. What boy doesn't dream of being a sheriff? Guns, car chases, and playing the hero. What more could a man ask for?"

He wasn't ready to share the deeper reasons with her. He'd keep his secrets for a little while longer.

Frustrated, Avery pressed the doorbell again.

"Come on," Cole finally said. "He's obviously not here. Let's go home. Monday's another day."

Avery kicked the closed door. She hoped Travis would tell them something confirming her Monsanto theory. Apparently, she had taken Cole's criticism to heart.

"Tomorrow at ten?" Cole asked.

"Tomorrow is Saturday. What's tomorrow at ten already?"

"Don't you remember? We're meeting Tyler and Pat at the beach. It'll do you good, a few hours by the water."

She was about to object when she realized that the prospect of spending a day outdoors without worrying about the case sounded great. "At ten you said?"

"Exactly. Just bring yourself, a bath towel, and a windproof jacket. This time of year the wind is pretty fierce by the sea."

"Will do. Do you want me to bring anything to eat?"

"Tyler and Pat are already doing that, dessert maybe?"

"Okay. Then I'll bring apples and caramel sauce."

"Sounds delicious. Bring enough for everyone. I'll bet that'll be popular."

Avery laughed. "All right. I know what I have to do tonight."

"You make them yourself?" asked Cole.

Avery nodded. "I told you that already."

Cole looked to the side. "Apparently, I forgot."

"I'm not very good at cooking. There are only a few isolated recipes that I have a handle on. Nothing great." She smiled. "One of them involves a knife, a fresh apple, and a can of peanut butter."

"*AAH*, the good old days. I lived on that for quite a while, too."

To avoid alerting the entire neighborhood to their presence, they had parked their cars one street over. As they walked slowly side by side, Cole gave Avery a sideways glance. *Is he going to ask me if I want to spend the evening together? Or if not, kiss me goodbye?*

Questions upon questions she didn't really have the answers to. Better she kept her distance. *After the case is closed, we'll have plenty of time to talk. We can revisit the discussion from ten years ago.* These occasional meetings, spread out over the year, were simply no longer enough.

Arriving at her car, Avery hurried to push the automatic door opener and slip behind the wheel. "See you tomorrow," she said.

Cole was sure she was feeling as awkward as he was. He nodded. "I'll pick you up. See you then."

Relieved, she watched him walk to his own car, still raising his hand in greeting as he did. She loved this man.

She had known that for ten years but unfortunately, she still didn't know how to reconcile their two lives. She sighed. Those were worries for another day. It was time to order pizza and watch the latest episode of *How To Get Away with Murder with Miss Marple*. And a day at the beach with friends was a nice prospect, too. Even in November. They were in California, after all.

CHAPTER ELEVEN

THE NEXT MORNING brought bright sunshine to Avery's bedroom. She still hadn't gotten around to buying curtains for her little house. *Interior decorating was never my strong suit.* She squinted against the bright light and turned in bed to feel for her alarm clock. It was only a quarter to eight. She moved her head back and forth. *No pain. No throbbing. Should have plenty of time for a good run this morning.*

Maybe that was a little ambitious, having only been two days after colliding with a wall and being in the hospital.

She stretched in bed. *I don't want to get up.* She pressed her nose into the pillow and caught a whiff of Cole's scent. The same aftershave he'd been wearing for years, mixed with the smell of leather and Cole.

Damn. Maybe I should clean instead of going jogging. Now that I can smell it, I think I need to. I'm not going to be able to go back to sleep, anyway.

She flipped back the covers and stumbled barefoot to Miss Marple's cage.

Avery couldn't spot her anywhere. *She's probably still asleep in one of her hiding places.* Since all the toys were again in a different place than yesterday, she assumed Miss Marple had a busy night. Avery chuckled. "My rat obviously has a greater talent for home improvement than I do. Miss Marple would have changed the curtains three times by now if she had any."

Carefully, she draped an old, dark-stained bed sheet over the converted closet to maintain the illusion of night a little longer.

In the kitchen, she put two bagel halves in the toaster and turned on her coffee maker. From the refrigerator she got orange juice and cream cheese. During the week, there was usually not enough time to eat a proper breakfast so she often limited herself to a coffee to go. She enjoyed the weekends even more when she was able to comfortably eat something and read the newspaper.

One bagel, one microwaved cinnamon bun, and two cups of coffee later, she looked at her watch. *OOPS*. If she actually wanted to clean up a little more, she had to hurry.

As she whizzed through the living room and kitchen with the vacuum cleaner, she noticed a car outside, driving slowly through the street. It was an inconspicuous gray sedan. At first she thought nothing of it.

It wasn't until she went up to the second floor to take a shower and saw the car again from the bathroom window that she snapped.

Taking two steps at a time, she sprinted downstairs. She grabbed her service weapon, which was on the kitchen table, and headed for the door.

She peered out the window.

Yes. Here it is again. Apparently, the car always goes around the block once. Only, what exactly are they watching? Gun firmly in her right hand, she opened the door with her left and pushed it open. *Crap. Now they're gone again.*

Patiently, she waited to see if the car would show up again.

Indeed, it did.

After barely a minute, it turned the corner in front of her place. *How dare they come to my neighborhood.*

Angrily, she stepped outside, fully intending to stop the car and confront the occupants or even take them to the nearest police station.

She realized she had left her phone inside. Pajamas were not suitable for police work, either.

The car came closer and slowed down. *Very good. That will make my job easier.* Determined, she walked toward the vehicle, her pistol firm in her right hand.

A window was lowered. She frowned.

She hadn't expected this much cooperation.

More like he was going to step on the gas and drive away, she thought.

To her horror she recognized the barrel of a gun.

She just managed to throw herself to the side as the first shots whistled overhead.

She ducked.

At the same time, she was aware of how futile the maneuver was.

Tires screeched. More shots rang out from a pistol.

One engine accelerated, then a second.

A second car? Who?

Carefully, she pushed off the grass and looked at the two vehicles. The one in back was Cole's car.

What's he doing here?

Then she remembered he was going to pick her up for their beach excursion.

She bent down to pick up one of the bullets stuck in the grass with the hem of her tee-shirt. She sighed. *So much for my leisurely Saturday. Better hurry and put some clothes on. Before long, the place will be swarming with detectives.*

Three hours later, the scare was over. Forensics had been through. Cole and she had made a statement to the local police. The computer department had checked the license plates. Sure enough, they were reported stolen.

Avery called Tyler and asked if they could speak that afternoon. The reason she gave centered around something about file studies. She didn't feel like having Independence's social media channels explode with wild stories again.

She turned around. Cole stood in her kitchen doorway, hands braced on the doorframe. The sun bathed his cropped, dark brown hair in golden light. His blue eyes were in shadow. Still, she could see the worried expression in them. "Are you okay?" he asked.

Avery smiled. "Sure. Yes. Just a workday like any other." She studied his face, so familiar to her, and frowned. "And what about you?"

He averted his eyes and ran his hand over his face. "Not really. When I realized you were about to be shot at, my heart almost stopped. I'm still rattled."

She froze. *Please don't. Please, please don't.* She was just starting to get used to him again. She couldn't endure another discussion about how being an agent was not for women. Tense, she waited for him to continue.

Thankfully, he changed the subject. "Do you have any idea what that was about?"

"Not sure," she said. "What happened with your pursuit?"

"Unfortunately, I lost the other car after a short chase. A group of children got in the way and I had to brake hard. We've got nothing but the model of the car and the license plates. Both seem to be a dead end."

Avery shrugged. Frustrated, she threw her hands in the air so that Miss Marple, who had just been sitting on her shoulder, hurriedly hid in the neck opening of her sweater. Only her little head with its black beady eyes peeked out. She did not like strong emotional outbursts at all. "What do I know? I'm afraid they didn't leave me a business card. Maybe someone who has an old score to settle?"

"Like the Monsanto brothers?" he asked.

"Believe me," she said. "If Alberto wants me dead, I'm dead. Since about the day before yesterday."

Cole conceded. "That's right. You're right again."

"Come on, let's go see our friends. After all, it's the weekend. Monday is still early enough for us to deal with the whole disaster."

"If we're still alive by then. Or rather, you are, considering the fact that those guys definitely had it in for you today," he said.

Avery chose to ignore his last comment. He wasn't entirely wrong, after all.

"Hey, what are you guys doing here?" Tyler stood outside her rented townhome in Carlsbad, a small town just north of San Diego, and only barely managed to spread her arms to catch Leslie, who literally flew toward her. "I'm glad to see you too, little one!" she laughed, hugging the girl. "But won't it be a while before school is out? I wasn't expecting you until just before Christmas."

Paula, who was a lot slower getting from the car to the front door, answered her question, "I took her out of school for two weeks. We've both had colds for ages. So I thought a staycation in sunny California would be just the thing for both of us now, before the big snow comes. Plus, we were eager to celebrate Christmas with family."

Paula was aware that she talked too much. This became clear when her sister Tyler raised an eyebrow in surprise and questioned her unusual communicativeness.

Leslie leaned over to Tyler and audibly whispered, "Nate and her had a fight. Now we've left until he calms down and thinks like a rational human being." She bit her lip. "Or until Paula's back to normal, Nate says," she added.

"Leslie! That's not helpful at all right now," Paula said.

"On the contrary, I find it very helpful," Tyler said. Most of all, she thought it was wonderful that, despite the situation, the girl didn't seem to care at all and seemed primarily to be enjoying her unexpected trip. That spoke highly of her confidence that she had her place with Paula, no matter what happened with Nate. "Thanks to Leslie, I have all the info right now. Otherwise, I would have had to painstakingly elicit it from you over the next few days. But tell me, how come none of this is on social media yet?"

Paula lit up. "Ha. Even the Diner Sisters don't have snitches on my farm. And since that was the place where he acted like a jerk, no one knows about it either."

"Kudos. No one else can do that."

Paula grinned. "I know. My brother moved a few states away specifically to get away from the rumor mill. And still, we in the mountains know about everything that's going on with him."

"Cole and Avery were supposed to be here any minute," Tyler said. "They were already going to be here for brunch, but something came up."

"On a Saturday?"

Tyler shrugged. "She was pretty distracted on the phone. She was mumbling something about studying files."

"Is this the new term for looking at your stamp collection together?" Paula laughed. "That's really strange."

"That's quite possible. Those two have never been able to let go of each other. I still don't understand why they broke up back then."

Leslie, while happy to see Paula again, didn't appear particularly interested in the background. "Can we go to the beach?" she asked, bouncing up and down on the spot. "Because I've never been to the ocean."

"Sure. Should we take Ranger, too?"

"Oh, yes, absolutely! I've been missing that pooch anyway. Should I go get him?" Without waiting for an answer, she jumped up the three steps and disappeared inside the house.

"Poor kid. She never gets a chance to pet an animal," Tyler said, trying not to grin.

Paula smirked. "A serious case of fur deprivation. You should have seen her the last three days. A road trip isn't really her thing. She finds everything totally exciting, but she'd prefer to stop and get out every thirty minutes and look around. And when we do stop and get off, it's not two seconds before she finds an alley cat or stumbles across a neglected dog."

Tyler stretched her neck and glanced in the direction of Paula's pickup. "How many fur babies did you bring?"

Guiltily, Paula ducked her head. "Um, two?"

Tyler said nothing. She didn't have to. The knowing smile that curled her lips was telling enough. "And what, may I ask?"

Paula turned without a word, walked to her pickup truck and pulled out a cardboard box from the back seat. Carefully, she carried it over and let her sister look inside. There, on an old blanket, were two little kittens. One dark tabby with a white tail and one red tabby with a white belly.

"Wow. Are they cute!" Carefully, Tyler stroked the darker one with her fingertips. In response, the kitten yawned and spread his claws, then blissfully went back to sleep. "Surely they can't be more than a few weeks old!"

"The vet we tracked down along the way said they were about four weeks old."

"That is…"

"Yes. Leslie feeds them cat milk substitute every few hours."

Full of affection, Tyler took her big sister in her arms sideways and gave her a hug. "This only happens to you. No sooner are you out of the house than your family expands by two members."

"I thought I'd take them to Kat so they could find a good home."

Tyler burst out laughing. "You don't believe that. After spending two weeks in close quarters with those two heartbreakers?"

Paula couldn't hold back a grin either. "Probably not. Oh well, what the heck. A ranch can always use a few more barn cats."

Tyler refrained from saying the two tiny ones would probably rather sleep in Paula's or Leslie's bed than join the barn cats. Her sister would notice soon enough.

At that moment, Leslie rumbled down the stairs behind Ranger. "Shall we go?"

"Yes, we're going. I just have to get the cooler bag from the kitchen. We can leave the car here. It's only three hundred yards to the beach."

"Can I leave the kittens at your house? It gets too hot in the car. You actually have summer temperatures here compared to Colorado." She pointed to her tee-shirt. "November and I'm running around in a tee-shirt."

"Well, welcome to California," Tyler said. "Do the two new additions actually have names yet?"

"Yup," Leslie said. "Jill and Jack."

"Well then, Jill and Jack, come on into the living room."

She held the door open for Paula to walk through with the box.

A short time later, they were on their way to the beach. Pat had also joined them. Leslie and Ranger ran ahead. The old shepherd was clearly happy to see his young friend again and did not leave her side.

Arriving at the shore, Leslie stared transfixed at the Pacific Ocean. The wind blew strong enough that the waves carried endless whitecaps. Only the upper part of the beach was sand. At the water's edge, a wide variety of stones of all colors and sizes made up the landscape. They hurried down to the water's edge.

Every time a wave washed over the shore and retreated back into the sea, the water made the stones rattle. "That sounds like music," Leslie said. She put her hand in the water. "Hey, that's warm. Or at least not as cold as I would have expected this time of year." She licked the water off her fingers. "And salty," she noted in amazement.

"You knew that, didn't you?"

"I did. But I couldn't imagine it."

Paula crouched down next to Leslie and also tasted the seawater. The same amazement that lit up Leslie's face spread across her own face.

At that moment, a larger wave rolled in and splashed them both wet.

Shrieking and laughing, they jumped back. Ranger, who saw it all as a big game, jumped around them barking joyfully.

"The water is warm, the air is warm, we're on vacation. Can I get in the water?" Leslie asked.

Paula laughed when she saw Leslie's hopeful look. "Can you even swim?" She actually didn't know.

"Sure," Leslie said.

"For now, just roll up your pant legs and bathe your feet. We don't have a bathing suit with us."

"She can borrow one of mine," offered Tyler, who had joined them.

Paula looked down at her smaller and very petite sister. Her swimsuit might actually fit Leslie. "Fine with me."

"Yay!" Leslie said. "Can I have the house key? I'll go back and get it."

Tyler held it out to her. "You'll find the swimming stuff in the closet in the bathroom. You should find towels there, too. Take Ranger with you. And don't forget to watch the street lights. This isn't Independence."

Leslie rolled her eyes and grabbed the key. "Come on, Ranger. Let's go." The dog didn't need to be told twice.

The adults looked after her. "She was going crazy," Tyler said.

"Yeah. She was," Paula said, a happy glow on her face.

"Are you going to tell me what's going on with you and Nate?" she asked.

Sisters. A memory like an elephant. Paula didn't want to talk about it now. Fortunately, at that moment, Cole and Avery appeared on the cliff leading to the beach and waved.

Tyler waved back, and the two started moving to join them. "Just don't think you can get around the conversation, big sister. Postponed is not abandoned."

Paula was tempted to do the same as Leslie had done, rolling her eyes. As if she didn't know Tyler wouldn't forget; but later was better than now. She just didn't feel like talking about her stubborn "friend" at all.

Later, as Avery lay with her head on Cole's belly, watching the pelicans migrate across the sky, she decided the day had definitely ramped up. Her belly was full of pork ribs, potato salad, and Paula's chocolate mousse, which she had whipped up sometime during the afternoon at Tyler's house.

She felt delightfully relaxed. Perhaps that had something to do with Cole playing with her hair. Still, she couldn't quite shake the nagging worry about who might have been behind the shooting that morning. The fact that there was a killer out there added to her anxiety.

Cole sat up. "What's wrong?"

She blinked at him, "Why do you think something's wrong?"

"A minute ago you were relaxed. Now you're not." Before Avery could digest the fact that he knew her so well, he continued, "Are you still thinking about the shooting?"

She shrugged. "Worried is the wrong word. Angry is. And I am. Heavens, I live in a quiet residential neighborhood. There could have been kids on the street. If someone's going to kill me, they'd better find a better place to do it."

Cole smirked. "Maybe you should put a sign in the backyard."

"That's not a bad idea," she said.

"Who knows what that roommate Travis will tell us Monday," he said.

"That's right. We'll visit him again and hopefully he'll be home this time," she said.

"Yeah," he said. "We could use a breakthrough."

"You said it."

Avery jumped up and pulled Cole up with her. "Come on. Let's go play Frisbee with the kid and dog. We can brood about work later."

CHAPTER TWELVE

"Did you take care of the problem?" Alberto asked.

Tony closed his eyes. *Not again. Couldn't his brother finally mind his own business?* Without letting his anger show, he turned to Alberto. "Of course. Want a drink?"

"Then why don't I know about it yet?" asked Alberto, ignoring the question.

"I don't know. Maybe your sources aren't what they used to be?" Before his brother could explode, which was imminent if he interpreted the stony expression correctly, he said, "After all, it's the weekend. Sunday, to be exact."

Alberto just glared at him.

"Anything else?" Tony asked.

Alberto gave him a nasty look and disappeared without a word.

"You have a good night too, bro," Tony said sarcastically, toasting the spot where his brother had been standing. "Jerk." He drained his drink in one go and slammed the glass down on the tabletop. He desperately needed a distraction.

Unfortunately, his brother's nagging voice did not disappear with him when he left, but remained in his head. He picked up his phone. Dialed. "Did you get the job done?" he barked.

The man on the other end of the line hesitated. "Just about."

Icy fear of his brother's wrath filled Tony. "What do you mean 'just about'? Either the rat is dead or she's not." He winced. He still couldn't really believe that his little friend was an agent. He still thought of her with affection, but his brother's word was law in such matters. It was regretful, but there was nothing he could do.

"We'll take care of it. Tomorrow."

"You better," he growled into the phone and hung up.

He reached for his coat, made from the finest Italian wool, of course, and left the room.

More than ever, he needed distraction.

That idiot. Shortly before midnight, Alberto stood in a dark corner of the bar where he had followed his brother. Shuddering, he looked around. It pained him to see his brother like this. Didn't he know what he was risking? Disappointment and bitterness sprouted in his heart and wound its way through his entire body until his thoughts grew darker and darker. He could feel disgust spreading through him. If he interpreted the situation correctly, he would soon have to clean up after him again. He had more important things to do. The business was running smoothly and demanded his full attention. The fact that he had escaped the clutches of the feds for so long was no coincidence but no, instead he had to deal with family problems. *Nothing I can do today. Tomorrow, then.*

Disgusted, he turned his back on the goings-on and disappeared into the night.

Monday morning, Avery and Cole were at Travis Bolt's door shortly before eight. For once, it was raining. The cloudy, gray sky didn't help lift Avery's spirits. Impatiently, she pressed the doorbell for the second time.

"I hope he's at least here if we're going to bother showing up this early in the morning," she said ungraciously. She was many things. A morning person, however, she was not.

Footsteps could be heard behind the door. It opened a crack and Travis's face emerged. His eyes were bloodshot. He looked at them in confusion.

Is he suffering some bad grief? Avery wondered. Then his alcohol-soaked breath hit her. More like a hangover. Had he turned to alcohol to forget or to celebrate? She wasn't sure. "Had a long night?"

Travis nodded, not yet fully awake.

"May we come in?" Cole asked in a friendly but firm manner.

Without an answer, he opened the door and let them in. Still silent, he stumbled into the kitchen and turned on the coffee maker.

"Coffee?" He looked at Cole. He avoided Avery's gaze as much as possible.

Right, that's what they had told me, she thoughts. *He has a problem with women. Great. Then I'll have to leave all the work to Cole.*

Both shook their heads "no" to the offer. "We'd like to ask you a few more questions," Avery said, pulling out her smartphone to record the interview. She held it up for Travis to see.

He shrugged indifferently, as if he didn't care why they were here. Still he did not look at them. "That's what I assumed. I don't know what else you want from me. I already told you people everything I know."

"We just want you to look at some photos and tell us if one of them might be the..." she searched for a word as innocuous as possible. In vain. There simply wasn't one. "...was your partner's lover?"

Travis flinched as his gaze flitted nervously to Cole and then to Avery. *Strange.* Avery glanced at Cole. He nodded, so he'd seen it, too. What was that all about?

"Is the lover the murderer, then?" Travis's eyes widened in shock. Now he was completely focused on Cole again.

Avery inwardly rolled her eyes.

"Right now, we're just trying to talk to everyone who saw your partner before he died," Cole countered. "That includes, by your own admission, the new lover."

As a result, Travis visibly relaxed and sighed. "All right. I can take a look at the photos."

Avery pulled up a chair. She put the photos in front of him and stepped back from the table. Cole reacted immediately and took over the questioning.

They had selected five men who looked alike. "Look at the photos at your leisure."

Travis's gaze slid over the first two men, neither of them Monsantos. His gaze lingered on Tony's picture for a moment, then he tore himself away without saying anything. He didn't really pay attention to the fourth picture, but bristled at the last one.

No wonder. Alberto and Tony looked a lot alike, too. In the end, however, he looked up and shook his head. "I'm sorry but he's not in any of these pictures."

Avery stared at him. "Are you sure?" she asked.

Travis shuddered as if he were bracing himself against a physical blow. Geez. Hardened drug dealers were definitely more her thing than sensitive suspects.

Cole talked soothingly to him in a low voice. Alternately, Travis nodded or shook his head, but in the end, he vehemently denied recognizing any of the men.

Cole gave up.

Avery signaled to him. Cole joined her and leaned down so she could whisper something to him. Her breath tickled his face. Memories of other sensations rose in him. With great effort, he pushed her aside and tried to concentrate on her words.

"Ask him if he would agree to a Miss Marple apartment search. If I ask him, he'll freak out before I even say the word 'rat'."

He nodded and briefly squeezed her arm to express his approval. He trusted her judgment. Cole stood and said, "We'd like to search your apartment. Maybe your partner left something here that will help us find his killer."

Travis looked like he was about to decline.

"Surely you want the killer caught, too?" added Cole.

Avery pulled Miss Marple out of her jacket and put her on her arm.

Travis saw the movement out of the corner of his eye and cast a furtive glance in that direction. As soon as he caught sight of the rat, a fascinating transformation took place. "Is that a Norway rat?"

Completely taken aback by the sudden direct address, Avery acknowledged it with a nod. "Why, yes. She is."

The same man who would not even look in her direction before came across the room with three big steps. "What a beauty!"

Beauty? Avery thought, puzzled. She looked at Cole, but he also shrugged in perplexity.

"Can I pet her?" asked Travis.

"Uh, yeah sure."

Carefully, he stroked the rat's back. Miss Marple's presence obviously helped him to block out the fact that a woman was present.

"This is Miss Marple, a sleuth," Avery explained. "If I may, I'd like to send her out to look for evidence."

"Is that, like, her job?" he asked, visibly intrigued.

"Exactly."

"Sure. That's exciting. How interesting," Travis said.

He obviously wasn't concerned that Miss Marple might find something incriminating. Or he underestimated the rodent's abilities. That happened quite often but Avery was pretty sure that the former was true. "You like rats?" she asked.

"Rats, dogs, cats, snakes...Everything. I love all animals."

That made him almost sympathetic, even though she was pretty sure he had lied to her about the photos. She feigned a smile.

Systematically, she sent Miss Marple through the apartment. Fortunately, she was not that big. Searching was just as exhausting for a rat as it was for a dog. Avery made sure to include little breaks so she could recover.

Finally, she ended the search disappointed. They had found nothing. On an impulse, she asked Travis to put his wallet on the table. Pleased as a little child that he could somehow help in the search, he complied with her request without hesitation.

Gently, she placed her little helper on the table. Miss Marple passed the coffee cup, a newspaper, and the fruit basket. Only when she reached the wallet did she stop, sit down on her hind legs, and whistle.

Immediately, Avery clicked. On the spot, Miss Marple ran to collect her reward from her mistress.

"Fascinating. Great class. Now what did she find in my wallet?" asked Travis.

"One of the things she's trained to do is to detect monetary bills." Avery put on gloves and reached for his wallet.

"What are the other things?"

"Gunpowder residue and drugs, mostly."

At the last word Travis suddenly turned pale and averted his eyes as if something had occurred to him.

Cole gave him a reassuring look. "Don't worry. We're not here for a little recreational drug use. We're not DEA."

Avery rolled her eyes and continued to search the wallet. She bristled at the bills. All were new and practically hot off the press. That was unusual, but of course not a crime. She came across a narrow paper folded several times. A quick glance showed her that Travis had regained his composure and was in the process of admiring Miss Marple. And paying her no attention whatsoever.

Carefully she unfolded the paper. White powder trickled out. *AHA.* Now she had probably found the reason for Travis's sudden nervousness.

She folded the paper tightly again and held it up. "I'm sure you won't mind if we take care of the disposal?"

Travis hesitated, then nodded. "*UM*, Of course."

She put the folded paper in an evidence bag and stuffed it in her jacket pocket. Cole stood up and collected the photos. Before pocketing them, he approached Travis again. "You're sure you don't recognize any of them?"

"For sure." To give his words more weight, Travis shook his head vehemently.

Cole gave up. They wouldn't get any more out of him that day.

They said goodbye, Cole with a handshake, Avery with a curt nod. At the last moment, Avery hesitated. Spontaneously, she said to Cole, "Ask him where he was last night."

She sensed his questioning look.

Cole turned to Travis and asked casually, as if it had just occurred to him, "Last night."

"Yes?"

"Where were you?"

"Oh my God! Has there been another murder?" Before Cole could say anything, he continued, "I was at Bellini's. You know. A gay club. Wanted to get my mind off things. There are witnesses!" At the last sentence, his eyes flitted to the table, to the place where the photos had been earlier. Interesting but he said nothing more. The ensuing silence was abrupt.

Cole and Avery exchanged a look.

"Don't freak out. It was just a routine question," Cole assured him. "Have a nice day."

When the policemen had gone, Travis leaned against the door and closed his eyes. Finally they were gone. He had nothing to hide, he told himself. Not really. He just didn't feel like airing his private affairs in front of the FBI but he couldn't shake the uneasy feeling in the pit of his stomach.

Avery was glad when they got back to the office. She felt she was returning from the interrogation with more questions than answers.

After greeting the others, she pressed the bag with the folded paper into Valentina's hand. "Can you take this to the lab, please? I'd like a drug test including the exact composition. I want to know if it matches the drugs we found on the dead bodies."

"All right," Valentina said. "I'll drop it off later today."

"Big A, you got a minute?" Avery asked.

The big man rose from his chair and came over to her. "Sure, what's up?"

"Travis Bolt stated that he was at Bellini's yesterday," she said. "I would like to know if Bellini's has surveillance cameras inside. If so, I want a copy of the tapes."

"You got it."

Exhausted, she dropped into her chair. Miss Marple poked her head out of her jacket curiously. Avery tickled her under the chin. "Good job, little one." Gently, she lifted the rat out of her jacket and set her on the table. Miss Marple ran to the cardboard box that served as her living room whenever they were in the office. There, water and food were waiting, as well as a sleeping den. She'd first eat, then drink, before finally curling up for the next few hours. She'd earned as much.

The group sat around the large table in the conference room. Cole projected the previous results of the investigation on the screen and continuously added the new findings.

"We're pretty sure Travis recognized Tony or Alberto or both. The question, though, is whether that links either of them to the murder. Since we found drugs on Travis, albeit a small amount, it's entirely possible he knew the Monsanto brothers, or even just one of them, but neither was his dead partner's lover. If it proves necessary, we can question him again. I suggest, however, that only men be present when we do so. As he did last time, he reacted very negatively to women."

"How is that relevant to our case?" asked Valentina.

"We don't want him to have any extra defenses up. I think it was Tony who fled the victim's apartment, but I'm not sure," Avery said.

Big A pulled out his phone and took a call. "From the bar? All right. We'll send someone there to pick it up."

"I can do that," Valentina volunteered. "Be back in half an hour."

"Take my car," Avery said, tossing Valentina the key. "It's downstairs in front of the door. You won't have to go to the garage."

"Will do. See you later."

As soon as Valentina was out the door, Avery saw Valentina's badge and service weapon lying on the desk. She would need the badge when she showed up at Bellini's. The service weapon probably not, but they *were* on the trail of a killer. That's where it paid to be armed. Avery jumped up, grabbing the items. She glanced at the elevator, which was still in process of moving downward. So she would take the stairs. That way she was faster and would catch up with Valentina sooner.

As she'd hoped, she got through the stairwell, lobby, and through the door leading outside in time to see Valentina standing by the car. "Valentina!"

Valentina turned around, the automatic door opener between her fingers, and asked with a smile, "Is something wrong?"

The world exploded around them.

Avery was thrown backward.

Car parts flew through the air. The front window shattered. *Not my head again*, she thought, before her colleague came to mind. *Valentina. I have to get to Valentina*, was her last thought. Then everything went black.

A loud bang shook the whole building.

Cole and Big A gave each other a horrified look.

Visibly distraught, Miss Marple ran in circles in her box. Her claws scratched over the box. After each lap, she stopped, climbed up the side of the box on her hind legs, and sniffed nervously over the edge.

"What the heck?" Cole said and ran to the window. Big A followed.

Black smoke rose to the eighth floor, where their offices were located. A siren wailed. They tried to make out what was going on downstairs. To no avail. Big A tried to open the window, but Cole tugged at his sleeve. "Down. We're going down!"

Running, he pulled out his cell phone and dialed 911.

"Possible explosion on Justice Boulevard. I repeat, possible explosion. We need the fire department and an ambulance." Without waiting for a response, he ran down the stairs, taking several steps at a time.

Big A followed just a few steps behind. "Coming through!"

"Gotcha," Cole said.

Other agents streamed anxiously into the stairwell. The mere fact that only trained professionals were in the building prevented mass panic.

Cole and Big A ruthlessly made their way down. They made it to the ground level door. "This is it," Big A said.

Without thinking about whether anyone was behind the door, Cole slammed it open so hard the knob left a hole in the wall.

They rushed through and stood in the foyer. "It's like a war zone," Cole said.

"Indeed," Big A said.

The extent of the destruction was clearly visible. Shards of glass were scattered throughout the lot outside. Black smoke poured in through the broken lobby windows, making breathing difficult and obscuring the view.

"Let's get out of here," Big A said.

"Which way?" Cole asked.

After a brief moment of disorientation, Big A shouted, "There!" and pointed toward a lit exit sign. They ran toward it.

"Can't believe that sign still works," Cole said.

"Probably not for long," Big A said. "Go!"

They did and went through the emergency exit door.

On the sidewalk, Cole almost tripped over Avery. "Whoah!" he said.

She'd collapsed against one of the metal pillars. Knees drawn up, head resting in her hands, she was shaken by coughing. She was just regaining consciousness and trying to get her bearings.

"Hey." Cole stopped her with a hand on her shoulder as she tried to get up to rush to Valentina. "Wait a minute and catch your breath first," he said. "Big A will take care of her."

Big A stopped short when he heard his name called and glanced at his partner. "Are you okay?"

"So far, yes. You take care of Valentina. Go," Cole gestured to him. "Check on her."

The big man nodded briefly, his dark eyes almost black with worry, and ran to the car. Or rather, to what was left of it. Stinking vapors rose from the car skeleton. The interior was completely destroyed, the roof lay in the middle of the road. Looking for Valentina, Big A let his eyes wander. Finally, he spotted her.

Valentina lay prone on the asphalt of the sidewalk. His heart contracted painfully. Two long steps brought him to her side. A cold, leaden feeling spread through him like poison.

"Oh, God. Please don't. Please, please not Valentina," he said out loud. Big A dropped to his knees beside her. With a trembling hand, he felt for a pulse, striving to ignore the charred back of her jacket.

Time seemed to stand still. Not even the wail of approaching fire sirens filtered through. Finally, he found the right spot. Her pulse t was strong and regular. He almost burst into tears of relief. Carefully, he stroked the singed hair from her forehead. She looked as if she was asleep; blood oozed from under her face.

"How is she?" asked Avery, who had dragged herself over.

"She's alive." He looked up. "But she took quite a beating. I don't dare move her."

Cole, who had an arm around Avery's waist for support, looked in the direction of the siren, which grew louder. "Good call. The paramedics will take care of it."

A few minutes later, the fire department arrived at the scene, closely followed by an ambulance. Firefighters and paramedics jumped out of their vehicles and attended to the victims.

The officers in charge surveyed the scene. The car in which the bomb had gone off was declared a danger zone and cordoned off.

The paramedics shooed the three friends aside and carefully loaded Valentina onto a stretcher.

"Where are you taking her?" demanded Avery.

"To San Diego General." He glanced at her. "You should get checked out, too, ma'am. The cough indicates possible smoke inhalation."

"Don't worry, I'll get her there," Cole assured him.

Avery gave him a murderous look. It was with great difficulty that she restrained herself from telling him what she thought.

When the ambulance with Big A and Valentina finally left, she turned to Cole, eager to fight. Unfortunately, the quick movement made her feel sick immediately, and she had to take a few deep breaths in a row to avoid spitting up on Cole's feet.

"I'm not going to the hospital," she said, despite her condition.

"You know the protocol as well as I do," he said calmly. "Anyone injured in the line of duty gets a doctor's certificate that either puts them on sick leave or declares them fit for duty."

"You're not the boss of me."

"You've just gotten a head injury for the umpteenth time."

Why am I wasting my energy even talking to this stubborn man? I'll just go alone. He can talk his head off as long as he wants. She had only gone two steps when she stopped. Frustrated, she groaned. Not only did her head and stomach revolt with every step, she didn't even have a car.

Cole caught up with her. "Something wrong?"

"Nothing's wrong." She threw her hands in the air. The next moment she held onto his upper arm feeling dizzy again.

He supported her, which she loved and hated at the same time. Loved because it felt wonderful and she would love to drown in the feeling. Hated it because she definitely didn't want to appear weak in front of him, otherwise it'd confirm in his opinion she needed to go to the hospital. Or even worse, tell her again she wasn't made for this job.

"We have a serial killer on the loose, an assassin who targeted me and got Valentina instead, and a totaled car. It feels like a herd of buffalo is tap dancing in my head." *OOPS.* She probably should have kept that last part quiet considering her refusal to go to the doctor.

"Ideally, you should be put under police protection although I understand the urge to keep working. However it's getting personal, because the killer or the Monsantos or whoever has picked one of our own as a target."

"Maybe so, but we can't snooze on this stuff," Avery said. "Time is of the essence. The trail could go cold fast."

"Tell you what," Cole said. "We'll go and get the USB drive with the surveillance camera footage at Bellini's. On the way back, let's stop by the emergency room and have your injuries looked at. After that, I'll take you back to my place. We'll take the files with us."

Relief flooded through her. Exhausted by the events, she let her head fall against his chest. Immediately, his arms wrapped around her and gently pulled her closer until her entire upper body rested against him.

"Much better already," she murmured. After a few seconds, Avery regained her composure and stepped back away. "We should get moving."

Cold pulled out his keys. "I'll get my car from the garage. Along the way, I'll let Jerry know about what happened. We can make our statements tomorrow. Right now, let's get forensics working on your car."

"Okay. Will you bring me Miss Marple?"

"Sure." He raised a hand and touched her cheek. "Try not to get shot or blown up while waiting here."

She rolled her eyes and said, "*HAHA*. Very funny."

CHAPTER THIRTEEN

"EVEN IF WE FORGET all the other questions, Tony fits your profile very well," Cole said.

They sat on the carpet on the floor in his living room. Take-out boxes from the Chinese restaurant littered the floor, but even their aroma wasn't enough to get rid of the bitter smell of smoke in her nose. She wore sweatpants and one of Cole's old sweatshirts, far too big.

The laptop ran footage of the bar at Bellini's. As Cole dug through the files, trying to find connections between the cases and the victims, she studied the comings and goings of the patrons. Friday night had been a bust. Saturday, too. She was viewing Sunday night in hopes of finding something pertinent.

"The only problem is our suspect's not gay," Avery said.

"We don't know that for sure," Cole said. "He paid you no attention at all, in that regard."

That elicited a weak smile from her. "My undercover outfits didn't directly invite any such reactions, either."

"I sorta liked that somber look on you," he said.

The corners of her mouth twitched as her gaze remained fixed on the screen. "Tony thought I was a teenager. Besides, he only lets himself be seen with models."

"Models? Is that what they call them nowadays?" he asked, winking.

"Models. Influencers. Whatever. You know what I mean." She blinked as her brain, slowed by the pain pills, tried to process what she'd just seen. She moved the cursor and clicked the stop button. Then she rewound the recording until a man walked in the door and headed for the bar.

"I don't believe it," she said. Cole looked up and slid closer to her so he could look at the screen.

She pointed to the figure. "Here. That's actually Tony."

"See, I told you so. Your profile hit the nail on the head."

"Well, except for the fact of his homosexuality," she said.

"Since we're talking about an Italian family that upholds tradition in its screwed-up way, I think maybe he's thinking twice about coming out," Cole said.

"That would be a pretty strong motive to kill his lovers. I guess being on the receiving end of blackmail doesn't appeal to him much," she reflected.

"Right." Cole rubbed his hands together. "Finally, this case is coming together."

"Look," Avery said. "Travis Bolt. I was wondering if and when he'd show up. The next scene explains the strange look on Travis's face the morning during questioning, as he walked purposefully up to Tony and engaged him in conversation. Tony looked confused, initially, but after a few minutes, appeared genuinely interested."

"Spot on," Cole said. "You've nailed it." He continued to follow the action on the screen. "Now they're even leaving the bar together. I don't believe it!"

"The next interrogation will probably be a lot more exciting." She drummed her fingers on the tabletop. "On the positive side, we've now established an actual connection with the murders and someone in the Monsanto family."

"And a possible motive was concluded."

"...and yet the whole thing remains mysterious."

"What's mysterious about it? A man lives out his repressed sexuality and gets rid of troublesome witnesses because he thinks he's untouchable. Case solved."

Avery reached for her beer on the table. "I don't know. It's all too easy if you ask me."

Cole found it increasingly difficult to concentrate on his files. Avery at his home, in his clothes, freshly showered. Also, she was really cute when she was absorbed in her work. He was smart enough not to say that out loud, though. He suspected she wouldn't take such a statement as a compliment.

He'd almost lost her again—the scene flashed through his mind. It could just as easily have been her. After all, it was her car, which suggested the hit had been meant for her.

Valentina was in the hospital and would remain there for a few days. The leather jacket she always wore had prevented worse burns on her back. The back of her legs had taken quite a beating. No burns, but severe bruising appeared where she had hit the car door. The left side of her face was scraped up and her eye was swollen shut.

Cole knew Big A had stayed with her. He would probably charm the nurses into allowing him to stay overnight. Valentina's family had been informed, but since they lived several hours away north of Los Angeles, they wouldn't come until the next day.

He brushed a strand of Avery's hair behind her ear.

At his caress, she tilted her head and smiled at him.

She tapped the screen with a pencil. At the sound, Miss Marple, who had just finished an exploratory tour of Cole's apartment, looked up and darted across the floor toward Avery. Absently, she reached into the bag of pumpkin seeds sitting on the table and fed the rat a few. "Don't you find the encounter strange? Almost as if Travis Bolt had sought out the conversation, not the other way around."

Cole shrugged and lowered his hand. "It's hard to judge without sound."

"And what about the attempts on my life? There have been two, both within a few days."

"I don't know. Maybe you were right and the two things are unrelated. Or maybe Tony actually recognized you on the day we were going to search the last victim's apartment, and he's trying to solve another outstanding problem."

Avery shook her head. "It's just not a good match. Especially not with Tony's personality."

"Is that your professional opinion as a profiler?" asked Cole.

"Good question." She wrinkled her nose and considered. "Both," she finally said. "For one thing, it doesn't quite fit the psychological profile. He clearly has narcissistic traits, but at the same time he's very purposeful and, as I said, quite sensitive. If the victims had been poisoned or, in my case, shot, I could imagine that, but with a knife? That's far too intimate an act. You get incredibly dirty. He'd have to be in mortal danger to react that way."

"What next?" Cole asked, grabbing her hand. Miss Marple saw the gesture and sat demonstratively on Avery's lap. She did not like to share her owner. She was very territorial in that respect. *Well. She was out of luck this time. She would have to get used to him in intimate* proximity.

"My gut," Avery answered.

"Can you rely on your gut?"

That earned him a critical look.

She realized his question was serious. She sighed. "For the most part, yes. It's served me well throughout my undercover investigations. I have to admit, though, that I've never been in a situation where a person I already know was involved. That makes it difficult for me to judge whether I can rely on my gut feeling."

He groaned and buried his face in his hands. He raised his head and looked at her. "I must admit that I find it very tempting to close this case soon. Then perhaps we could move on to more important matters."

"More important things?" she asked, alarmed by his serious tone. She wasn't sure she was ready for serious talk. Especially *that* conversation.

Cole ignored her question and leaned over until the tip of his nose touched hers. "Yeah. More important things. Like you, for instance. And me. Us."

He brought up a whole world of different possibilities, each more beautiful than the other but also exciting and frightening. She wasn't sure she was ready for those alternatives. Having his lips so close to hers, on the other hand, she found it wonderful.

She leaned forward and whispered, "First the case. Then the important things."

He recognized her evasive tactic but if it earned him a kiss or two, he wouldn't complain. Light as a feather, he touched her lips.

Avery grabbed the back of his neck and brought him closer to her. Then she kissed him. Strong.

Evasive tactics were perfectly acceptable, Cole decided, before focusing on the task of returning her kiss.

Miss Marple, who had fled indignantly when the kiss became more intense, ran to her box and jumped in. She curled up, hid her nose under her small blanket, and blanked out what was happening in the room. People sure were strange.

Later, with Avery in his arms and asleep, Cole laid awake for a long time. He felt like he had come to a crossroads in his life. Not in terms of what he wanted. What he wanted was currently snuggled up against him in his bed. If he didn't get a handle on his concern for her soon, nothing would come of it. That had become clear to him over the last ten years. He realized it had been rather chauvinistic of him to even suggest she choose another profession.

I'm really afraid of losing her. Afraid something might happen to her during a mission. I couldn't bear it. Of course, he hadn't told her. Being afraid, even for someone else, was definitely not cool.

Even if he had, it wouldn't have made any difference. She would have been right to ask him what she should say. Something could happen to him as well as to her. That was also clear to him. Emotionally, it was something completely different. For him but not for her. In the last ten years, during which they had seen each other only sporadically and he had followed her career with the DEA from a distance, he had convinced himself that he was over this fear but the experiences of the last few days had shattered that conviction rather quickly. If he listened carefully inside himself, his feelings hadn't changed at all. The only question was how he would deal with it in the future.

He slipped his free arm under his head and stared into the darkness. As he let his mind wander through the last ten years, he realized that he would learn to cope no matter what it cost him. Another ten years without Avery by his side was not an option. She murmured something in her sleep, snuggling closer to him and confirming how he felt about her.

The next morning he woke in an empty bed. Not yet fully awake, he gazed around the room. For the first time since he had been living there, he noticed how dreary his apartment was. Beige walls, a brown bed, light-colored carpets. No photos, no pictures, let alone plants. The latter was better that way. The last plant—a cactus!—hadn't survived its stay with him. When he had told Avery, she'd burst out laughing and asked him, "How did you manage to kill a plant that survives in Death Valley?"

"I have no idea," he said. "I'm just going to keep my hands off anything green."

In any case, he found it telling he'd not made his apartment a home. His home was with Avery, wherever she was. Anything else was just a temporary solution. How they were going to figure it out work-wise, he didn't know but he was confident they could handle that problem, too.

On bare feet, he walked into the living room. There Avery and Miss Marple sat at the table—Avery in the chair, Miss Marple on the table—eating cereal. Avery with milk, the rodent without.

Should I object to having a rat sitting on the dining room table? Nah. They're too cute to object.

"Morning," he grumbled.

Avery, who was busy with her smartphone, gave him a fleeting smile. "You didn't call home or inform our friends yesterday, either?"

He shook his head in denial. "Take a look at your social media. There's all kinds of speculation about our whereabouts. Some think we ran off to Las Vegas to get married, others think we were blown up. The explosion obviously made it into the media."

"Shoot."

"Yeah, I'll call my mom then," Cole said.

"Do that. I already told my grandfather. I'm sure he's passed on the good news that we're still alive, though still unmarried, to your parents but it certainly makes sense to call them yourself."

"Absolutely. Otherwise, Mom will lynch me the next time I show up in Independence," Cole said.

Avery just shook her head.

"Indeed," Cole added and dialed his mom. While waiting for his mother to pick up, he said, "Vegas isn't the worst idea."

"What?"

"I'm just saying. If we're going to get married, why not do it in Vegas? At least then everyone won't know who drank what or who went home early or late with whom."

"Are you talking about us?"

He pressed the off button. This was an interesting development. He didn't want any distractions. "For example. Why not?"

"Why not?" she asked. "Without going into the umpteen reasons why the two of us shouldn't get married at all, there's no way we're getting married in Las Vegas, should we ever think of getting married."

After her proclamation, she felt a little dizzy. She suspected it was more from using the word "marry" three times in one sentence, and in connection with Cole. That would make any woman lightheaded.

Not just because he was definitely a great catch, but because he was equally impossible. They'd broken up ten years ago over irreconcilable differences, and then, without discussing those differences, he was talking about getting married. *And in Vegas, with no family or friends. Men! Unbelievable.*

Her inner princess left her alone when she chased the bad guys as an agent, but not when she was off the clock. Because she didn't have much else in the way of flowers and bows in her life, she intended to marry in style, should things ever come to that.

Fortunately, at that moment, Cole's phone rang. His mother was calling back.

CHAPTER FOURTEEN

After a short visit to the hospital, Avery and Cole drove straight to the office on Justice Boulevard. Workmen were already replacing the large glass window panes. The glass fragments had been swept away and the damaged car towed to the garage at the forensics department where it could be meticulously examined.

The stench of burnt rubber still hung in the air. Avery swallowed to quell the rising nausea.

Cole, who hadn't missed it, gave her arm a quick squeeze. "You okay?"

She nodded curtly. "Almost." The last thing she wanted was to talk about it. He seemed to understand and let it go.

They had barely arrived at the reception desk of their floor when their boss, Special Agent Jerry Smith, ordered them into his office. "We need to speak. Pronto," he said.

"Aye-aye," Avery said. They followed him.

At his door, Avery gave Cole a questioning look. "I don't know what he wants. Maybe a briefing from what happened yesterday?"

Avery frowned. "Well, he can read about that in the report. We made our statements yesterday, typed them up in the evening, and uploaded it to the server," she said. "Actually, I don't feel like telling it all over again. After all, we already made our statements."

"He rarely sets foot in the premises of his subordinates. He's a good supervisor but he enjoys his status very much," Cole said. "So, this must be important."

"I'll make a mental note of this fact. Nothing against Jerry, but status-conscious people are often very receptive to bribes." She straightened her shoulders and pushed open the door.

Cole followed her.

To her amazement, not only Jerry was waiting for her, but her own boss, Sondra Brown.

"Pleasure seeing you two this morning," Sondra said. "Thanks for coming in."

Before Sondra could say anything, Jerry spoke up. "Special Agent Wilkinson, Special Agent Carter, please have a seat."

The two exchanged a look and complied with the request.

"To make a long story short, since yesterday, the circumstantial evidence we have seems to prove a connection between the Monsanto family and the murders. That, and the fact that yesterday was already the second attempt on your life, unfortunately forces me to take you off the case."

Shocked, Avery glanced at Cole. *He looked just as surprised as she was. Either he's a very good actor, or he really didn't know about this decision.* She turned back to Jerry.

"No problem," Avery said. "After all, my involvement with the FBI was only meant as an interlude anyway. If you'd like, I'll continue to keep you informed of the latest developments on the case. I imagine I will, after all, continue to follow the case in my capacity as a narcotics investigator, anyway."

"Um..." Sondra said. "I'm afraid that won't be possible."

"What do you mean, it won't be possible?"

"You'll be given a new assignment," Sondra said. "Sorry. It's just too risky. As it is, your cover has been blown. That alone puts you in danger. The Monsanto family isn't squeamish about traitors."

"But...the case isn't solved yet!"

"Just about, it is," Jerry interjected. "We'll bring Tony in for questioning in the next few days. It's only a matter of time before he confesses to everything."

She glared at Sondra in disbelief. "I knew this would happen. Alberto will provide Travis Bolt with ten of his best lawyers and that'll be that. Don't you agree?"

"All I know is I don't feel like fishing one of my best agents out of the harbor next week. Or to collect the pieces when the next car bomb hits its target."

"That's a good argument. Still, it goes against who I am to just give up at this point in the investigation." Seeking backup, she turned to Cole. He stared blankly at the wall behind the desk. "Was that your doing?" she hissed as it dawned on her the development probably suited him just fine.

Surprised, he looked at her. "Excuse me? Where did you get that idea?"

"Because I know your opinion on the subject."

"Sorry, but you have no idea what I think about this."

Undecided whether she could trust him, she stared at him.

"Do you mind?" interrupted Jerry. He held out his hand to Avery in farewell. Woodenly, she shook it. "Today you're off to pack. Tomorrow you're off to Michigan," her boss informed her.

First her case was taken away, then she was also transferred from mild San Diego to Michigan. Suddenly, she was fed up with other people always telling her what to do. Acting on that impulse, she pulled out her gun and badge and slammed both down on the table. "You know what? I don't give a hoot about Michigan. I quit."

Jerry stared at the objects on his desk as if he had never seen a gun and a badge before.

Sondra tried to placate her. "That's a little extreme now, don't you think?"

Avery stubbornly remained silent.

Sondra struck a different, tighter tone. "I'm assuming that the day off today is enough for you to get over it. I'll expect you in the office tomorrow before the eight o'clock flight."

Avery didn't even think about it. She just knew she had to get out of here, safety deficit or not. Even if everyone else disagreed, she had a case to solve. She turned on her heel and stormed out of the office.

Cole tried to grab her by the sleeve, but only earned a nasty look before she resolutely broke free and slammed the door behind her with a loud bang.

"Quite the spirited one," Jerry said.

Sondra raised an eyebrow. "I would appreciate it if you would treat my agent with the respect she deserves."

"Then why did you take her off the case?" interjected Cole. He was getting angry. "Her cover was blown either way. If that's the reason to take the case away from her, you shouldn't have given it to her in the first place. We know where the danger is coming from. At least here we can protect her. After all, we're the FBI. Who knows what she'll get into now if she's on her own?"

"She'll come around," Sondra said. "And I doubt that the arms of the Monsanto family reach all the way to Michigan."

"Oh. And you're sure about that?"

"Agent Carter. Get a grip on yourself!" Jerry ordered.

Disgusted, Cole shook his head and wordlessly left the room.

With long strides, he hurried into their shared office. No sign of Avery. All her papers were gone. Miss Marple's box was gone, too. She couldn't have gone far, though. She didn't have a car, after all—it'd been blown up.

He went to his desk to get his keys. Maybe he could drive her somewhere.

A minute later, he realized that he wasn't going to drive her anywhere. She was, in fact, driving *his* car. Although annoyed, he couldn't help but admire her ingenuity. He just hoped she wasn't doing anything rash.

"Is that what you call 'taking care of a problem'?" Alberto's voice sounded hoarse.

Tony shrank in his chair, with no trace of his usual pomposity.

"A shooting in broad daylight?" Alberto asked. "No results. The next best thing you can think of is a car bomb? This isn't the Middle East. Not only did it hit the wrong agent, but the explosion was in the media. In other words, the pressure on the authorities to solve the case is growing. So they're going to look more closely."

Tony winced and pulled his head in a little more.

The phone rang. Alberto answered, putting it on speaker. "What?" he barked.

"I just wanted to give you the happy news that the agent in question has been taken off the case."

"I'm glad," Alberto said, not sure if that was enough for him.

"Then I assume that the failed attempts on her life will come to an end?" the mysterious caller asked. "Not good for the image of this city."

"I don't know what you're talking about," Alberto said. "I suggest you choose your tone wisely"

"I apologize for wording it in such a way," the mystery person said. "But the sentiment is the same. This must be low profile as it endangers us all."

"Understood." The caller hung up and Tony squirmed under his brother's gaze. "I suggest you take care of the problem yourself this time. Here's a tracking device. Put that on her car." Theatrically, he grabbed his own forehead. "Oh, no. You can't do that! She doesn't have a car anymore. So you're going to have to come up with something else."

Alberto's eyes glittered mischievously, as if he was unexpectedly enjoying the whole thing. *Of course he is,* Tony thought, annoyed. *Always putting down his little brother. It's always been this way.* Reluctantly, he picked up the coin-sized piece. "And what does that do for me?"

"If you know where she is, you can wait for the appropriate moment." Alberto made to leave. In the doorway, he turned around. "What are your plans tonight?"

What business was it of his? But Tony knew better than to challenge his brother when he was in this mood. So he reluctantly said, "I'm on the boat. A business dinner."

"Oh, that's what they call it now?" Alberto said as he left.

Thank God he's finally gone! Tony turned the tracking device around in his hands. He had no idea what he was supposed to do with the thing.

What was Alberto thinking? That he would walk up to her and stuff this device in her jacket pocket? Annoyed, he shoved the thing into his own pocket. He glanced at his watch. Only a few hours left until his meeting. He felt better.

Maybe he would stop by Maria's house in the meantime. She was still Maria to him, even if she looked very different. She probably always would. Until now, he had not found it so tragic she had been an informer. After all, she was just doing her job, like everyone else. And he had always enjoyed the company of the dark girl with the unusual pet.

However, if she continued to cause him problems with his brother, that would change in no time. He gritted his teeth as he thought of the telling off he'd just received.

He rubbed his eyes. Maybe tonight's date wasn't such a good idea after all. With his index and middle fingers, he loosened the collar of his shirt, which suddenly seemed much too tight. He reached for his phone.

After the third ring, Travis Bolt answered on the other end.

"Hey."

"Hey."

"Tony?"

"Yes."

There was silence for a moment, during which Tony tried to sort out his thoughts.

"Did you want to cancel our meeting?" Travis asked.

He sounded so disappointed that Tony cringed. "No, no. Absolutely not. I just have a few...things to do."

"Yes?" This time the voice resonated upward with hope.

"Is it okay if I just come by later?"

"Of course," Travis answered hastily. "I don't care what time it is, just come on over."

"Alright, see you later."

Exhausted, he ran his hand through his coiffed and gelled hair. That hadn't quite gone according to plan. On the other hand, he was able to meet his brother's needs as well as his own. He only hoped that the other would not fall head over heels in love with him right away. People in love were always difficult to get rid of. He didn't need any more complications at the moment. Accompanied by a deep sigh, he pulled out his agenda and dealt with the current deliveries for the first time in a long time.

Alberto, who had stopped outside the room, had overheard the phone call. On the one hand, he was pleased that his brother seemed to finally want to take care of his problems. On the other hand, he felt nauseous when he thought about how his brother wanted to end the evening. *How sick is that? Just sick.* Disgusted, he shook his head and left.

Avery seethed with anger as she steered Cole's car down Justice Boulevard away from the office. She still couldn't believe it. Being pulled off an ongoing case just like that had never happened to her before. *I wonder if Cole had a hand in it. I wouldn't put it past him. He doesn't think I'm strong enough to be in this line of work and that I'm not quite suited to be an agent.*

In La Jolla, she pulled into one of the parking lots above the beach and got out. She had never been to this stretch of beach before. It seemed fitting to her to look for a new place.

A strong wind ruffled her hair. She pulled a hair tie from her pocket and gathered the unruly strands into a ponytail. The wind forced her to take a deep breath. She put her head back, closed her eyes, and held her face up to the winter sun. The rhythmic sound of the surf calmed her racing thoughts a little. She wandered a short distance along the beach until she found a small, sandy cliff overlooking the rocks that served as breakwaters. There she settled down with a deep sigh.

Miss Marple, who had noticed that they were taking a break, curiously poked her little head out of the collar of Avery's jacket.

Avery gently stroked her head with the tip of her finger. "You've had enough excitement the last few days, too, haven't you?"

The rodent looked at her unimpressed and struggled out of the jacket.

Avery laughed. "I can see you want to explore." Gently, she set her companion on the ground and released her. "Watch out for the seagulls," she warned, but Miss Marple was already gone.

Somehow she had to get herself a new vehicle, since a company car was probably no longer an option. Unless, of course, she reported to her boss tomorrow at the latest and went to Michigan. She listened to herself and tried to figure out how she liked this idea. She didn't. Still. If it was going to be cold and snowy, it had to be back home in Colorado. She laughed.

Suddenly, she felt freer than she had in a long time. She had just quit her job, including pension benefits. Instead of worrying about what to do next, she couldn't wait to find out what life had in store for her in the future.

Obviously puzzled by her caregiver's uncharacteristic outburst of merriment, Miss Marple returned and sat on her hind legs in front of her.

Avery lifted her up and nuzzled her cheek against her.

"Don't worry. You won't be out of a job. I'm sure there's demand for your skills all over the world. Either we'll become the local high school scare in Independence and assist Jake in his war on drugs, or we'll retrain you to be a mold-sniffing rat. What do you think?" she asked her companion, nudging her with her nose.

Miss Marple didn't understand the dilemma. She returned the look from her black beady eyes and fidgeted impatiently with her little paws.

"Okay, okay. I'll put you down already."

The rat had obviously explored enough and tried to climb into the jacket pocket where the food was stowed. Amused, she put the little one in her jacket and gave it some oatmeal to nibble on. Thus satisfied, Miss Marple made herself comfortable in the inside pocket.

Mentally, she made a list of all the things she wanted to do before she left for Independence. First, she would go to the hospital and see how Valentina was doing. Surely the agent was bored and would be happy to get a visit. Next, she would pay a visit to one of the Monsanto warehouses. She'd always wanted to search them during her undercover time, but never got the okay from her superiors to do so.

She was no longer bound to such idiotic rules. If she found anything, she would simply send the evidence anonymously to her old team at the drug squad. They'd do the rest.

What was going to happen with the murders? She didn't know yet. Cole would certainly stay on the case. Even though she resented his decision to exclude her from the investigation, she had no intention of jeopardizing it.

She noticed black dots on the rocks and in the water. She leaned forward and squinted.

Seals! Or were they sea lions? No matter. Either way, she wanted to get closer and watch them play and sunbathe.

Avery braced herself and knocked the sand off her pants. After a glance at the sand, she got rid of her shoes and socks and set off barefoot.

The antics of the younger animals made her smile ear to ear. There was diving, racing, and splashing for all it was worth. The older ones sunbathed on the rocks, an indulgent smile on their faces.

She really had to tell Tyler. *Speaking of Tyler?* The best thing she could do was drive by and ask her to go with her to the car dealership. Cole could just pick up his car from his sister later.

She watched the seals for a few more minutes. Then she got up and headed back.

On the way, she collected her shoes. Arriving at her car, she wrote Tyler a short text.

Would love to come by. Do you have time? It's Avery.
Sure. Now?
In half an hour. Just got into La Jolla.
Is this an official visit with sirens and blue lights?
No, why?
Because with traffic you're not going to make it in thirty minutes. At least not legally.
**lol* It doesn't matter today.*
???

Avery shook her head with a grin when she saw the three question marks. Tyler would have to wait the half an hour for her explanation. The story was definitely too long to cover in a text message.

CHAPTER FIFTEEN

Fifty minutes later, Avery pulled up to Tyler's house. As she got out, she heard Ranger barking. She smiled, happy to see him. *This dog's really something special.* Belatedly, it occurred to her that she didn't even know if Paula and Leslie were still there. No matter. She would find out in a moment. Either way, it didn't matter.

The door opened and Tyler came out. Well-mannered as he was, Ranger dutifully stayed by Tyler's side until she signaled for him to greet Avery. He jumped down the few steps from the porch and pressed himself against her legs, tail wagging.

Avery greeted him first, then hugged Tyler, who had joined them.

"Are you okay?" Tyler asked.

Avery shook her head and asked, "Did Cole call?"

"Yes. He's worried about you."

Avery snorted. "More likely about his car. After all, the rest is right up his alley."

Tyler frowned. "He didn't sound like that, though."

"Which part do you mean? The part about the car or the other bit?"

Tyler ducked her head. "He actually misses his car."

"I knew it. What else did he say?"

"Let's go inside first," Tyler said. "Then I'll be happy to tell you everything. In exchange, I want to know all the details about your wedding in Vegas." She concluded with a wink.

Avery rolled her eyes and followed the two into the house.

As they sat at the table with a glass of fruit juice, Tyler related how Cole had been upset on the phone about Avery being suspended.

"I find that hard to believe. Honestly, I assumed the idea came from him."

Tyler frowned when she heard Avery's vehement tone. "I hardly think so. He even got into it with his boss and yours over it."

She remembered the shocked look in Cole's eyes when she had accused him of exactly that. Suddenly, she doubted her theory. Had she done him wrong?

Tyler, who seemed to sense her stress, added, "I would definitely recommend you talk to him again before you do anything rash."

"Maybe tomorrow." Avery would certainly not let him in on her nightly plans. There was no way he would approve of those. Not willing to elaborate with Tyler, she changed the subject. "Do you have plans for the next two hours? Are Paula and Leslie still here? Or do you have to work?"

"Paula and Leslie left yesterday. Much to Ranger's chagrin. This time he'll miss not only his girlfriend Leslie, but also Jack and Jill. He sort of adopted those two."

"How sweet!"

"That's what we thought," Tyler said. "Every morning he would carry them down from the second floor and lick them thoroughly clean with his big tongue."

"*UGH*. What did the little ones think?"

Tyler shrugged. "Oh, they just surrendered to their fate. Didn't leave them much else to do."

"Work?" Avery asked.

"Unfortunately, no. It's been frustrating. Although I already clarified as much as possible from Colorado, it seems that there are now problems with the approval of the dance group. So it's going to drag on for another week or two. If things continue at this pace, Pat will have finished building his houses and we'll be on our way back to Independence without me having had a chance to start my project."

"Sounds pretty tedious."

"It is. Especially since I know it would be a real asset to the kids in the area."

"Then it's a good thing I'm here to take your mind off things. How would you feel about helping me buy a car?"

Tyler's eyes widened. "You want to buy a car? Now? Just like that?" She glanced out the window where Cole's car was parked. "I was wondering why you were driving my brother's car. Unfortunately, he wasn't very forthcoming when I asked him why on the phone."

"Let's just say mine had an unfortunate run-in with explosives."

"Explosives?" Tyler visibly struggled to maintain her composure but she didn't quite succeed, which was easy to see from her hands flapping wildly in the air. "Are you hurt?"

"No, no," Avery reassured her. "I just hit my head. Again."

"That seems to be turning into a bad habit," Tyler said.

"My teammate Valentina wasn't quite as fortunate. She's in the hospital at the moment. From that point of view, I'm quite happy with my luck."

"Geez. Slowly but surely, I don't think the idea of your suspension is such a bad idea."

"Says the woman who was stalked by a psycho for weeks and kidnapped at the end."

Tyler, who was about to launch into a tirade, shut her mouth just in case.

"I thought so," Avery said. "What about now? Are you coming?"

"Where?"

"To the car dealer."

A few hours later, Avery was the proud owner of a red, four-year-old Corvette. Perhaps not the most practical car for the mountains but at least she had remembered to get winter wheels put on it and got some chains. If she was heading to the Rockies in a few days, she had no desire to be caught off guard by snow.

She hugged Tyler goodbye and squeezed her tightly. "I'm going to miss you. I loved that we finally got to see each other more."

"Me, too."

"And good luck with your project. Maybe I'll see you in Independence for Christmas."

"If you're still around then, absolutely," Tyler said. "Mom would never forgive you if were there but didn't stop in."

"We'll see. I actually don't know what I'm going to do next at the moment," Avery confessed. "For now, I'm unemployed, which is a whole new experience for me, and sorting out my thoughts."

"Then it's a good thing you're going to Independence. There's no better place to reorient yourself."

"*HA*. I doubt that, with all the interference that takes place there from "benevolent" souls. In your case, it had more to do with your dream man, if I remember correctly."

Tyler smiled. "I guess so, but Cole's coming to Independence for Christmas, too."

"Whether he has the same miraculous effect as Pat remains to be seen," she joked. "From experience, Cole and I tend to fight like cats and dogs."

"What's the saying? What teases each other..."

"Yeah. It's okay."

Avery waved and drove off.

Tyler watched her go, her right hand resting on Ranger's head. "What do you think, big guy? Are they going to make it this time?"

Ranger tilted his head and wagged the tip of his tail. She knelt next to him and put her arm around the dog.

"You're right, who knows." Knowing her brother was worried about Avery, she pulled her phone out and dialed him. He picked up on the first ring.

"Tyler? Any word from Avery?" Cole asked.

"I guess you could say that. Her new love interest is bright red and has just over 400 hp under the hood."

Cole laughed. "If it weren't for the serious circumstances, I'd guess she was happy about having an excuse to buy a new car."

"Let's put it this way: that was her bright spot today."

"How is she doing?"

"*HMM*. I think the events have taken more out of her than she lets on. Not in the sense that she's scared, though. She's mulling over the fact that she was deprived of the opportunity to keep working on the case and solving it. She's taking the attack very personally."

"It doesn't get much more personal than having a bomb in your car. The fact that a colleague was injured in the process doesn't help. I can understand she's angry. I tried to get our superiors to change their minds but as usual, everything is strictly according to protocol." His frustration was clearly audible.

"I suspected as much and told her so," Tyler said.

"I imagine she didn't believe a word you said."

"I wouldn't put it that way. She actually seemed to understand."

"Is she still with you?"

"No. She left five minutes ago. From what I understand, she's headed to Independence to restart her life."

Cole groaned audibly. "Well, that's just wonderful. I can already see our first marital crisis playing out on social media."

"You two are also so wonderfully suited as a topic of conversation. You're both interesting personalities with exciting professions and a common past. No wonder the speculation is running hot. Plus, it's convenient you're so far away and can't confirm or refute any of the rumors."

"Can do. I've been kind enough to hold off until now," Cole grumbled. "If this keeps up, though, I'll soon change my mind. Hacking a social media account is one of my easiest exercises."

Tyler laughed. "I don't think I want to know exactly what the technical possibilities are. Especially since I suspect even a pimply thirteen-year-old could do it."

"Yes, unfortunately that's the case."

"No. Please don't destroy my last illusions about safety on the net," she said.

Cole grinned. "All right, sis. I love you. So, I won't call her until she's already in Colorado. Give her some peace. There's a better chance she'll actually listen to me if I give her some space first. In the meantime, I'll do my best here to solve the case."

"Do that. And Cole?"

"Yes?"

"I have my fingers crossed for you. I think having Avery as a quasi-sister would be really, really great."

"I'll keep that in mind. Regards to Pat."

"Bye."

No sooner had they hung up than her eyes fell on the car in her driveway. She pressed redial on the phone.

"Yes?" Cole asked.

"It's me again. How are you getting to your car now?" Tyler asked.

"My car. Right." He thought for a moment, then said, "I'll have a patrolman bring me to you."

"Good. And if you want to stay for dinner, just let me know."

"Thank you. I'll be happy to do so."

CHAPTER SIXTEEN

Avery peered in the rearview mirror. She was sitting in her new, but not very inconspicuous, Corvette in front of one of the many warehouses the Monsanto brothers had rented. For her mission, she had dressed all in black. A cliché, to be sure, but somehow it seemed fitting for her first foray into the world of burglary. *Does it count as burglary when crooks stole from crooks?* she asked herself as she waited for the last employees to leave the warehouse.

Just then, the lights went out.

She counted the seconds that passed.

When she reached one hundred twenty, three men left the building laughing and chatting. One raised his hand in greeting and separated from the other two. Of course, he was coming in her direction, of all the places.

She sent a quick prayer of thanks to the patron saint of thieves that she'd remembered to turn off the headlights. *I have no idea who you are, patron saint of thieves, but I hope my prayer gets to you in time!*

Avery remained very still as the employee approached. She did not dare to breathe.

When the man stopped to admire the fast car, she bitterly regretted not having chosen one of the boring gray sedans.

The man at least seemed to be in a hurry to get home. He stopped just long enough to let his gaze travel once from the front to the back. Then he whistled softly through his front teeth and continued on his way.

Relieved, she sat up again. For safety's sake, she'd wait another five minutes before she and Miss Marple turned their attention to the hall and the boxes inside.

She looked forward to doing some tangible investigative work together with her rodent. They hadn't done that in a long time. *It's a pity, really, because we're a great team. Miss Marple's successful in almost every case.*

Her four-legged partner sensed the rising tension and stuck her head out, whiskers vibrating.

As Avery expected, a private security guard circled the building. At the corner, he looked around leisurely before continuing his patrol. According to her observations in comparable places, she should have at least ten minutes until he came again. Maybe even more if he took a little break. However, unpredictable breaks were of no use to her. He didn't have a dog with him to distract.

Finally, the three hundred seconds were up. Relieved to be able to do something instead of sitting around and waiting, she got out.

She put one hand protectively over her little helper. Without locking the car, she slipped the key into her pocket. *After all, you never knew when a quick exit might become necessary. Best to be prepared.*

She had chosen the warehouse because she'd overheard snippets of conversation about it more than once. As she understood it, drugs were moved there under Tony's direction. It was something like his journeyman job. If he reliably took care of one branch of the business and had everything under control, Alberto would make him a full partner. She shook her head at the thought. *As if Alberto would ever relinquish even part of his rigid control.*

Approaching the entrance, she pushed her hair out of her face. With a practiced grip, she disarmed the security system at the gate. She pressed a few buttons in the control box, located on the outside of the wall, and cut two cables. She didn't dare cut the power to the entire building. The risk there was still someone somewhere in the building was too high.

Avery hadn't seen any more light anywhere, but she knew from other warehouses of this type that there were windowless areas inside. If someone was still there, she certainly didn't want to alert them by suddenly having the lights go out. It was more complicated, but it was worth investing a few extra moves.

She glanced at her watch and checked the elapsed time. *Five minutes. Good.* She was still within the time limit.

Miss Marple suddenly turned her head. Alarmed by her rat's sudden movement, she gingerly closed the fuse box and ducked into the shade of the nearby dumpster. Just in time. The security guard was just coming around the corner. Adrenaline shot through her veins, making her heart beat faster. She made an effort to breathe calmly and evenly to block out the stench rising from the collected trash.

As he passed her, she was startled to realize that it was not the same man as before.

That could mean two things. Either she had shown up for the shift change, or there were two of them. That would be very bad. She'd have to pay double attention and have only half as much time between intervals. Avery sighed, relieved as he disappeared behind the building.

Should she wait until he or his buddy came around again? It would be more sensible. She was deeply reluctant to waste any more time. Better she made sure she got in.

She crept up to the gate, picked the surprisingly simple lock with the lockpick she had brought with her. She'd read out the numerical code earlier with a small device via the fuse box. *Sometimes it pays to keep up with the latest technology*, she thought with satisfaction.

Sixty feet and two doors down, she found herself inside the warehouse. She waited a moment for her eyes to adjust to the darkness. In front of her stretched long rows of wooden crates. Pairs were stacked on top of each other but she needed one standing individually if she was going to look inside. Since using the forklift was out of the question—she didn't want to alert the night watch with the noise—she could only hope to find a single crate. Otherwise, it was a matter of climbing.

Slowly, she paced the rows, but soon gave up her search and put Miss Marple on the floor. There was no point in wasting time looking for the perfect box when she didn't even know if there was anything interesting inside.

She crouched down on the floor and signaled Miss Marple to search.

The rat scampered toward the first box.

Wrong.

Disappointed, Avery let herself roll back from her tiptoes to her heels. Miss Marple wasn't giving up so easily. Determined, she scurried to the next, climbing up the first crate until she reached the top of the second. There she indicated a find.

Avery clicked and Miss Marple dashed back to her to collect her reward. She smiled broadly. *HA!* If only they'd listened to her weeks ago. But no. Instead, she was taken off one case, put on the next, and finally suspended. She would show them!

Her cell phone vibrated in her pants pocket. She slid her hand inside and pressed a button to suppress the telltale sound. In the silence of the abandoned warehouse, it was uncomfortably loud and clear.

Holding her breath, she waited a moment, fearing she was about to be caught but everything remained quiet.

She repeated the search operation in different places. Miss Marple always found what she was looking for. However, she did so only at the higher boxes. They passed a few individual ones, but those seemed to serve as camouflage and were likely filled with innocuous material. Or at least materials with things to which Miss Marple attached no importance. Avery sighed. She would have no choice but to pry open a few of the upper boxes and check the contents.

Suddenly it occurred that it would be nice to have Cole with her. Many things were easier when there were two of them.

Pull yourself together, she reminded herself silently. *There's no time to think like that. Stay focused. You can manage on your own just fine.*

After checking again that she was alone, she retrieved a crowbar from the wall. Looking up at one of the towering stacks, she pushed the heavy piece of metal into the crate and climbed up, using it as leverage.

Tony parked his car in front of the gate, without heeding the no-stopping signs, and got out. It annoyed him immensely that he had to take care of business in his personal time, so to speak. He had already paid a visit to two unreliable dealers—it was to be expected they'd be very reliable in the future—and collected protection money from some store owners. Doing so was beneath him, but Alberto insisted he take care of it personally.

Since Alberto managed all the money, he was in the passenger's seat, but that would soon change. Tony would fork out a nice chunk from the next deal. Then his brother could see where he stood.

After all, this was the last stop before he could meet up with Travis. He could feel his blood rising at the thought of the guy. Fresh meat was a wonderful thing. First work, then pleasure.

He was about to enter the security code when he was taken aback. The gate was open a crack.

Alarmed, he looked around. No one was seen or heard. He was about to dismiss it as the mistake of a careless employee when a conspicuous car on the side of the road caught his eye.

Tony squinted. What was *he* doing here? His gaze drifted back to the gate. Was there a connection between the two things?

A man from security came around the corner.

"Hey!" shouted Tony, waving the man over.

Suspiciously, the man came closer. Only when he was almost upon him did the man recognize Tony. "Oh, it's you, boss. What's up?"

"The gate was open. And there's a car over there that doesn't belong here."

"Everything's been quiet," the guard said. "I didn't see or hear anyone."

"Good. I'd like to check the stock, make sure things are in order. Go in and get everything ready. I'll take a look at this car."

The guard said, "Sure," turned, and walked toward the warehouse.

Tony jogged over to the red Corvette in his expensive Italian shoes. When he got there, he realized the futility of his venture. It was unlikely the owner had left his business card anywhere. In order to run the license plate, he didn't have the right contacts on hand. If he called Alberto for help because there was a strange car near the warehouse, he would have to listen to his taunts forever. So that wasn't an option.

He was about to turn away when his gaze fell on the passenger seat. There lay a cardboard box that he knew all too well.

"Oh, it's you, isn't it? Why aren't I surprised? Just you wait," he said. The fact that Maria was there could only mean one thing: she was there to cause trouble.

Since trouble with Maria meant trouble with the drug squad, he couldn't have it at all. Anger rose, and he reached into his jacket pocket and pulled out the tracking device. Suddenly he was grateful for his brother's foresight. Even though he had no intention of letting her get away alive, he placed the transmitter under the car body. After the fiasco of the last few days, he preferred to play it safe.

In the meantime, the security guard discovered the two door locks had been picked. "Was there anything unusual about the car?" he inquired.

"You could say that. The car belongs to an agent of the DEA."

The security guard turned pale. He took a step back.

Tony grabbed him tightly by the arm. "Now, if you love your job, you're going to get to that warehouse before I do. You shoot at anything that moves. Understand?" he said.

The man swallowed and nodded reluctantly. "Understood." He pushed open the door. In one hand he held the pistol as instructed, while in the other he lit the way with the flashlight.

Unaware of what was happening outside the warehouse, Avery and Miss Marple continued to work diligently. They had already opened six containers. Contrary to their expectations, they had found no drugs. Instead, countless weapons. Some new, others obviously already used. Miss Marple was trained, among other things, to detect gunshot residue on a weapon that had already been fired. Avery felt giddy when she thought of how many pistols and rifles were here. Enough to equip a small army. She had carefully documented everything. The photos she had taken were already uploaded to the server. She closed the latest box, which she had just examined.

With a low whistle, she called Miss Marple to her. Obediently, the rat arrived and picked up a pumpkin seed. She grabbed the rodent and stowed her in her jacket. She took out her cell phone, intending to inform her colleagues in the drug squad but then reconsidered, since she had found weapons, not drugs. Those were the responsibility of the FBI.

She pressed a speed dial button.

"Avery! Where are you?" Cole asked after the first ring.

"I don't have much time. Get something to write with and listen."

The urgency in her voice was impossible to ignore. Although a thousand questions burned on his tongue after they had not spoken since her suspension, he kept his mouth shut and leaned across the table to reach for paper and pencil. "Shoot."

"I am located in warehouse 233A in old port section C."

"Yes. Got it. Go on," he said.

"Send a team, preferably tonight. There's a big shipment of weapons here. At least ten thousand pieces."

"Avery," he said. "Are you there?

"It doesn't matter. By the time you get here, I'll be gone. You can find the evidence on my server. The access code is MissMarple06051987."

"My birth date?" he asked, surprised.

"Cole!" came Avery's reply. "Can you focus here for a minute, please?"

"And with the name of your rat?" He didn't know whether to be flattered or offended.

He heard rumbling.

"I have to go," she whispered. Then she disconnected the connection.

"Avery?"

But Cole heard only the beeping of the phone line.

He dialed Jerry, while with the other hand, he booted up his computer to access the data in Avery's Cloud.

His eyes grew wide when he saw the photos.

When he didn't reach anyone at Jerry's, he dialed the next number. This couldn't wait. Especially not if Avery was in trouble, as he feared. She was such a stubborn person. Despite his concern for her, he couldn't help but feel proud of her at the same time. Perhaps not entirely legally, she had accomplished in one evening what both the FBI and the DEA had been trying to do for months. All he had to do was find a judge who wasn't in the Monsantos' employ and organize a search warrant. He knew who he would call.

He uploaded the photos to his account on the FBI's server. Then he grabbed the car keys. Luckily, he'd picked up his car from Tyler after work.

Avery wasted no time. Silently, she slid along the crates to the floor, glad she'd vowed to keep up her strength training until she was old and gray. Indeed, one never knew when it would come in handy; this was one of those times. Reaching into her jacket, she made sure Miss Marple was safe. Then she ducked behind the long row of boxes. Thanks to the intruder's flashlight, she knew where they were. *Two people, at least. Maybe security guards?* Cautiously, she stuck her head out from behind the crate.

"Up ahead. Shoot! Now shoot!"

Was that Tony? She pulled her head back just in time when a bullet whistled past her ears.

Time to run.

She grabbed the crowbar and ran through the next row and didn't turn until the far aisle.

If the one was indeed Tony, she thought he wouldn't try too hard. She focused on the location of the door, which appeared as a bright rectangle at the far end. Unfortunately, that was the only exit she knew for sure would be unlocked. Perhaps she should have planned her actions more thoroughly. It would have been helpful if she'd studied the floor plan beforehand.

To buy a little time, she threw the crowbar across the row into the nearest aisle. In the resulting noise, she ran as fast as she could toward the exit.

Behind her, she heard the men cursing. The glow of the flashlight panned back and forth frantically.

She stayed crouched and pricked up her ears. Her heart was pounding up to her throat.

At that moment, she would have absolutely not minded having Cole by her side, if only for the chance to argue with him. At least that would take her mind off this precarious situation for a bit. Since that option was not available, she consoled herself with the thought he had already pulled out all the stops to set up a raid.

For her though, the agents would arrive too late. If she judged the footsteps behind her correctly, there was no time to wait for the cavalry. She could hide in one of the crates, of course. Only, she had carefully locked them all again. Unlocking one would make too much noise to serve as a safe hiding place. Moreover, the thought of being locked in such a confined space for so long made her feel queasy.

Avery calculated the distance to the door. *Patience*, she thought, and crept forward. She dreaded the idea the two men might have split up. At any moment she expected to be grabbed.

But she was lucky until the last few feet.

Arriving at the end of the long line, she looked back—directly into the bright beam of the flashlight. Dazzled, she blinked and quickly pushed her way around the corner of the crate.

"Now we have you!"

You wish, she thought, and sprinted off.

Toward the door, through it, and to her car.

She would have liked to lock them behind but they were too close for that. If they reached the door before she had engaged the lock, she'd have no chance of keeping the door shut. Better she concentrated on the final destination, her car.

The soles of her sneakers slapped the asphalt. She came to a skidding halt in front of the car, yanked open the car door, and dropped into the seat. Before she had even trained her left leg into the car, she started the engine and drove off with squealing tires, grateful for her Corvette's horsepower.

Good thing I chose something impractical, she thought. *Probably just practically saved my life.* The Corvette was simply much better suited than a Fiesta for making a quick exit. She glanced in the rearview mirror. Astonished, she saw them watching her drive away and making no effort to follow. *Are they on foot? Environmentally conscious gangsters who were using public transportation?* A nervous giggle escaped.

She desperately needed a few hours of sleep before she set out on the long road to Independence. With a practiced flick of her wrist, she pulled Miss Marple from inside her jacket and placed her in the cardboard box on the passenger seat. "Well, little one? Did you survive the excitement?"

The rat blinked at her, unimpressed, and held out a little paw, her way of begging for food.

"Got it, of course, immediately after the excellent job you did back there."

Tired, Cole returned to his apartment at four-thirty in the morning. He unloaded his pistol and other gear and placed it all on the kitchen table.

The raid had been a complete success. Big A had left Valentina's sickbed and led the operation together with him.

All the weapons had been seized. Piles of paper identified Tony as the owner of the cargo. E-mails with clear, incriminating correspondence had been found on the computers in the offices. Even with an armada of lawyers, he would have a hard time getting his head out of the noose this time.

What had been missing until then was proof of Alberto's involvement in the whole thing. Being Tony's brother was not punishable. And there was no trace of Tony himself.

Cole went to the refrigerator and pulled out a carton of orange juice. He drank in large gulps until the carton was empty. His gaze fell on a bag of rat food sitting neatly on the counter.

He raised an eyebrow and went to his bedroom. Without turning on the light, he peered into his room. Sure enough, Avery was in his bed, just like Snow White. Despite their disagreement that morning, she had sought refuge with him. They might still have some hurdles ahead, but for the first time he was confident they would find a way together.

CHAPTER SEVENTEEN

AVERY TURNED INTO THE DRIVEWAY of her grandfather's house. She had been on the road continuously for two days, had traveled over one thousand six hundred miles, and felt every one of them in her bones. At least it hadn't snowed.

Several times during the trip, she'd had the feeling of being followed, but she never located her tail.

Although admittedly, she had been too tired to pay much attention. Her plan had been to sneak out of Cole's apartment unnoticed. She hadn't expected to wake up tightly wrapped in his arms. Thus sneaking away had been impossible. As soon as she moved, he'd woken up.

The following hours together had been wonderful, but were no substitute for sleep. The memory still made her feel hot in various places. *He's the only man in my life who's ever left a...lasting impression.*

It probably wasn't very smart to think such thoughts after a passionate night. The sex between them had never been the problem. It was all the rest that hadn't worked out so well. She pushed down her feelings. *It's not the time to deal with them. I successfully repressed them for the last ten years. A few days or weeks more won't matter.*

Since nearing Independence, she took several detours to avoid leading her pursuer directly to her grandfather. True, he was fit and had a nimble finger on the trigger of his shotgun, as well as almost one hundred percent marksmanship, but she wanted to spend a quiet evening and a restful night before dealing with any more action.

Avery sighed. She didn't know how Tony had done it, but she was pretty sure he'd bugged her car. The temptation to find and remove the tracking device was strong but it could wait until tomorrow. Hopefully by then she'd come up with a bright idea of how to use the tracking device to her own advantage.

She swung her heavy travel bag over her shoulder and lifted Miss Marple's box out of the car. She'd be happy not being locked up in her box after such a long trip.

Her grandfather was already waiting for her in the doorway of his log cabin. The term log cabin was not quite correct, though. More of an understatement. Even though the entire house was made from solid wooden beams, it was two stories high with huge picture windows reaching from the ground floor to the roof, offering an unobstructed view down the valley all the way to the center of Independence.

George Wilkinson had been very successful professionally. He was still a partner and consultant in changing ventures. "Otherwise, I get bored. A rolling stone gathers no moss," was his motto. He had an alert mind and a weakness for beautiful things, such as his log house.

Her grandfather was already over seventy and an impressive figure with his tall stature and silver hair. When he was out and about, he carried his walking stick with its chiseled silver handle. Not because he needed it. At least not to walk. He wasn't above giving someone a nudge with it, however, if he thought they desperately needed one. "Helps you think," he said.

Avery beamed when she saw him. Every time she came, she wished she hadn't let so much time pass without visiting him. This time was no different.

"Hello, Miss Wilkinson. Or should I say Mrs. Carter?" Grandpa George said, teasing.

Avery blushed. "As always, you get right to the point, George." Ever since she was little, she had always called him by his first name. She'd started doing it as a little girl and no one had had the heart to tell her that Grandpa or Grandfather would be more appropriate.

He laughed, amused. "Of course. I'm too old to beat around the bush. I'll be in the ground soon enough, so I'm not wasting any time."

"You'll outlive all of us," Avery said.

"That very well might be, especially if you keep playing with bullets and car bombs," he said dryly, but without accusation in his voice.

That's what she loved about him. His acceptance. He took her as she was.

"I see you're up to speed," she said, winking. "Let's go inside. Miss Marple can't wait to let off some steam in the living room."

Her grandfather looked to the side. "We'll have to see how it goes with her."

"Have you suddenly developed an aversion to rats?" she asked in wonder.

"Of course not," he said. "Miss Marple and I are friends."

"Well, what is it then?"

"I have a new roommate. Smiri."

"Smiri?" repeated Avery, still not understanding what the problem was. Most importantly, couldn't they discuss this inside? She was tired, she was cold, and something to eat wouldn't go amiss. When George made no effort to explain himself in the next few seconds, she resignedly dropped the heavy bag on the floor.

"Who is Smiri? Your girlfriend? Do I know her?"

He was still fumbling around, uncharacteristically. However, she was also surprised he had a girlfriend. He'd always been more the type to flirt with all the women at once and never really let anyone get close to him but well, if he had found someone, she would heartily support him.

"Whoever it is, I'm sure I'll love them. At least if I can take a seat at your table within the next minute and get something to eat."

"Smiri is a cat."

Avery's eyes widened. All through their youth, he had vehemently resisted a cat. Impossible critters, he'd called them. She'd wanted one for years and hadn't gotten one. No wonder he was acting like this.

"A cat? How did you get one? I thought you couldn't stand cats?"

"Actually, I can't either." He cleared his throat. "I made the mistake of visiting Kat," he grumbled.

Avery burst out laughing. "Well, looks like you've met your match." Kat ran the only local animal shelter in the area. She was extremely successful at placing her charges in new homes. When she was convinced she'd found a suitable candidate, she was not easily dissuaded. Avery admired her greatly. On the other hand, she was also glad to have Miss Marple as a good excuse why she couldn't take in another animal.

"How old is Smiri, then?"

"Just ten weeks."

"Then, yes, there's a chance that the two will get along. At the moment, Miss Marple will probably be almost taller than she is."

"That's right," he said with relief, finally pushing open the door.

Avery bent down and swung the bag back over her shoulder. "Well, little one," she said to Miss Marple, peering over the edge of her box. "It almost looks like there are more adventures waiting for us here."

Inside the cozy log cabin, it smelled temptingly like stew. Avery's mouth watered. The open kitchen adjoined the living room, separated only by a kitchen island. She maneuvered her bag onto the landing and set the box down on the kitchen table. After getting rid of her scarf and thick jacket, she took Miss Marple out of the box and set her on the floor. In a flash, the rat ran under the nearest sofa.

"Whoa. I think Miss Marple has already caught on that all is not as it should be here. Where's Smiri the kitten?"

George grinned. "I'm sure she'll be here any minute. She always naps in my office at this time of day. The office chair is her favorite place."

"What if you want to do some work?"

"Oh, I either sit her on my lap or I work from the couch."

"I can see she's already got you completely covered," Avery said.

"That's a kitten for you," he said. Moments later, the small tabby cat with a white belly and legs stuck its head into the living room. Like any self-respecting cat, she paused in the doorway for a moment, tail twitching, before deciding to join them in the living room. She marched confidently into the kitchen, sat in front of her bowl, and meowed.

"You're a little early, young lady," George said to Smiri.

Smiri ignored George and continued meowing. Avery had to stop herself from laughing. She was pretty sure George usually gave the kitten something immediately when she opened her mouth, but didn't want to embarrass herself.

Miss Marple ventured out from under the sofa. Either curiosity had lured her out or she had seen the kitten and decided that it was not an enemy to be taken seriously. Nevertheless, she sat at an appropriate distance.

Smiri took one look at the newcomer, arched her back, ruffled her fur, and hissed for all she was worth. Then she retreated and hurried toward the stairs.

Equally frightened to death, Miss Marple jumped and climbed up Avery's trouser leg. Avery picked her up and placed her in the crook of her arm. The rodent's whiskers trembled indignantly. "I can see we have some getting used to there. I'm just not sure yet who we need to watch more. Do you eat little cats? Or is the feral cat more likely to eat you?"

Miss Marple did not answer, but pushed her little head between a fold of Avery's sweatshirt.

The next morning, Avery parked her car in the large parking lot in front of the community center. Actually, she had wanted to sleep in but for some reason she'd woken up bright and early and had not been able to get back to sleep, so she drove downtown.

Her morning social media search on Independence's page had revealed that Aileen had since opened her patisserie called *Sweets.* Comments on it were mixed. Some welcomed the much-needed gastronomic expansion. The diner was fantastic, and much the comforting establishment people enjoyed. Others felt they had to show solidarity with the Diner Sisters and were strongly opposed. As far as Avery could tell, Miss Minnie and Miss Daisy were proud of their relative Aileen, who was only three blocks away, and praised her to the skies. The only thing they complained about was that they had more work to do, since Aileen had taken a lot of the load off them while working for them over the last six months.

She would definitely pay Sweets a visit. The photos on the beautifully designed webpage were promising. So promising, in fact, that she couldn't wait to try one of the delicacies. The profiteroles with their creamy filling called her name as soon as she saw them.

But she knew better than to go directly to Sweets. First she had to report to the Diner Sisters if she didn't want to mess things up with them—and she definitely didn't want to do that. After all, the diner was still the only place downtown that served hot meals. If she didn't want to have to rely on her own poor cooking skills or her grandfather, she better remain in good standing with Miss Minnie and Miss Daisy.

Miss Marple on her shoulder, she stepped into the diner. Normally she would have left her at home with her grandfather but since he was also out that morning, she hadn't dared. Smiri was small, but after what she'd seen yesterday, also infected with delusions of grandeur. She didn't want to risk anyone—*Miss Marple!*—getting hurt out of sheer hubris. Although Miss Marple could hold her own and might even show Smiri a thing or two!

Miss Minnie was pouring coffee for Jake and his deputies and thrust the pot into the hand of the nearest person when she caught sight of Avery rushing to meet her. The rat was just barely able to escape into the hood of her jacket as Miss Minnie pressed Avery to her expansive bosom. Out of experience, Avery didn't resist the hug, which was quite tight. It wouldn't have done any good, anyway. Only after a few long seconds did she let go of her. Miss Minnie took Avery's face in both hands and said, "Child. What a worry you have caused us! It's time for you to get married and have children!"

Avery would normally have been mortally annoyed by her remark, but she saw the mischievousness flashing in Miss Minnie's eyes.

"I'm fine, as you can see."

"Thank goodness." She let go of her face and reached for her hand. "But what do I see there? No ring? Then my information was wrong?" She looked honestly dismayed.

Avery bit back a laugh. "I thought I'd stop by for a minute to calm this bubbling rumor mill a bit. It might keep the absurd bets in check a little."

Miss Minnie didn't seem to be comfortable with that either. "How boring."

"But necessary," Avery reminded her, "unless you've started making fictional bets?"

"Oh my goodness. Of course we don't, but maybe you could...embellish your life a little? The way you put it, it doesn't sound very exciting any longer." She glanced out the window. "At least you bought a hot new car. I was beginning to think they'd completely softened you up in California."

Amused, Avery shook her head. If car bombs were less exciting than a used Corvette, she didn't know either. "Do I get breakfast in exchange for information?"

Miss Minnie's look became calculating. "Full story? Including the juicy details?"

Avery called upon her undercover training and fibbed without batting an eye. "Sure. Anything you want."

Tony stood outside in the cold under a large canopy as Avery left the diner. About time she got out of there. He was cold. When he'd left in such a hurry, he hadn't expected to end up in these darn mountains of all places. His suit from Armani looked good, but it was not warm. He had neither a coat nor a scarf. He had been tempted to buy a coat at the local feed store but the sight of the padded lumberjack shirts had made him feel quite queasy, and he had retreated.

The men who went in and out of there, on the other hand, were another matter. If he had known that they grew into such doozies thanks to the mountain air, he would have moved his hunting grounds to Vail or Aspen years ago but what was not, could still become.

He was hungry, too, he thought, as Avery stopped once again to talk to a passerby. Did she know half the town? With only one restaurant in this hick town, he had no choice but to wait until she finally left. He didn't want her to see him. The time was not yet ripe.

Out of the corner of her eye, Avery saw Tony shaking from one foot to the other. She almost laughed out loud. The city boy looked pretty lost. Served him right. She wouldn't let his presence rattle her. She didn't think he was that stupid to shoot at her in broad daylight. The way she saw it, she clearly had the home field advantage.

She went to the right and turned onto the main street. Sidewalks lined the street and led past various stores. The houses were older and built close together, the overhanging balconies forming a kind of arcade, so that one could window-shop even in bad weather. This was especially important for the stores that specialized in tourists.

Avery passed the old dance studio, which housed Jaz's yoga studio on the upper floor and was used by Pat and Tyler as a joint training space for dance and martial arts on the lower floor. She tried to peek inside, but the frosted window that stretched across the width prevented her from doing so. Maybe she'd peek in on Jaz later. If she was lucky, even Cammie was there. The thought of the little bundle of joy warmed her heart. The Carters were family people. Probably the population of Independence would double because of their family alone, if the children continued in the pattern of their parents. The fact that she would be involved, if she pursued the matter with Cole, was something that she tried not to think about.

Two steps forward and Avery already arrived at the patisserie. She could have found her way blind. The smell of freshly ground coffee beans and melted chocolate hung in the cold winter air for blocks. The building, which used to be totally run-down, had been given a new coat of paint. The broken window panes had been replaced, and Christmas lights gave the patisserie-slash-café an inviting touch.

She pushed open the door. A bright chime sounded.

Inside, she pulled her gloves from her fingers and stuffed them into the pockets of her jacket. Miss Marple climbed out of the hood and onto her neck, sticking her white muzzle out from under her chin-length bob. Hastily, Avery shoved her back into the hood. She had no idea what Aileen would think of rats in her sanctuary. The health department would have a fit, that was for sure, but they weren't on site. The only question was whether the owner would see it that way, too. Rats were always a tricky subject. Many people were fundamentally disgusted by the cute animals. Moreover, they were still associated with vermin and epidemics. Which, of course, was complete nonsense for a well-cared-for pet like Miss Marple. Unfortunately, not all people gave her enough time to explain.

Avery looked around the medium-sized room. It was, of course, much smaller than the diner but the space was used optimally. A long bench ran along the wall. In front of it were small, round tables, each with a chair on the other side. Small, square glass vases in which ferns grew adorned the tables. She felt strongly reminded of the cafés in Paris.

"Can I help you?"

The voice belonged to a tall, slender woman with clear features, dark eyes and short, dark curls that framed her head like a cap. She was dressed all in black, black blouse, black pants. Over this she wore a dark red apron decorated with gold lettering. Her hands, which she had placed loosely on the counter, were unadorned. She wore a long golden chain. She exuded a natural elegance that Avery immediately envied. Avery had many talents; effortless elegance, unfortunately, was not one of them. Oh well. At least she could take a gun apart and put it back together in a few seconds, she consoled herself. And train rats.

She extended her hand across the counter to the woman. "Hi. You must be Aileen. I'm Avery. You probably know my grandfather, George. George Wilkinson."

Aileen's eyes glittered with amusement. "Hello, Avery. Pleased to meet you. Sure I know Mr. Wilkinson, the old charmer."

Avery smirked. "I can see you haven't been spared either."

"Oh, I actually find him very charming. He always behaves himself. Even when he's buttering me up."

"I'm sure he does. That's why he gets away with it." She rolled her eyes.

"Are you just here out of curiosity or did you want something to eat?"

"You've got to be kidding me. Has that ever actually happened, someone coming in and leaving empty-handed?" Avery laughed and cast a longing glance at the baked goods on display: cupcakes, profiteroles, tarte au citron, macarons, savory quiches—there was no end to the delicacies—not to mention the various breads.

"Now that you mention it, no, I don't think anyone ever has come in without getting something." Aileen clapped her hands. "You could say my little bakery is a success. You made my day with that comment. In return, you get to choose something now, too. On the house, of course."

"You'll never stay in the black if you're going to give freebies away like that," a voice behind them jokingly interjected.

Aileen's eyes lit up. *Interesting,* Avery thought. The voice behind her sounded familiar, but she couldn't place it.

"Oh, my daily delivery of cheerfulness is here. I'll be right there. Just let me get some food and drink for Avery." Aileen took a plate from the stack and loaded it with a variety of things.

Avery, meanwhile, turned to the person who had joined them. "You're Lily from the flower store, right?"

"Right. And you're...?"

"Avery. George Wilkinson's granddaughter."

"That's right. I remember now. But the fact that you're...what? Four? Five?...years older than me, I couldn't place you right away."

"For me, it was much easier. I've bought flowers from you many times before."

"Speaking of flowers," Aileen cut in, handing Avery a plate that was almost invisible among all the goodies and a cup of steaming coffee.

"Thank you."

"You're welcome."

Aileen turned to Lily. "What nice thing did you bring me today?"

Lily blushed slightly. "I thought it would be a good idea to start getting the decorations a little more Christmassy. After all, it's only a few more weeks."

Avery watched the exchange between the two with interest. It looked as if two people had found each other. *I wonder if they already knew that*, she thought. She hadn't known that Lily was interested in women. How could she? Unless she wanted something from the person in question, she didn't give a darn about the love life of the others.

"I'm going to sit over there. Nice meeting you, Aileen. And to see you again, Lily."

Both waved absentmindedly at her. Obviously, the delightful arrangements of prickly holly leaves, red berries, and white flowers of a winter plant Avery didn't know about required their full attention. Or more likely, the opportunity for them to be together, she thought with amusement. She knew this condition. It had been no different for her in recent weeks with Cole.

Cole. She should probably call him. Bring him up to speed. Especially about Tony's presence in Independence.

Lost in thought, she bit into an éclair. And moaned. That was *sooo* delicious. Nothing against Miss Daisy's cooking but this was in a class of its own.

"Can you tell me why you didn't open a bakery in New York? What's a genius like you doing in our humble Independence?"

Aileen laughed. "A lot of people ask that but you can't imagine how much money it takes to open a new business in New York. I really wanted to do that, though. Continuing to work for others was not an option. So I had to find a place where I could afford it. So when I found out the Diner Sisters were here, it was an easy decision." She let her gaze drift to Lily. "It was definitely worth it."

Embarrassed, Lily averted her eyes. "I'll go and get the rest of the arrangements from the car."

"Looks like you have some convincing to do," Avery groped. She didn't know Lily very well but at least better and longer than Aileen. She didn't want Lily to get hurt. She already knew she couldn't stop it, and that it was none of her business. Still, she could feel a little ahead.

CHAPTER EIGHTEEN

"It's worth fighting for the good things in life," Avery said. Was it true of her and Cole, too? Had she given up too soon? Should she have tried longer to explain her point of view to him? She didn't know. She was pretty sure she hadn't given him a real chance yet again. However, the various DEA cases had also kept her on her toes.

Speaking of which, it was time she got back into some work. She may no longer be "officially" working with the DEA, but neither was she going to forget the cases she'd dedicated so much time to. And the fact that Tony was nearby...well, the sooner this was all solved, the sooner she could spend time with Cole and seriously deal with the fact that she no longer had a job—but first things first.

A few hours earlier, she'd talked with Valentina on the phone. She had been pleased to hear her teammate was on the road to recovery. She'd been discharged only that morning. Big A put her up at his house, despite her protests. She was taking a break for the day, but she would be back at work the next morning.

Tony Monsanto kept Avery busy all day. She'd driven her car to Mike's garage after the heavenly experience at Sweets. There she had taken the trouble to look for the transmitter and had found it. After a ten-second internal struggle not to trample it with her heel, she borrowed another car, drove two hours out to Cloudy Peak, and hid it there.

It was a beautiful viewpoint in the middle of the Rockies and far from any civilization. She grinned. *I hope Tony filled up his rental car before setting off on his wild goose chase.* Either way, she was pretty sure he wouldn't bother her again that day. She would have loved to see the reception the people at the diner had given him. Italian designer fashion wasn't something you saw too often in town.

When she got home, Avery grabbed the murder case files and snuggled into her blanket on the sofa. She would use the afternoon to start from scratch again and profile the killer. Hopefully, the work would distract her a bit. The spinning thoughts about Cole were getting her nowhere. She wanted to call him, but if she did, she wanted to be able to offer some new insight. *Well,* she thought. *It looks like I'm still trying to prove myself to him. Another issue I should finally address.*

Two hours and a hot chocolate later, she sat up abruptly. How could she have missed that? Tony fit her profile only part of the way. For someone else, however, it was perfect. Even the motive was there. Excitedly, she reached for her phone. *Where's the stupid thing when I need it?* It rang and vibrated at the same time, revealing its whereabouts to her. She reached under her butt, where it had slipped, and pulled it out.

Cole calling, the display read. *What a coincidence.* "I'm glad you called," she blurted out.

"You won't believe this, but..."

"You have a new body."

Silence on the other end of the phone for a moment.

"How do you know?" he asked.

"Because I know who the killer is."

"You know who the killer is?" repeated Cole.

"Have you turned into a parrot since I left?"

"Uh, no. Of course not. I'm just a little surprised that you'd trump my news like that, out of the blue."

"That's because I'm good," Avery said without any false modesty.

"It sure looks that way. Not that it's a new insight."

Wasn't it? she thought. No matter. She would think about it later. Now she had to share her news first. "I've done another profile with all the new info we've gathered in the meantime."

"Don't keep me in suspense."

"Is the dead man Travis?"

"Yes. Unfortunately."

"Crap." She felt a twinge in her heart, as she always did when she had failed to save someone from a horrible fate. "If only I had thought of the solution sooner."

"Let it go," Cole said. "It won't do any good."

She swallowed. "I know. Still."

"Yes," he agreed with her. "We feel responsible. I feel the same way. So, let's nail this bastard. Who is it?"

"Alberto Monsanto."

"Alberto? Are you sure?"

"Very sure. It's the only thing that makes sense. Especially since we made a connection between Tony and the dead bodies that keep piling up. Tony just doesn't have the chops for such atrocity. Besides, what sense does it make to constantly kill your new lover right away?"

"Afraid of discovery?"

"Possibly, but he'd be more likely to hire someone else to do the dirty work. You've seen how successful that was with their failed attempts on my life."

"Wait a minute. You think Tony is behind the attacks on you?"

"I suspect the man who knocked me down outside Travis's partner's apartment was Alberto. I believe he came back to cover any tracks that could lead to him or Tony. In the process, he must have recognized me. The man didn't become successful because he's an idiot. Once he recognized me, it must have dawned on him that Maria and I were the same person," Avery said. "So, I had to be eliminated. Since Tony had dragged me into the family, it was also Tony's responsibility to get me out of the way. Fortunately for me, Tony doesn't like to get his own hands dirty, which supports my theory that he can't be the killer."

"But what motive does Alberto have? I can't imagine he's a trophy hunter. As you just said, legal or illegal, he's a very successful businessman. Why would he put all that at risk to kill a few people? As far as I can tell, none of the victims ever had anything to do with him personally."

"The family is extremely Catholic and family honor is paramount. I'm assuming he found out Tony was gay and then tried...I don't know, but if I have to guess... *damage control.*"

"*HMM.* Okay. In a strange way, it makes sense," Cole admitted. "And you're sure it couldn't have been Tony? In a Dr. Jekyll-and-Mr. Hyde kind of way?"

Avery chewed on her lower lip as she considered. "When did Travis's murder take place?"

"Two days ago. So, one day after your stunt in the warehouse. The whole team sends their love to Miss Marple, by the way."

"Glad the troop knows who is responsible for the success of this investigation up until now." Avery smirked. "But anyway, Tony couldn't possibly have killed Travis. At the time, he was crossing the Arizona-Colorado border a few cars behind me."

"Tony did what?" Cole said. "And you're just mentioning this now? Is he in Independence?"

Avery held the phone a little farther from her ear. There was no reason to suffer hearing damage just because the man couldn't control himself. She let him rant on for a few moments until she decided to cut it short. "Now calm down. I've got everything under control."

"No wonder we can't find him. The prosecution wants to talk to him urgently."

"She's welcome to, but first? I still need him." Avery shook her head.

"Do you really still need him? What for, please?"

The distrust in his voice pained Avery. Did he really trust her so little? Oh well. At least that answered the question of whether she should have tried harder to convince him of the rightness of her career decision ten years ago. If he still hadn't figured it out, it was hopeless.

"Knowing who the killer is and proving it are two completely different things."

"I realize that, too."

Avery rolled her eyes and was tempted to slap her phone against the wall. Better yet, to smack Cole with it. It was too bad he was so far away. "I will get you the evidence you need."

"But…"

"Sorry, the connection…*kkkrcchz*…mountains…"

She pressed the phone's off button.

The conversation had not gone quite as she'd imagined. Well, he had been suitably impressed by her new profile and seemed to agree with her conclusions in principle, but the rest she could have done without. *He would probably prefer to lock her up in a tower,* she thought angrily.

Where was Miss Marple, anyway? She looked around the room. Alarmed, she realized she couldn't spot her anywhere. Shoot. Hopefully there hadn't been a confrontation with Smiri.

Avery put her notes aside and kicked off a wool blanket. Wearing socks, she walked across the smooth wooden floor to the kitchen. No sign. No pink rat tail in sight, either.

Finally, she pushed open the door to her grandfather's office. Smiri's tail tip hung over the edge of the chair. Still no sign of Miss Marple.

She went to the desk to pet the kitten. When she got there, she stopped, stunned. Miss Marple and Smiri were nestled close together on the cushion of the chair. Both blinked at her in wonder, as if they didn't quite know what all the fuss was about.

Okay. Apparently she had worried for nothing.

Perplexed about what to do after she'd solved a difficult case and had no one to celebrate with, she took out her phone and scrolled through the contacts. Surely someone would be able to be found with whom she could celebrate a little. Tyler? She was still in sunny California, lucky girl. In Independence, snow was forecast for the next day. The first snow was always special, but she knew that by the third day of shoveling the driveway, she'd be longing for spring.

Astrid? She had played volleyball with Astrid in high school. However, she was at the university in Denver writing her doctoral thesis. Besides, she hadn't had any contact with her for ages.

Paula? Paula was definitely a good person to chat with. With her, she could complain about Cole, too. Paula wouldn't take it personally, even if it was about her brother, but would she had time? Now that she had a child, so to speak? Avery shrugged unconsciously. There was no harm in calling, after all. She simply couldn't think of anyone else to ask. Pretty sad, she knew. On the other hand, she had always been someone who had a few good friends instead of many superficial ones.

Cole looked at his phone in disbelief. Had Avery actually hung up on him? She couldn't be serious about the age-old trick of faking a bad connection. Which led him to conclude that she had definitely hung up on him. On purpose. And that was two seconds after she told him a criminal on record with ties to the Mafia was hot on her heels.

That's no way to make me stop worrying about her, is it? Determined to do something, he picked up the phone and called Big A.

"Cole. What's wrong?" Big A asked.

Cole wasn't surprised that Big A knew right away that this wasn't a normal call between friends. They had been working together for quite a while. "Can you do me a favor?"

"Always. What's it about?"

"It's about Avery. Apparently, she didn't drive to Independence alone. Tony must have put a tracker on her car. Now our prime suspect is sitting in the Rocky Mountains plotting Avery's imminent demise."

"What are you waiting for? Go. Valentina and I will take care of the rest of the investigation here in San Diego."

"Thanks, man," Cole said. "I knew I could count on you."

"Can we skip the emotional stuff? You have more important things to do now. Saving your future wife, for example."

"The only question is whether she even wants to be rescued," Cole grumbled sullenly. *Did he just refer to Avery as my future wife? Is everyone in on this, or what?*

"You're on your own with that particular problem," Big A hastened to add, laughing a smidge. "Maybe ask her what her plan is first. That usually helps."

"Don't make me laugh. If she has a plan, I sure don't like it."

"Listen, Cole, you're a great partner, but when it comes to Avery, you're as stubborn as a mule. If I remember correctly, that strategy cost you a lot last time."

"It's okay, Dr. Love," Cole said. "You know I can't stand it when you analyze me. Especially when you're right. I need to introduce you to my mother because you're both always right. You'd get along well."

Big A cracked up. "Whatever. Your funeral, buddy."

"On second thought? Not a great idea about you and my mom. Too dangerous. Within two days, the two of you would be plotting to take over the world, and within another twenty-four hours, it'd work!"

"Just come on in," Paula called from inside as Avery stood on the porch of the big ranch house knocking on the door. Inside, the dogs were going crazy, yapping at the top of their lungs. How Paula put up with that racket was a mystery to her. She knew that in two minutes the dogs would have calmed down, but until then, it was incredibly loud.

She stepped into the house and was immediately greeted by a cloud of aromatic scents. She identified oregano, thyme, and rosemary.

"When I said we could have pizza, of course I had meant to call the pizza place," Avery called out as she pet the dogs.

Paula grinned and shook her head. "Girl, you've been living in the big city too long. This is Independence. Not San Diego. We don't have a pizza express here."

"That had actually slipped my mind. After all, I brought wine with me. However, I stole it from George."

"Then I know at least it's good."

Avery laughed. "Definitely it is! Only the best for my grandfather." She looked around the kitchen. "Where's Leslie? In the barn?"

"No. She's with Nate and Shauna. She's spending the night there."

"That's great."

"Sure," Paula grumbled, then added something that sounded like "little traitor."

"Trouble in Paradise?"

"For that question, I need a glass of wine first. Or whiskey. Whichever you prefer."

"*AHH*, I think I'd better start with the wine for once. If the evening calls for it, we can always upgrade to whiskey."

"Reasonable."

Paula pointed to a round rolled-out dough and pushed some small glass bowls toward her, filled with various things.

"Here. Tomato sauce, mozzarella, and assorted garnishes." Paula pointed to the bowl in the center. "These are roasted vegetables. We've got olives, ham, chorizo, pineapple, mushrooms...are we missing anything?"

Overwhelmed, Avery sat at the table. "That's more than enough different ingredients. Everything looks so delicious. I'm just going to make a pizza with everything."

"That's the right attitude. First we eat and drink. Then we're sufficiently fortified for the serious conversations of life." Paula winked at Avery. "Where did you leave Miss Marple?"

"At home. She fell madly in love with George's cat. When I left, they were sleeping side by side in harmony. I didn't have the heart to wake her," Avery said. "Besides, I don't trust your two scrounges." She threw a pointed glance at the two dogs, who rested peacefully under the table.

"Maybe that's for the best."

Later that evening, the two women sat on the living room sofa. Avery poured her heart out to Paula. Maybe Paula had some inside information about her brother with the macho problem. She was pretty sure she wasn't slurring her words. Not yet. It had definitely been easier to string words together in the correct order before all the wine, though.

"He just doesn't trust me with anything," Avery said. "He probably figures I should have gone to the nearest police station and left everything to the local guys once my suspicions were confirmed."

"Now, just slow down. I think you're confusing things," Paula said. "How would you feel if he were in your situation?"

"Of course I would be worried, too, but at the same time? I would trust him to do his job well," she said.

"Really? So you wouldn't be tempted for a moment to rush to his aid?"

"Yes, I would, of course I would," Avery said. "Makes sense to have backup, after all."

"Oh." That was all Paula said. She didn't need to say anything more.

"That's very different," Avery asserted as it dawned on her what she had just said.

"It's not and you know it. He's just worried about you. Granted, a little more tact wouldn't hurt him but you'll get that through his skull, too."

Avery closed her eyes. Not a good idea, she realized as the room began to spin. She snapped her eyes open.

"What's going on with you and Nate, anyway? And don't try to shove me off with empty platitudes," Avery warned her friend.

Paula sighed. "His view and mine of how certain things should go are very different."

"You mentioned something about marriage?"

"I know. Leslie once again couldn't keep her mouth shut." Despite the harsh words, her mouth twisted into a loving smile.

"It's understandable, with a subject like that. Is she happy about it?"

"About what?"

"Well, that you're getting married soon."

"We're not."

"Wait...what?" Avery asked. Somehow, she was having a hard time following the thread of the conversation.

"Nate would have to ask me first."

"But...I thought he had already proposed?"

"No. He didn't." Paula raised her whiskey glass and took a sip. "He informed me that it would not make sense to get married after all."

"Now what?"

"Exactly. I'm waiting for him to come to his senses."

"So, do you still want to marry him?"

A moment passed before Paula answered. Roo snored as Paula swirled her drink, making the ice cubes tinkle.

"Yes, I do, but I could never have imagined it before. But with Nate? I can imagine it. Very well, in fact. The kids would be delighted, too."

"Then what's the problem?"

Paula snorted. "As unromantic as I usually am, I'd still quite like to be asked."

Avery laughed. Only when she realized Paula wasn't joining in the laughter did she catch herself. "Oh my God. You're serious. He hasn't actually proposed yet?" she asked, her eyes wide.

Paula nodded.

"Geez. Well, let's see how long it takes him to figure out what he did wrong."

"This could be a long time coming."

Avery agreed wholeheartedly. All you had to do was look at her and Cole. Ten years had passed and they still hadn't solved their problems. Would they ever?

Paula turned her head toward her so that their faces were very close. "We're already a couple, aren't we? We both have great men—if they weren't such clueless jerks from time to time."

"I blame their screwed-up chromosomes," Avery said.

"Ha. That would explain it, but I can't take care of everything. He's going to have to take care of that issue on his own and get out of his comfort zone."

"Are Leslie and Shauna helping Nate get on the right track?" Avery asked. "Maybe I could put them on Cole, too?" She laughed and took another gulp.

"I'm definitely glad I got to vent my anger about my future husband to you today, even if he is your brother." *Shoot. Did I just refer to him as my future husband? Talk about a Freudian slip!*

"Unfortunately, that doesn't stop him from acting like a temporary idiot."

Avery chuckled. "Apparently not."

"Are you going to tell me about your plan now?" Paula asked.

"Sure. Like I said, having backup is always good. I would have let Cole in on my plan, too, if he hadn't been so busy yelling at me."

And then she let Paula in on her plan.

CHAPTER NINETEEN

WHERE'S TONY?

Alberto looked down from his office window at the hustle and bustle of the harbor. Ever since he took care of his brother's last misstep, Tony disappeared off the face of the earth. So, he was beginning to worry. During Tony's...*escapades*, he'd never stayed out overnight.

He appreciated the comforts their shared home offered. From the food their chef prepared, to the top-notch wines and spirits, to his comfortable bed—and his brother's bank account.

The FBI had already questioned him twice to find out where Tony was. No wonder, after the disaster at the warehouse. Against his lawyer's instructions, he had cooperated. He felt that being as forthcoming as possible would only benefit him in the long run.

Since he had no idea where his brother was, they were welcome to question him as long as they wanted. He was just glad he had wisely kept his business and Tony's separate from the start. The only problem were the customers. They didn't care at all whether Alberto and Tony filed taxes separately or together. They simply wanted their goods. Which couldn't be delivered because the FBI had confiscated them.

Fortunately, he could rely on his middlemen. A new shipment of weapons was already on its way. Still, his customers did not like to wait.

I want to wring his neck. Hope he's finally put an end to this undercover agent, because it had all started with the little snake.

Should he send a private detective after his brother? After careful consideration, he decided against it. He'd wait two more days. There was no need for outsiders to know about the rift running through the family.

If the behavior continued, he might do the unthinkable and get rid of his brother. It was not what he wanted, but he also had to be realistic. With all the problems Tony was bringing and causing to the business, he was becoming a serious liability.

Cole waited for his suitcase at baggage claim. He would have preferred to travel with just a carry-on but he wouldn't have been able to take his service weapon with him. He hadn't had enough time to apply for a special permit, so it had to be in a checked suitcase. Under no circumstances would he set out in pursuit of Tony unarmed.

Finally he caught sight of the battered suitcase. He took a step toward the baggage carousel and impatiently pulled it off. All he needed was a rental car and he'd be at Avery's in a few hours.

He wasn't sure how she'd receive him. In retrospect, he had to admit that he had not handled the situation very well, but when he had heard that Tony was on her heels, one or a dozen fuses had blown. *Justifiable,* he thought. *After all, Tony had already tried to kill her three times. The fact that he'd never tried to do it himself was no proof he wouldn't eventually. Desperate people don't act logically.*

There it was. *I just better not overdo it when I see her. She's not into having a man...any man...try and save her. She doesn't need saving. Still, I can't help being worried.*

Tony woke up in a bad mood in what he'd describe as a shabby bed-and-breakfast. He spent the previous day trying to follow the GPS signal. In vain. Somewhere in the mountains, he lost the signal. Well, not exactly lost. The signal was still there, but no sign of Maria or her flashy Corvette. Didn't make sense. However, his technical understanding had never been his strong suit. If the position of the signal hadn't changed, he'd go home. His brother could stay away. There was no way he would go through another conflict like yesterday. First, he got lost on the way back. The country roads all looked the same, with nothing but rocks and boulders on either side, trees below and snow above. How anyone could voluntarily live in such a place was beyond his understanding.

Then his car died. The tank was empty. Shaking, he made the long way down into the valley. His expensive shoes were ruined. His salvation had been a taciturn old man with a huge beard who had spoken exactly four words. "Ran out of gas?"

Tony nodded, hoping that maybe the man had a filled spare canister in his crowded truck but he had only held open the passenger door and said, "Damn tourists."

Reluctantly, he accepted the invitation to get in.

Soon he had to realize that his assumption that the guy would drive him directly to the next gas station and back to his car was completely wrong. He had important things to do first. Like bringing the still warm liver of the deer he had shot to his sick friend. Of course, the sick friend lived on the next mountain, far away from any gas station.

It continued in this manner until Tony almost lost his nerve. He would have loved to shoot the old man. He was surprised at how bloodthirsty he had been lately. Well, he corrected himself, bloodthirsty was the wrong word. A gun was a pretty neat thing after all. Only the idea he'd never, ever find his way back to his car kept him from giving in to his urge. By the time he had arrived back in Independence, it was nine o'clock. So he postponed dealing with Maria for another day.

He glanced at his cell phone. It was almost eleven. Without much hope, he checked the GPS signal. What he saw gave him pause. Had it moved? Indeed it had. Maybe his patience was worth it after all. Tony checked his messages.

His good mood immediately vanished again. *A dozen missed calls from Alberto. Since when is my brother such a mother hen? He should be thrilled I chased Maria away from the warehouse, but it was just like always. No matter what I do, it's never good enough.* Tony rubbed the back of his neck and tossed the phone aside.

Cole tracked down Avery through the customers at the diner, Jake, and his mother, who relayed she'd gone to Paula's ranch. Sometimes nosey residents have their good points, he had to admit.

He drove to Paula's ranch. She'd be staying on the western part of the property, away from the main house. A narrow dirt road led directly to an old cabin. He parked his rented Toyota Corolla at the turnoff behind some trees. *At least my rental's black and not pink*, he thought as he got out. He walked the rest of the way. He didn't want to risk alerting anyone.

Hidden in the shade of a tree, he found Avery. She was lying on the ground, a rifle pressed to her cheek. He glanced toward the cabin and spotted a black Mercedes parked next to her red Corvette. Both great cars. No Toyota Corolla for the mob. Or for Avery, but that was another topic.

Tony was there, sitting in the car and seeming to be mulling something over. Cole hoped the pondering would last a moment, at least until he informed Avery of his presence. Careful not to make any noise, he approached her from behind.

Avery's neck prickled. She took her attention off Tony for a moment, who was still sitting in the car, making no move to get out. *What was he waiting for? For a written invitation?* She skimmed the surroundings in a semicircle, but couldn't spot anything that warranted the tingle. Concentrating, she turned her head a little. At that moment, the wind shifted and carried to her a scent she knew all too well. Sometimes it haunted her even in her dreams. Admittedly, the scent was heavenly. If she could bottle it and sell it, she was guaranteed to win a prize. Nevertheless, it was highly undesirable right then.

She closed her eyes in annoyance and counted to ten. "What are you doing here?" she hissed.

"*UM*. Needed to see you?" he said, although Cole seemed to realize the response didn't seem appropriate, especially since it looked like Avery had everything well in hand.

Tony, finally getting out of his car, deprived him of an answer.

They watched as he circled the cabin once. Hesitantly, he approached the door and pushed down the handle.

"Looks like he suspects a trap," Cole whispered.

"It's not like he's completely stupid, just desperate," she said, starting to move.

"Do you need help?" he asked, hurrying to follow her.

"What do you think?" she said.

Cole looked appropriately contrite.

"Anyway, no, I don't need any help. Watch and be impressed." Carefully, she crept up to the cabin. Cole waved goodbye to her, and she waved back, stopping herself from rolling her eyes. *I don't need a knight in shining armor to handle this.*

She pushed open the front door, following behind Tony. From inside, Tony's deep voice muttered. Good. He was busy with himself and wouldn't hear her slip into the room behind. She'd sprayed the hinges of the door with WD-40 as a precaution before the action and had plenty of time to prepare herself.

"Well, well, well. My little Maria," Tony said when he saw the woman sitting at the kitchen table. He pulled his pistol from his waistband. "No goth clothes today?"

She didn't turn around.

Tony continued in a jovial tone, "Sure, I forgot you aged fifteen years overnight and now you drive a Corvette. That looks better on you than the black eyeliner, anyway. More fitting for your age."

Avery shook her head in amusement. That was actually pretty funny, what he just said. Unfortunately, from her vantage, she also saw him holding the gun. He was shaking badly. Not a good sign. Moreover, he was already very close to Paula, who was sitting at the table with a black wig.

She had no more time to lose. Taking a big step forward, she thrust the barrel of her gun into his back. "Drop your weapon."

Obviously confused, Tony tried to turn around.

"Maria?"

"That's right. Maria. Turning around is still a bad idea."

"Very bad, in fact," Paula butted into the conversation, standing up in one fluid motion, turning around, and unceremoniously snatching the gun from him while pointing at him with a shotgun.

Tony looked from one woman to the other. He looked so stunned to find two of them that he didn't offer any resistance when Avery expertly handcuffed him and read him his rights.

Cole almost couldn't stand it outside anymore. *What was going on inside?* Apart from a few snatches of conversation, nothing could be heard. Were they having a darn tea party there or what?

He was all the more surprised when, a few seconds later, Avery came out with Tony in handcuffs. His sister Paula followed them. In one hand she held a black wig, while in the other? Her shotgun named Betty.

"We did good," she told Avery.

"Definitely. We're a dream team. Thank you so much for your help. I couldn't have done it without you."

"Don't mention it. The problem will be more that Jake won't want to give you up."

Jake? What did his brother have to do with all this? Cole thought, irritated. She asked Jake for help and not him?

"Can someone explain to me what's actually going on here?" Cole asked. As soon as the words were out, he wished he'd bitten his tongue. Damn.

Avery gave him an annoyed look. "I think that's pretty self-explanatory? Wanted felon, handcuffs, law enforcement, arrest?"

"You don't work for the DEA anymore," Cole said. "How...?"

"You're right. I don't. But as of today, I work for the sheriff of Independence," she said with a smug grin. "I was officially made a temporary deputy a few hours ago."

Cole blew an appreciative whistle. "Smart move. I'm impressed." Oh, that's where his brother came in. That made sense. Smart of Avery to hedge her bets. That way Tony's lawyer wouldn't have any leeway in getting the bastard released. He loved watching her work. It turned him on beyond belief. Something he should consider before he freaked out the next time he was worried.

Avery stopped in place, her grip on Tony tight, and stared at Cole as if he had grown two heads. "Just like that? No moralizing?"

He shrugged. "Why should I? That was a textbook bust. You obviously thought this through." His look revealed even more than his words could. "I have all the respect in the world for you."

She smiled and bit her lower lip; he recognized the expression in her eyes.

Cole looked at her, and the world around him disappeared.

"Can you guys maybe slobber on each other later? I'd like to finally get into my cell, or at least into a police car," Tony grumbled, interrupting the intimate connection. "This place is freezing."

"Quiet," Avery said, giving him a good shove. "Nobody asked you."

"Hey, that's police violence. In front of witnesses," Tony cried.

Paula burst out laughing. "Far from it. Standard operating procedure when restraining and transporting a violent suspect, I'm afraid."

Horrified, Tony stared at her. "Honestly?"

"Don't push it," Paula said, tapping the side of Betty the shotgun.

He shook his head in disbelief and said, "Fine. Fine. No problems from me."

Jake drove up in his police car.

"Finally," Avery called out. "You sure took your time. I was beginning to think I'd have to listen to this creep for ages."

"Oh, I knew you guys had that covered." Jake smiled, eyeing a handcuffed Tony.

"And what if things hadn't gone smoothly?" Cole asked, which earned him an irritated look from the two women.

"What happened to being proud of us!" Avery yelled.

"I am. That has nothing to do with it!"

"No?" she asked.

"No offense, but I'd still like to ship my detainee to the police station now," Jake interjected. "We can work out questions of morality and principle later."

Tony willingly let himself be led to Jake's car and got in.

Avery gave Paula a hug. "Thanks again. And we'll do another night like last night soon."

"Absolutely. I have a lot of free time in the evenings right now," she said with a smile that didn't quite reach her eyes.

"You wait and see. Maybe your time off will come to an abrupt end." She glanced to the side, where Cole stood. "Sometimes the jerks surprise you, after all," she whispered rather loudly. "Despite themselves."

Cole cleared his throat behind them. "I heard that."

"Good. I meant for you too," Avery said without turning to face him.

Cole really liked this version of Avery. Keeping his eyes on her ass, he grinned. He liked it very much, in fact, even if she had just called him a jerk. He'd convince her otherwise in time. He liked this view so much that he started whistling.

Jake was already in the car when he rolled down the window and called out, "Meet me at the station? I assume you'll want to talk to him, too, after I'm done with him."

Avery and Cole nodded in unison. "Gladly. And please, remember: take your time with the official report. I still need his help on another case. So it would be good if the arrest could remain our secret for now," Avery said.

"*HMM*. Of course, I'll be silent as the grave," Jake said. "On the other hand, of course people will talk."

"Oh really? I wouldn't have thought so," she teased. More seriously, she continued, "I'm more concerned with police channels than local gossip. If the FBI gets wind that Tony Monsanto is in your cell, you'll get a medal and an immediate visit from the FBI."

"I know that. That's what we talked about."

"Right. I just wanted to make sure."

"Got it."

Cole, still standing off to the side with nothing to add to the conversation, felt himself getting upset again that Avery had discussed all this with Jake instead of him. Nice view or not.

Finally Jake drove off, and he relaxed a little.

Paula hugged them both goodbye. "I have to go. See you later. And please do me a favor: If you're going to kill each other, you'd better not do it on my land. It always makes such a mess."

Cole put his arm around Avery's shoulder. "Don't worry. We'll go across the street on public land."

"Good idea. So, bye you two."

When Paula left, Cole spun around to face Avery. "And now for you, Deputy Wilkinson. If I've put this all together correctly, this was only the first part."

"*HMM*. Yes." She stifled a grin.

"I want to hear every detail, but first? I have to get something done that can't wait."

"What...?"

Cole put one hand on the back of her neck, the other nestled her right cheek.

And then he kissed her.

Seconds or minutes later—who knew for sure?— they broke away from each other.

"What was that for?" she asked.

"You don't know how attractive you are when you're in full work mode. I'd love to stop time then and drag you into the nearest dark corner," he said.

"Really?" she asked. "Work mode?"

"It's hot. You know exactly what you're doing, you don't take crap from anyone, and you're very confident in your demeanor."

She backed away a little to get a better look at him.

Cole wasn't done with his list. "Those jeans, top, and boots don't hurt either. Especially not with your insane body."

She gave him a playful shove. "I knew there were motives at play in your statement." But she smiled as she said it and pulled him a little closer by the waist.

Cole closed his eyes and just enjoyed her closeness for a moment. Then he opened them again and said, "We really should talk quietly for once. I'd hate to lose what's so obviously between us a second time."

She said, "Yes. Okay."

Whereupon he kissed her again.

Finally, she pulled away from him. "As much as I'm enjoying this, we don't have time to waste. Let's go to Independence, check out the new patisserie, and discuss the rest of my plan. Then you'll be prepared."

"I'd love to. Is the patisserie as good as people rave?"

"Better. Much better."

CHAPTER TWENTY

With a plate full of heavenly sweets in front of her—she hadn't been able to decide between the bright red cupcakes or a slice of the espresso chocolate cake so she ordered both—Avery set about explaining her plan to Cole.

At first, though, she looked with pity at his little lemon tart. "Do you want me to wait until you get a refill?"

"Why? That's plenty. Not everyone is a glutton like you."

"That may well be but you speak from pure ignorance. Try it and then we'll talk further."

Cole shrugged. He didn't understand all the excitement about Sweets. Sure, a little variety in Independence was great. In fact, when he compared the place to Breckenridge, Independence was something of a culinary desert. Except for the Silver Lodge, which was a bit out of town, the diner was the only place to eat, but food was food. It was either good or it wasn't. The subtleties usually eluded him. He only made an exception for a good steak. There were very real differences. Starting with the meat, to the method of production, to the spice, everything played a decisive role. Absently, he bit into his lemon tart. He chewed, widened his eyes, chewed some more, swallowed, and devoured the rest of the tart with a second bite. Determined, he stood up. "Be right back."

Avery grinned. "I knew it!"

When he came back to the table, she said, "You see, it's well worth listening to me."

"Yeah, yeah. Go ahead and ride it. Speaking of listening to you: I'd love it if you'd let me in on what you're up to."

His gaze bore into hers.

She narrowed her eyes to slits and appraised him. *So he wanted to argue?* Fine. He was welcome to it.

Not noticing the change in her attitude, or perhaps he had simply chosen to ignore it, he continued, "Partners work together. You don't go on a late-night recon tour without taking your partner with you, or at least informing him."

"I wasn't your partner at that point," she shot back.

"That's bull-doggy. A mere formality, and you know it. You don't just stop being partners."

Crap. He was kind of right about that. She glanced to the side, rolling the arguments back and forth in her head. Finally, she said, "Have you ever considered that maybe this is related to your reactions to my plans?"

"My reactions?"

"Yes."

He rubbed his hand over his face. "You mean like yesterday? When I almost jumped through the phone?"

At least he sounded reasonably contrite, Avery thought. "Exactly. I wanted to let you in on my plans yesterday but you were far too busy yelling at me."

"So, you thought just hanging up would solve the problem?"

He raised his eyebrows and stared at her challengingly.

"Honestly, yes. On my side, at least, it was obvious you weren't in the mood to listen, for whatever reason. I wasn't in the mood to be yelled at. Certainly not ten minutes after I practically cracked the case. Since I only have control of my emotions, it seemed the most sensible thing to do was to hang up."

Now it was Cole's turn to look aside, embarrassed.

Avery gave him time. Better because she didn't know what else to say. From her side, pretty much everything had been said.

"Shit. Listen. When it comes to you, sometimes I just blow fuses." Cole looked ashamed.

"I noticed," she said pointedly. She just couldn't help herself. After all, she had been dragging the feelings around with her for ten years. The fact that the same discussions were being repeated did nothing to help her forgive and forget.

"You are very, very important to me. I just worry about you." Avery was about to flare up, but he stopped her with a placating hand gesture. "Please. Listen to me. After this, you can get all worked up if you want."

She kept mum and listened.

Cole went on. "What you don't understand is that my concern for you is not because I don't trust you with anything. On the contrary. I know you're an outstanding agent. Having you as a teammate is a dream. We work well together, we always have, and that's incredibly valuable, as you know yourself. That said, I don't want anything to happen to you. And before you come back with the fact that you could also fall off a ladder at home tomorrow or get under a bus, I know all that. Nonetheless, the fact is that we put ourselves in potentially dangerous situations day in and day out."

"Looks like I won't be doing anything dangerous like window washing in the future," quipped Avery, overwhelmed by the intensity of his words.

"*HAHA*. Do you understand my concern has nothing to do with your abilities?"

Avery tugged at the flower arrangement that was on the table. Lily had been there again, it seemed. She pulled herself together and focused again on the man in front of her.

"You say that now but at the time you actually thought women had no business in narcotics."

The tips of Cole's ears turned red. "What can I say? I was young and arrogant. And selfish. I wanted you to stay close to me. You flat out refused the FBI, though, and that's what I wanted to do. I hoped to convince you to study something else and go to Quantico with me. In my youthful delusion, I couldn't think of anything else to say but 'you can't do it.'" He raised his eyes and looked directly at her. "Believe me. I've regretted that sentence countless times. And I'm really sorry if it gave you the impression that I didn't appreciate your work."

Avery was surprised to realize how thoughtful and mature his words were. Apparently she'd been carrying around even more old grudges than she'd thought possible. But she still wouldn't let him off the hook quite so easily. "And yesterday? That's when it slipped your mind on short notice that I'm a trained agent? If anyone could have heard you, I'm sure they would have thought you were talking to a teenager who wanted to play a baby detective."

"The thought that Tony Monsanto, only a few minutes earlier our prime suspect in multiple murders and proven responsible for two or even three specific attempts on your life, was after you just, drove me half crazy. Especially since I was over 1,500 miles away and had no way to support you."

Avery remembered Paula's question about how she would feel if the roles were reversed. She had to admit, the chance that she would have freaked out for a moment was realistically quite high. "Why didn't you at least call me back later when you had calmed down a bit?"

Cole ducked his head a little. "Uh, I've been busy arranging my flight to Denver, talking Jerry into letting me fly here, and getting all my stuff in order."

"And all this is just to dissuade me from what I'm trying to do?"

"No," Cole said. "Of course not. I was just scared something might happen to you."

"I appreciate that, and that you took the time to actually fly here," she said. "But you could have just called me."

"Is it so bad that I'm here?" he asked.

Surprised, she looked at him. "Not at all. I just would have preferred it without all the drama."

He rolled his eyes and ducked his head a little. "Just don't let Jake hear you say that. Or Paula. Better yet, none of my family. I'll be hearing that for the rest of my life. Cole, the drama queen."

She laughed. "That may well be. Is everything good between us now?"

"I don't know. Is it?"

She nodded. "It is. Absolutely, tough guy."

A broad glow stretched across his face. Spellbound, she stared at him, fascinated by the transformation it brought about in his expression. She would try to make him laugh more often in the future.

Cole brought her amazement to an abrupt end as he reached across the table and grabbed her hand. "Tell me about your plan so we can get started because I'd like to finally close this chapter and get back to you and me."

Damn it. She finally had to stop always assuming the worst right away. "Okay," she said.

He stroked her fingers with his thumb. "It's time we found out if we can bring the magic of ten years ago back to life."

"I would love that," she said. Relieved, she squeezed his hand. "All right. Let's go to Jake's so I won't have to go over everything twice. "

Everyone had gathered in the largest room, the break room, because there was no actual meeting room at the police station. Jake was there, his deputies, Polly Miners the former cop who had actually retired and was now doing the office work, and of course Cole. Astonished, Avery saw Ace was there, too. What was the chief of the local fire department doing there?

Jake pointed to Ace. "I called Ace in because, as a former SEAL, he's seen a few hostage handovers. If, contrary to expectations, everything doesn't go according to plan."

This elicited great laughter; from experience, nothing ever went according to plan. It was more a question of how much would go wrong.

The sheriff waited until the laughter died down. "I'm glad for any extra help. Now I'm going to turn the floor over to Special Agent Wilkinson."

Avery rolled her eyes. "Based on the fact that most of you have known me since I was in high school, I am Avery to you. There's no need for formality. Isn't that right, Sheriff? Besides, strictly speaking, I'm not a special agent anymore, I'm a deputy sheriff."

Jake raised an eyebrow.

Avery took a deep breath and brought everyone up to speed. She gave a rough overview of her work as an undercover agent and how she had subsequently been transferred to Cole's team at the FBI to profile the serial killer because of her knowledge of the Monsanto family.

She only dealt superficially with the attempts on her life. She was of the opinion they were only marginally related to the investigation.

Jake stepped in. "Tony was actually stupid enough to complain loudly that this was all your fault. He's not at all pleased that you so consistently refuse to die."

"I can well imagine that but, as you know, weeds don't die." She laughed.

Cole grinned. "In any case, this means we already have his confession for the attempts on Avery's life. That makes our case a lot easier."

"When will he be transferred to California?" Polly asked; she was handling logistics.

"Good question," Avery said. "Not just yet. First, we want to catch his brother."

"His brother? What does he have to do with all this?" asked Toby, one of the deputies.

"We now suspect that he is behind the murders. Our problem is that we can't prove it."

"Now I understand," Ace said. "You want a confession."

"Exactly."

"Ingenious, but risky," he said and nodded.

Cole frowned. "And how are you going to get that?"

"By making him an irresistible offer. His brother's life in exchange for information."

"And you think he cares that much about his brother's life?"

Avery shrugged. "If I pitch it correctly, yes. At least I hope so. The fact that I'm unemployed and no longer working for a government agency should help, too."

"I thought you were a deputy?" he teased her.

"*HAHA*. Normally Alberto Monsanto is very well-informed but I doubt that his feelers reach all the way inside the Independence Police Department. However, I will specifically scatter information to make sure he learns the right things."

"What do you need from our side?" Jake asked. "We know the broad outlines of your plan, but how do you envision putting it into practice?"

"How many do we have? Polly, you, and four deputies? So six. Ace, Cole and me, that's nine."

"I'm sure Big A will come if I ask," Cole said.

"And Valentina?" Avery asked.

"I'm pretty sure she'll go with Big A," Cole said. "Believe it or not, they still consider you as part of the team."

Avery smiled. "Amazing. Okay. That makes eleven of us. Plus, I still need to ask Jeff and Jarvis for help. I need the Silver Lodge for my meeting with Alberto."

Cole whistled softly through his teeth. "Now I understand. You're not just baiting him with his brother, you're giving him a proper environment where he'll be tempted to brag about what he's done."

"Exactly. He'll think I want money in exchange for his brother to make a nice life for me in South America. This business transaction will take place in the upscale setting of Silver Lodge," Avery said. "If I do it right, he'll practically be eating out of my hand."

"Let's not get cocky," Cole warned. "Let's not make the mistake of underestimating the man. He's killed seven men without getting caught."

"Of course. That's why I'll need half of you as extras in the restaurant. The meeting will take place on a day the lodge is closed. So I need guests, not many, but a few, and of course appropriate service personnel to make it look authentic." At the last sentence, she wiggled her eyebrows and looked at Cole expectantly.

"No, no," Cole said. "Absolutely not. I'll be outside just monitoring the situation."

Avery laughed. She had suspected that was how he'd react. "Whatever. We can decide that later. In any case, your total secrecy is important. Keep it off social media, texts...anywhere it might be leaked." She looked around urgently.

Jake folded his arms in front of his chest. "Now you just have to be careful not to offend us. You're talking to capable police officers here, not some provincial sheriff."

She raised her hands. "I'm well aware of that. It's just that I know the gossip potential of certain fellow citizens. Believe me, I know what I'm talking about."

"You still haven't shown us any photos of Vegas," Toby said.

Avery ignored him.

"When is this going to take place?" Toby asked, changing tact.

Avery looked from Cole to Jake and back again. "We need a few days for the preparations. Then the people have to come here first. In a week?" She turned to Polly. "When does the lodge have its day off?"

"Usually on Monday."

"That's the day after tomorrow. That's too short notice. Then we'll have to postpone it until next Monday."

Cole made a mental note. "I'll talk to Jeff and Jarvis. If the day they're closed is mentioned on their homepage, we need to delete that right away. I don't want Alberto looking at the site and getting suspicious."

"Good idea. Alberto always does his homework very conscientiously. He hasn't been so successful because he's stupid, that's for sure."

"Then we just have to be careful that some unsuspecting mountain people don't stumble into the situation," Cole said.

"My guys can take care of that," Ace intervened.

"Really? Great," Jake said.

"Do you think that's smart? That means more people we have to rely on," Cole mused. "I understand the question may feel a little disrespectful, but we just have to make sure everything's out in the open and be realistic."

"I understand your concern but what Jake said applies to the guys in the fire department, too," Ace said resolutely. "Avery's safety comes first."

Jake pulled his phone out and checked his messages. He looked up. "Everyone, listen up. Momma Brenda's inviting us over for dinner."

"All of us?" the others asked.

"All of us," Jake confirmed. He glanced at his brother. "That's especially true for you, bro, and your girlfriend."

Avery ducked her head. Maybe she should bring Grandpa George along. He could provide a distraction, if need be. Maybe. If he didn't gang up on Brenda. Possibly she could hide out with Paula?

"Is your sister coming, too?"

"Yes, she is."

Crap, Avery thought. *So much for an escape plan. The only thing to do is grin and bear it and hope we survive the excess of friendly, concerned interference.*

CHAPTER TWENTY-ONE

"Paige? Are you ready to go? We're about to leave."

Paige ignored Kat's call. There was no way she could go. Sam's mother had invited them to the big family-and-friends dinner. Kat decided the friends-part extended to her, too. Paige was anything but sure. So, she had decided to have a quiet evening at home. The latest newsletter for *Safe Haven* was due soon and the photos of the new arrivals she took a few days prior needed to be uploaded to the shelter's social media accounts. She had more than enough work to keep her busy for a few hours.

Maybellene, the schipperke dog she had adopted, stood expectantly in the doorway, wagging. "I'm sorry to disappoint you but we're not going there today."

The dog stared at her for a few seconds, unblinking. When she realized that Paige would not move as expected, she turned and ran down the stairs, yelping.

Paige sighed. That dog was an old tattletale.

Someone showed up at her door moments later. She hadn't even heard any footsteps. However, it wasn't Kat, as Paige had expected, but her boyfriend Sam. Surprised, she blinked. "What are you doing here?"

Admittedly, not exactly the friendliest greeting. After all, they were getting along reasonably well ever since she'd fixed things up with Paula and Leslie, and Kat had so reliably helped out with publicity and all the administration. Nevertheless, there was still a certain tension between them.

And now he was there.

He nodded. "My family would be very happy if you came," he said, not unkindly.

Paige tilted her head. "Is that so? Why do I find that hard to believe?"

"Honestly." He grinned, and Paige realized once again why her friend had fallen in love with him.

"I'm sorry I've been giving you such a hard time. It was really great what you did for Leslie and Paula."

Paige shook her head. "Did you just say something nice about me?"

"Yes, I did," Sam said, laughing.

"*OOPS*. Did I just say that out loud?"

"You did." Sam was obviously very amused by her reaction.

"Maybe you can do it again? Then I'll make a video of it this time. Such memorable moments should be documented."

"*HAHA*. What now? Are you coming?"

Paige sighed. "All right, but I'll take my car. Then I can leave if it gets too much for me." Maybellene heard and raced into the room, sitting at Paige's feet expectantly.

That earned her a shrug from Sam. "Whatever you say."

She grabbed her thick down jacket and Maybellene's collar and slipped it on. That wasn't so easy. The little dog sensed that they were on the move and enthusiastically jumped up and down. They all left her room. She turned off the lights on the way out and they went downstairs.

Maybe it will be nice, she tried to reassure herself. On her way out, she hissed to Kat, "What did you put in your honeyboy's food?"

"Why?"

"He apologized to me."

"Wow. I wouldn't have thought so. I mean, I love him but sometimes he can be a really stubborn guy. Especially when it comes to his family."

You don't say, she thought. Out loud she said, "Yeah, right. Wow."

"All's well, then," Kat said, and the subject was closed.

Fifteen minutes later, they arrived at the Carter family home. When she saw the cars along the driveway, Paige wasn't so sure anymore whether it had been a good idea to come along. Tense, she buried her fingers in Maybellene's fur. The dog sat on her lap, as the trunk of the big Chevrolet Escalade was full with two full-grown mastiff dogs and Bella, the attack-dog-something mix Kat had rescued from certain death less than a year ago.

She hadn't been there then, but the story of how Kat had single-handedly broken up a dog-fighting ring was still fondly and frequently told in dramatic tones. Especially to newcomers. She must have heard the story half a dozen times. Pretty impressive, considering that people had only talked to her for the first few weeks. After that, she had become *persona non grata* virtually overnight.

Things improved somewhat, she had to admit. At the diner, she was served again, and someone even sat at her table from time to time. Maybe she was just too sensitive. Or still had a guilty conscience. She looked out the window.

They passed parked cars when she saw an old Jeep Wrangler. Ace was here. Heat rushed through her like a jolt of electricity. *Panic, pure panic,* she told herself. And knowing at the same time that she was lying to herself. Of all the responses, Ace's polite but permanent ignoring of her had been the treatment that had hurt the most. There had been a time when she thought there was a connection between the two of them. Since then, he'd made it clear more than once it was not so.

She tried to think of an excuse she could bring to go back home. Unfortunately, she could think of absolutely nothing, especially since she had given in at the end and had gone with Kat and Sam in the car.

Maybellene, sensing her inner turmoil, stretched and licked her chin. She suppressed a giggle. If someone had told her a year ago that her best friend would be a dog, she would have laughed.

Avery leaned against the wall next to Paula as she watched the colorful activity in the living room. The decision to stand next to Paula was a strategic one. She hoped to avoid Brenda's interrogation that way. At least, she suspected there would be an interrogation. If so, she would put her grandfather on it to take Cole to task. *Equal justice for all.* Knowing George, though, he would do so even without a specific invitation. She grinned.

Paula, who was currently holding a bubbling Cammie, looked at her. "That grin was pretty sneaky. Do I want to know why?"

"Oh, I was just thinking about concerned parents," Avery said. "Or grandparents. And that worrying never ends. No matter if you're sixteen or twenty-eight."

"That's probably why Jake ordered Jaz to produce a boy next," Paula said. "He said another girl would cost him too many nerves. He's already dreading the time when Cammie goes out with a boy for the first time."

Avery sighed. "Probably greets him for the first time with a shotgun and takes him on a tour of police headquarters."

"I think so, too. Speaking of parents? Here comes my mother. I think she wants to see you. Have fun!"

"Hey!" shouted Avery after Paula. "I needed you for moral support!"

"I'd love to. Later." Paula waved her off, obviously not ready to take on being her mother.

Avery wanted to ask about the kittens. Maybe she could distract Brenda by asking about Jill and Jack's welfare?

"It's nice to have you with us again. This time without a stalker in the family," Brenda opened the conversation as she casually leaned against the wall next to Avery.

Avery wasn't fooled. Brenda was always well-informed about what was going on with her five children. Nothing escaped her. She probably had psychic powers, or at least eyes in the back of her head, and ears like a lynx.

"I'm happy to be back, too," Avery said. "Every time I'm here, I'm struck by how much I missed Independence."

"Does that mean you'll be staying longer this time?" asked Cole's mother, casually.

"Uh, maybe. I don't know. It depends."

Brenda sighed. "Bummer."

Although she had expected the surprise attack, she was now a little caught off guard. Probably mostly because she didn't really know what the correct answer to the question was. If it was done with saying whether she would like to stay in Independence, the answer would be easy, but there was still one small detail to clarify: what would she do for work in the future?

"I would love to stay around. Most of all, I would also love to stay in one place for once and make a real home, but I just quit my job," she said, "or was let go, it's not really clear to me yet. In any case, I have no idea what I'm going to do next."

"I heard you were appointed deputy sheriff today?"

"That's right, but it's only temporary," she hastened to explain. "It was important for a case Jake was helping me with."

"I'm sure he'd be interested in making it something permanent."

"I thought there was also a budget issue and therefore a political issue?" Avery asked.

"Oh, if you could imagine it, I'm sure Jake could make the mayor understand the need."

"Wow. Okay. That's good to know but I think I need to sleep on it a few more nights first. I really don't know what I want to do yet."

"Sure, but it's always good to know as many options as possible."

"That's right. Thank you."

They sipped their drinks.

Brenda asked, "So, has my son finally come to his senses?"

Avery looked at her. "What do you mean?"

"Well, has he arrived in the twenty-first century by now and realized that women make just as good—if not better—Federal cops as men?"

"You know about our dispute then?"

"Girl, of course I knew that. He's my son, after all. Even though I love all my kids, that doesn't mean I'm blind to their faults."

Avery lowered her eyes and looked at the tips of her shoes. "I always thought you would blame me for us breaking up."

"It's not about guilt. It's about whether two people can find a way together. I can only trust that I've given my children enough common sense that they have the tools to do that. What they then do is beyond my control." She laughed softly. "In this specific case, unfortunately, he had decided to turn off his brain. So my question is, has he put it into operation in the meantime, as far as you're concerned?"

Completely dumbfounded, Avery just stared wordlessly at Brenda until she finally rolled her eyes and said, "Now don't tell me yours is out of commission, too? I had such high hopes for you."

"You had high hopes for me?"

"Of course. You're very good together, and you have enough fire that you'll stand up to him even if he overshoots the mark again."

"Or turn off his brain."

The corners of Brenda's mouth twitched. "Or that," she agreed.

Avery took a deep breath. "Then you'll be happy to know he's in the process of using his common sense." She looked over at Cole, who was laughing at a joke Leslie had just made.

Brenda watched Avery look at her son and nodded with satisfaction.

A murmur of voices came from the corner of the sofa. Leslie gestured wildly with her hands. Paula leaned down to the girl and was listening intently. Worry lines appeared on her forehead.

"Dolly was sweating and kept checking her belly. I got worried and told Shauna about it," Leslie said. "She thinks it's colic and her dad always says colic is really bad."

"Why didn't you say anything before we left?" Paula asked.

Leslie went on. "I wasn't sure how bad it really was. It wasn't until Shauna insisted on calling her dad that I realized what a terrible mistake I had made."

Paula frowned. "And did you call Nate?"

"Yes. He said he'd be there in twenty minutes."

"When was that?"

"Just now. I came to tell you right after I got the call."

Paula studied Leslie's expression for a moment. "Get Shauna and say goodbye to Brenda. We're leaving in two minutes."

Leslie bit her lower lip and nodded, her eyes on the ground. "Got it," she said before dashing off.

Paige slipped into the kitchen. The evening had gone surprisingly well so far. Everyone had been very nice and had included her in their conversations. It looked like she really just needed to let go of her guilt toward Paula and her resentment toward everyone else. It's just a bummer that it wasn't that easy to just let go.

Overwhelmed by all the people and her emotions riding a roller coaster, she needed a breather. Maybe she should try this yoga breathing she had learned during her first and, so far only, yoga class with Jaz? Probably that was the next thing, which sounded easy, but in reality was anything but.

The kitchen was dark, lit only by the light that burned in the hallway and the living room. To get a glass of water, it was enough. Without turning on the light, she went to the sink, took a glass from the draining rack and filled it with tap water. Greedily, she drank the whole glass in a few gulps and filled it again. There was simply nothing like the clear water of the Rocky Mountains.

Ace was sitting in the dark at the kitchen table. He had come here to see if there were any of Brenda's meatballs left. And to switch off a little. For the last few days he had been on his feet constantly, looking for wayward hikers. People were equipped as if they were going to climb Mount Everest, but listening to the weather report or taking a paper map with them was something few thought to do. After all, there was Google Maps. Unfortunately, there was no cell phone reception in many places in the area.

He found the meatballs. His peace, too. So he was not very pleased when someone came into the kitchen. From his point of view, his break could have lasted longer. He was even less pleased when he saw who it was. Paige, of all people, with the cheerful laugh, the quick-witted manner that betrayed her intelligence, and the body of a pin-up girl from the fifties.

He forced himself to forget that when it became clear what a mess she had thrown Paula's and Leslie's lives into because she had not kept her promise.

For Ace, it was irrelevant whether she had done it on purpose or not. The damage was done and she had been the trigger for it. For him, who put loyalty and honor above all else, hers was inexcusable behavior.

Then he'd watched the light go out in Paige's eyes as she realized the magnitude of her mistake and the people united against her. Against his will, compassion stirred in him. As a result, he had ignored her. Quite successfully, in fact. In the meantime, he had learned he was not allowed to look into her brown doe eyes under any circumstances. That helped enormously.

Ignoring her was difficult in a twenty-square-foot room. He kept very still and hoped she wouldn't see him if he didn't move.

Paige rinsed the glass, then looked around the kitchen for a dish towel. When she saw Ace's dark figure in the corner, she let out a small, strangled cry. "Jesus.

You scared me." She took a deep breath. When the fright slowly subsided and he still said nothing, she frowned.

"Who does something like that? Just sitting there silently and not saying anything when someone comes into the kitchen."

"Me, by the looks of it."

She rolled her eyes. "Behold, he speaks," she said, the sarcasm in her voice clearly audible.

The right corner of Ace's mouth twitched but he stopped himself from smiling. It would be much easier to ignore her if she wasn't so funny, he thought grumpily.

"What are you doing here all alone in the kitchen anyway?"

He considered not answering but that would have been rude. He could no more bring himself to be rude than to betray a friend. What she had done, he remembered sternly. So he would answer politely, but distantly. "The same as you, probably."

"And that would be?" she asked.

"Enjoying a moment of relative silence." The voices of the others were audible, but not as overwhelming as in the living room.

"I thought I was the only one who needed a breather."

"Why is that?" he asked, genuinely surprised at her statement.

"Well, until recently, no one talked to me at all. Now most people are talking to me again, but it's exhausting. I feel like I have to dodge hidden landmines all the time."

He shrugged. "What did you expect? That everything is forgiven and forgotten just because you straightened out your mistake? People have a long memory for such things. It will be quite a while before the people of Independence trust you again. Until then, you'll probably have to endure strained conversations and dodge landmines."

Paige flinched. "You fight hard, don't you?"

He shrugged again as if none of it mattered to him at all. "I like to call a spade a spade. Doesn't do much good to beat around the bush. Pure waste of time." As Ace listened to himself, he wondered when he had actually become so insensitive but his words had already hit their target. He could no longer take them back.

"Uh-huh," she said. "I get it." Paige eyed him wordlessly for a moment. Then she went to the door where she turned and asked, "You haven't answered my question yet. What's your excuse for hiding out in the kitchen?"

"Double shift at the fire department. Skiers who went off the trail. A missing boy. Ten years old."

"Did you find them?"

"Yes."

"So, it was worth it then. I'm happy for you. I'll leave you to your break, Mr. Tell-it-like-it-is." With these words, she turned around and disappeared into the hallway.

Ace sat for a while, staring at the spot where she'd been standing. That was the problem with Paige. Every time he thought he knew who she was, or what she was like, she surprised him all over again and he had to revise his image. Extremely annoying.

Why this annoyed him so much, he preferred not to think about it too hard.

CHAPTER TWENTY-TWO

With both children in the back seat of her truck, Paula drove home in silence. She glanced in the rearview mirror. Leslie and Shauna were silent, too. The two held hands. Probably out of concern for Dolly. Something still felt strange but she could not tell what it was. Perhaps simply concern for the pony.

After twenty minutes, she turned into the driveway to her ranch. Nate's truck was already parked by the barn. Good. Then there was a good chance he had already injected Dolly with a muscle relaxant. The drug worked reliably for colic. They would spend the rest of the night monitoring Dolly and taking short walks at regular intervals. The girls would certainly want to help out. Tomorrow was school, but she could write them an excuse for first period, after all. She felt that real-life experience definitely outweighed school.

She parked next to Nate's car. "So, girls, we're here. Please go in quietly. Don't want to scare Dolly and the other horses."

"Let's do it," said Leslie, who had already gotten out and was impatiently waiting for Shauna, still busy climbing out of the high truck.

Shaking her head, Paula watched the two of them run toward the barn. They braked just before the barn door and actually slipped slowly through the gap-width open gate. She opened the glove compartment, pulled out her gloves, and slipped them on. The hat, which was on the passenger seat, followed. Not exactly a fashion statement, but warm.

In the middle of a winter night in a barn somewhere in the Rocky Mountains, the need for warmth trumped the need for beauty every time. Wrapped up so warmly, she reached for the girls' hats and gloves. They had been left behind in all the excitement.

She crossed the frozen ground with long steps. All of Independence hoped it would snow soon. She glanced up at the starry night sky. *No snow today or tomorrow. Maybe we'll be lucky for Christmas.*

With her shoulder, she pushed the gate open a little farther. She stopped as if frozen. The picture inside the barn was different from what she had expected, and she was tempted to go out and back inside again. Maybe then she would end up in the right movie.

Nate was wearing his best boots, dark blue jeans, and a white shirt. He looked scrumptious. Maybe she should reconsider her sex moratorium she'd pronounced in the heat of the moment because of the stupid marriage topic.

Her gaze fell on the horses. All three were standing in line. Their coats shone and their manes were decorated with flowers. Dolly was no exception. Apparently she was in the best of health. At least, she thought, trying to make sense of the situation.

Nate held a bouquet of flowers, she belatedly noticed. His Newfoundland dog Nessy and her puppies Barns and Roo lay at his feet. Sensibly without floral decorations in their coats. Nessy didn't distinguish so well between edible and non-edible, only between chewable and indestructible. The only animals missing were the two cats and their two hundred head of cattle. Would probably have been a little crowded, though.

When her thoughts calmed down a bit, she suddenly felt hot. Was that supposed to mean...*Oh, no!* Panic rose in her at once. Did she really want this? Was she ready for it? Or had she better retreat while she still could?

But then her gaze fell upon the two girls who were standing at the side with expectant expressions and the same flowers in their hair as the horses, still holding hands. *I'd better think here and get my nerves under control before I disappoint everyone for no reason.* She swallowed as she realized the importance of this moment. Not just for herself but for the whole family. Her family.

Nate watched Paula closely. None of the many emotions that flashed across her face escaped him. So it was easy for him to tell when panic was setting in. He had expected it. After all, he knew her very well by now. So well that he wanted to marry her. He only hoped that despite the panic, she would come to the same decision as he did. For the first time, he began to have doubts about whether he had handled the whole thing the right way. Leslie and Shauna thought so, but now it all depended on Paula.

Paula was really struggling with herself. Until she saw the uncertainty flash in Nate's eyes, followed by a look of pure affection. She knew then that everything would be okay. Somehow, they would get through life. With everything that came with it. She broke out a wide smile.

A load fell from Nate's heart. Now everything would be all right. He walked over to Paula, the dogs on his heels, and knelt down in front of her.

On the side, the two girls giggled quietly to themselves, and their excitement was almost physically palpable.

Paula looked at the tall man at her feet and bit down hard on the inside of her cheek to keep from laughing out loud. Somehow it seemed wrong to her to see him there. She liked that he was big and strong and a worthy sparring partner. Her steadily rising tension didn't help her imminent burst of mirth, either.

"Paula, you know..." he began. He didn't get any further. Nessy, who was obviously deliriously happy that her master had finally joined her on the floor to play lunged at him. Under the onslaught of fifty pounds of accelerated Newfoundland, even Nate went down. Of course, Roo and Barns didn't want to miss any of the fun and joined in, yelping loudly.

It looked so funny that Paula couldn't hold back for the life of her and cracked up.

Shauna and Leslie, who had been trying to stifle their laughter behind their hands, laughed, too.

Paula took pity on Nate. She let out a short whistle. Roo and Barns stopped fussing and laid down on the spot. Unfortunately, they were a little close to Nate, who was still busy pushing the giant black dog off.

She grabbed Nessy by the collar and tugged it. With their combined efforts, they managed to push the dog aside so that Nate could stand up. Once he stood, Paula distracted the playful dog with a horse treat.

Nate patted the dust off his dark pants, only to realize after a few seconds it was a completely futile labor of love. He grinned wryly when Paula looked at him.

"That didn't really go according to plan," he said.

"You don't say," Paula said. "But you have to admit it suits us."

"And the best part is, we got it all on video!" cheered Shauna.

Leslie, who was older and thus knew very well that this announcement would probably not meet with much enthusiasm, tugged at her quasi-sister's sleeve. After a heated discussion, held in whispers, the two ducked into the feed room.

Paula walked over to Nate, put her arms around his neck, and ran the tip of her nose along his cheek. He let out a deep sigh. "What were you about to say when you were so blusteringly interrupted?"

He pressed his forehead to hers. "Paula. It's you. The woman for the rest of my life. You, Leslie, Shauna, and the whole four-legged pack."

She smiled and he smiled, too. "Was there a question hidden in that sentence?" she asked with an amused twinkle in her eye. Clearly, he needed a little jump-start. After he'd already taken on a wild fur monster for her, she thought he'd earned a little concession.

"I messed up again, didn't I?"

Paula laughed softly. "Depends."

"On what?"

"If the question ever comes out."

"Will you be my wife?" he said as if shot out of a pistol.

"Now that was prompt."

"I don't want to take any chances," he said. "I don't want you to change your mind."

"Change my mind? I haven't even answered yet."

He wrapped his arms tighter around her. "Please shoot me now. I've made such a complete fool of myself."

"Right? Maybe I will."

"You could finally say yes, woman!"

"Yes."

"Yes?"

"Told you. Now let's call in the kids and the dogs so we can spread the good news."

He grinned. Then he whistled loudly, causing an immediate invasion of children and dogs.

"What did she say?" Shauna asked, bouncing up and down beside him.

Leslie was more reserved. Paula walked over to her and wrapped her in her arms. She ignored Leslie's fidgeting.

"Congratulations," Paula said, her mouth on the top of her head. "You just got a sister." She glanced over the girl's head at Nate. "And a dad."

Nate heard them and nodded as he held a beaming Shauna, bobbing up and down in place with joy.

Leslie broke free and slipped between the poles to the horses, where she buried her head in Dolly's mane. A few of the blossoms sailed to the ground.

Nate made a worried face but Shauna patted his arm and said precociously, "Don't worry, Dad. She just needs to tell Dolly everything. She'll be fine after."

Two hours later, they had put the two completely overexcited girls to bed. Paula was tired, too. Exhausted, she flopped down on the sofa. Nate joined her and brought her a cup of tea. She accepted it with a grateful smile. As they sat comfortably leaning against each other, Paula said, "We should discuss all the logistics."

"*MMMH*," Nate agreed.

"But not now. Now I'm just going to call my mother. Not that she's still worried about Dolly." She reached for the cordless phone and dialed her parents' number.

Brenda picked up the phone. "Paula, dear. Congratulations!"

Paula took the device away from her ear and stared at it in confusion before turning her attention back to her mother.

"What was that, Mom? Did you just congratulate me? Before we even said hello?"

"Sure. To the proposal Nate finally made to you."

She held her hand over the mouthpiece before hissing, "Did Mom know about your plans?"

"Not from me. And the girls certainly didn't say anything."

"Then why the heck is she congratulating me on our upcoming wedding?"

He shrugged. "I don't know."

"Thanks, Mom," she said in response. "But will you tell me how you know?"

"Well, it was on social media. At first I was a little afraid for your husband when Nessy threw herself at him, but everything turned out all right."

"Okay. Good. Then you're informed. We'll talk again tomorrow."

"Sure. Sleep well."

As soon as she hung up, she pulled out her cell phone and opened Independence's social media pages. Indeed. "The whole thing has been posted."

"Wow. That was fast," Nate said.

"Those two kids. Their ears should be pulled long," she grumbled.

"Let me see."

Nate looked at it for a few seconds before he switched off the phone. "At least we have something to give our children and our children's children. Not everyone has such a great story to tell." He put a hand on the back of Paula's neck and pulled her close. "Now come on. Let's go upstairs. I assume the ban from your bedroom is lifted."

Paula smirked. "Oh, you don't want to sleep on the sofa?"

"Tomorrow, maybe, but not tonight," he growled and grabbed her. Then he lifted her up and carried her up the stairs to her bedroom, despite her protests.

There she stopped protesting.

CHAPTER TWENTY-THREE

Four days later, Cole knocked on George Wilkinson's front door bright and early. Most of the preparations for the trap they had planned for Alberto had been completed. Now it was a matter of waiting to see if Avery's message was received as they hoped it would be. If Alberto said he didn't give a hoot what happened to his brother, they were out of luck. Everything depended on Alberto's sense of family, which Avery assured them was exceptionally strong.

Avery. She was the reason he was there. While he was pleased with how the preparations for the big showdown were going, the fact that Avery and he never had time together frustrated him. So, he had thought of something special. He hoped she would like what he had planned.

He peered through the window. Was she still asleep? After all, it was half past seven. At seven, he had held back and waited another half hour. Now he knocked again, this time harder.

He heard murmuring voices behind the door.

The door was yanked open and Avery stood there. At least one question was answered immediately. Yes, she had still been asleep. No, she wasn't happy that he had gotten her out of bed. Her hair was all tousled and she was wearing oversized flannel pajamas. In one arm she carried a small cat, in the other Miss Marple sat sniffing curiously in the cold winter air.

"What are you doing here," she asked. "And come inside for your explanation. You're freezing to death out here."

Without waiting for an answer, she went back in.

Cole quickly followed her and closed the door behind him. Avery sat the cat and the rat side by side on the sofa and went over to the kitchen to make coffee.

"And you're sure they won't hurt each other?"

"Very sure. The two are one heart and soul."

Sure enough, the cat lay down, and Miss Marple curled up next to her. "If I hadn't seen it with my own eyes, I wouldn't believe it."

"It was the same for me. For the first few days, I kept Smiri and Miss Marple strictly separate. Until I started working on my perpetrator profile with a high level of concentration. When I'm so engrossed in my work, I tend to completely block out my surroundings. Miss Marple took advantage of that and introduced herself to the cat."

"Smiri. What kind of name is that?"

She grinned. "I asked my grandfather the same thing. Apparently it's the name of a gremlin in a children's book."

"Interesting choice for a man your grandfather's age."

"Oh, George is of the opinion that there are only good and bad books. So why shouldn't he read children's books if he likes them?"

"A Harry Potter fan?"

"Yes. That, too." She laughed. "We read them at the same time, and at night we discussed whether Harry or Hermione was more heroic."

"Harry, of course. It's logical. Otherwise the series wouldn't be named after him."

"Sure," Avery said, unmistakably disagreeing. "We'll discuss that later. I'm not awake enough for that debate yet. Coffee?" she asked.

"Uh, yeah, I'd love to," he replied distractedly. Her slim silhouette in the large pajamas brought back memories of how she felt in his arms. Maybe he should just throw out his plans for the day and drag her upstairs to the bedroom.

With a flourish, Avery put coffee in front of him. "No, we're not going back to bed. I'm already awake."

"Sleeping wasn't what I had in mind," he murmured, blowing gently into the hot drink.

Amused, she shook her head and poured herself a cup of the aromatic brew. "You don't say."

Cole watched her drink. The woman must have had a throat made of Kevlar armor. There was no other way to explain how she could down the piping hot liquid so easily.

Now in a much better mood thanks to the coffee, a smile played around the corners of her mouth. Cole found it really difficult to concentrate on the reason for his coming.

"If you don't stop staring at me so hungrily soon, I'm going to reconsider going back to bed."

Cole's face lit up at the prospect but he pulled himself together. Time together under the covers would have to wait. They had important things to discuss. And adventures to be had. All right. Maybe not exactly adventures but a lot of fun in any case.

"I was going to kidnap you."

"Kidnap?"

"There's snow in Vail. Much more than here."

It had snowed in Independence. One morning he had woken up and discovered the white splendor. Overnight, everything had been covered with a thin layer of powder snow. But in Independence, everything had already melted again due to the sunny days. "I thought we could grab our snowboards and hit the slopes."

"Snowboarding? Don't we have anything else to do today?"

"Not that I know of. Everything is prepared and agreed upon. Hopefully the informants in San Diego will take care of Alberto finding out about you and your offer. Instead of sitting around waiting for him to call like a lovesick teenager, I figured we could take a day off."

"Brilliant idea. I'll just let George know and we'll be on our way."

"Do you want to take Miss Marple with you?"

"No. It's cold outside. She'll be happier if she's allowed to stay here."

"Okay. How much time do you need to get ready?"

"Are we having breakfast on the way?"

Cole nodded.

"I just need ten minutes, then I'm ready to go. Make yourself comfortable here in the living room. Otherwise, you'll be shock-frozen before we even leave."

A short time later, they were on their way. After a lengthy discussion, they had taken Avery's Corvette.

"My car has super winter tires. In addition, it desperately needs a run."

"Be reasonable. Clearly a truck is much more appropriate than this sardine can."

At that, Avery had narrowed her eyes to slits and stubbornly started packing her things into the Corvette.

He had given in, though not without muttering that she just shouldn't be surprised if they ended up in the ditch.

To which Avery had sadly shook her head. "That's a whole new sound. What happened to 'no risk, no fun'?"

Wisely, he had said nothing in reply, but had taken his things out of the car and stowed them in her Corvette. He knew from the experience with the women in his family that there were moments when giving in was called for. It was definitely one of those moments. The snowboards barely fit, but he said nothing about that either. He would have to endure three-quarters of an hour on a narrow seat and the end of a snowboard in his face.

Seeing Avery only when he squinted under the snowboard, he soon gave up trying to have a conversation. It was more important to him anyway that she pay attention to the road as it serpentined up the mountain.

Avery was a good driver. It was just that he preferred to be in the driver's seat when there was a steep cliff on one side and it was downhill on the other.

Cole had to admit that despite the cramped seat and his initial skepticism, Avery was a joy to ride with.

She drove safely and calmly without taking unnecessary risks. Every now and then she would call his attention to something she noticed in the landscape. A particular rock formation, the sun breaking through the clouds and promising a gorgeous day, or a fox strolling through the snow some distance from the roadside.

He had always liked her ability to take pleasure in the little things she encountered every day.

Avery pulled into the parking lot near the ski lift. There, they peeled out of the car, dragged out their snowboards and packed up their things. Even close to Christmas, it was considered off-season. At least during the week. So they were at the checkout in no time. She pulled out her purse to pay for her ticket, but Cole beat her to it. "My idea, my money."

"Really? Thank you."

"You're welcome. It's not entirely altruistic. The ski slope was the only place I could think of where I was reasonably sure no one would steal you away from me." He wrapped an arm around her waist and pulled her close until they were belly to belly. "For weeks we've been talking about wanting to talk and never finding the time. Now the final showdown is coming up and I wanted the chance to spend some time with you. Just you and me. Before one of us gets shot." The last sentence had actually been intended as a joke but somehow his voice lacked lightness.

Avery's arms closed tighter around him. "What is this fixation you have about getting shot? I have no intention of getting shot. You?" she asked, looking at him challengingly.

"Of course not."

"All's well, then. Come on, let's go. The powder is calling."

The Rocky Mountains were not considered an absolute snowboard paradise for nothing. Thanks to the dry air, there were usually ideal conditions on the slopes and even powder snow. Avery could hardly wait. It had been ages since she'd last stood on her board. She turned to Cole. "Do you know the last time I was on the slopes was with you?"

"Really?"

She looked out the window of the cable car. "I was always on the road so much. Then when I was here, it was to visit friends and spend time with George. And it wouldn't have been the same without you."

He grabbed her hand. "Wise decision. I've tried it. Hit the slopes with others."

"So, how was it?"

"It was okay with my buddies. That's what I used to do."

She looked at him sharply. "And with women?"

He grinned. "Jealous?"

"Sure. Snowboarding with you is mine!"

"You can relax. It was horrible with everyone else."

That astonished Avery. "Terrible? Why is that?"

"Either it was too cold for them, or too steep, or too difficult, or, something. It was always very, very exhausting."

They got off the cable car and walked to the edge of the slope with their snowboards under their arms, where they sat and fixed their boards.

"What do you mean?" echoed Avery.

"No one was the same as you," was all he said.

Avery couldn't help a self-conscious grin. "I could have told you that."

"*HAHA*. Come on, whoever gets to the bluff first, wins."

And away he went.

The bluff was an overhanging rock slightly outside the slope. From up there, they had a first-class view over the whole valley, with the surrounding majestic peaks on the horizon. On sunny days, with a little luck, one might even see birds of prey circling.

Cole waited for her halfway down the slope. He looked toward Avery, who boarded gracefully toward him, eyes flashing and cheeks flushed from the cold. He let her pass him and followed at a more sedate pace.

Finally, they reached the bluff. The clouds had cleared in the meantime. The sun warmed the tip of her cold nose as she lifted her face to the sky. Behind her, Cole caught up. With practiced movements, he unstrapped his snowboard and laid it upside down in the snow to create a dry place to sit. Avery did the same.

When they were both seated, he pulled a thermos of hot, sweetened tea from his small backpack, followed by two apples and a bar of chocolate.

Avery snatched an apple and the chocolate from his hand.

"Hey, the chocolate isn't yours."

She laughed her loud, unabashed laugh; no nervous giggling from Avery. "It is now, by the looks of it."

"Well, wait." He set the thermos aside and pounced on her.

The moment she was lying on her back, above her, the chocolate was forgotten. An intense look passed between them before he lowered his mouth to hers.

Eventually they broke away from each other, mainly to catch their breath a little.

"Wow. Why on earth did we give that up?" he asked.

A shadow passed over Avery's face. She scrambled up out of the snow so that he had to move aside and release her. "Primarily because you were an idiot."

He started to say something, but she held up a gloved hand to stop him. "And, what's more, we were very young." She let her gaze wander over the wide valley. "We were too young to say what we thought and hear what the other was saying." She looked him in the eye. "I've thought about it a lot. It doesn't make your idiocy any less, though," she warned him, "but it certainly wasn't the only reason. I think people just aren't made to meet their soulmate so early in life." She paused. "And that's what you are to me. My soulmate."

"Wow." He was stunned. He hadn't expected an opening like that. He had thought he'd have to coax the smallest concessions out of her. At the same time, he wondered why he had thought that. After all, he knew Avery. She might have been stubborn at times, but she never held back her opinions.

He tried to reach for her hand, but she stopped him. "Stop. Let me finish first. I wasn't finished."

He withdrew his hand and looked at her intently.

"Soulmate or not, I can only be with you if you let me be me."

"But..."

"Wait. I'm not a woman who crochets blankets or spends hours trying to find the perfect recipe. I love the thrill of the chase, the thrill of driving too fast, and I love skydiving."

"Is that a complete list?" He tried to lighten the mood.

Avery continued with the same intensity as before. "In order for me to be happy with you, I have to be able to be happy with myself. And I can only do that if you trust me to do these things, to go along with some and just stay home with others, knowing what I'm doing. What I don't need is discussions before every potentially dangerous mission or horror visions of what could happen. I understand that you're worried about me. I feel the same way about you but these worries must not get out of hand. And most importantly, they must not lead to you telling me how to live my life."

Cole shrugged. "And that would be exactly the idiotic part of our breakup. My part. I'm well aware of that. I think I'm cured of that for good."

At her skeptical look, he hurried to say, "I love you just the way you are. Always have. It's just that my worries about you have led me to want to clip your wings. I don't want that anymore. I may try to put up a net now and then, just in case, but I want to fly next to you, chase the adrenaline rush with you, and jump off the cliff together. I can't promise you I'll never fall into old patterns of behavior again. There's something about you that makes me mutate into a caveman in no time. Probably because you're mine and I never want to give you up." He rested his forehead against hers.

Avery smiled. "That's not always a bad thing. I'm certainly willing to compromise, too. Just not when it comes to rules for my life. Then I get stubborn."

"Understandable."

He handed her the apple that had fallen into the snow earlier in the heat of the moment. "Here. Let's eat. We can discuss how things should go forward. You're facing some changes right now. Maybe we can find an alternative together."

"Are you actually considering quitting the FBI?"

"For quite some time, if I'm honest. Your resignation pretty much woke me up. I've been wondering why I didn't do the same thing a long time ago." He stared at the glistening snow at his feet.

"Wow. I didn't know that." That was a surprise but one with an extreme amount of potential. She spun that information back and forth in her head a few times until she grinned broadly, "Well, let's see what wild ideas we can come up with together."

"Good idea," he said, leaning forward to kiss her again. "And if I might make a suggestion...?"

"*MMMH.*"

"Let's figure out something else we can do to stay close. Going snowboarding together is something I don't want to wait to do again for another ten years."

Avery laughed. "Okay. I'll include that when brainstorming."

"Good," was his curt reply before he kissed her again.

CHAPTER TWENTY-FOUR

Tension was rising in the makeshift command center. Yesterday, Alberto had finally contacted Avery. Logically, he had not been very pleased that she wanted to blackmail him but apparently Tony was important enough to him that he got involved.

"Even if it's just so *he* can kill him," Avery had said when the conversation ended.

Jake was instructing Jeff and Jarvis, the owners of Silver Lodge, on how to proceed. They had not been able to avoid involving them in the plan. For one thing, the men refused to simply make their restaurant available without being part of the action, and for another, among all the agents and police officers, male and female, there was simply no one who could cook nearly as well.

Alberto was known for his obsession with good food. Their plan would be busted immediately if he didn't get the food he expected in a place like Silver Lodge.

Big A and Valentina had arrived two days prior. Valentina had recovered amazingly well in such a short time. Avery was very happy to see that she was already feeling much better. Indirectly, she felt guilty; after all, the bomb had been meant for her. The rational side of her brain knew that was bull-doggy, of course. It hadn't helped at all when she had visited her new friend in the hospital.

Valentina conferred with Ace. They and Polly Miners would represent the few other guests at the lodge. Fortunately, the guest room was quite manageable, so it would still look realistic, even if only two other tables were occupied.

Toby and Marc, two of Jake's deputies, had been assigned to serve. Yesterday they had helped out all day at the lodge and had been instructed by Jeff in the finer points of the hospitality business.

"From now on, the staff will get more tips from me," Marc moaned at the end of the long workday. "That's really hard work people are doing."

The presence of so many people posed a risk. On the other hand, they would all be able to act as witnesses, should they be lucky enough that Alberto somehow gave himself away, because Avery did not dare to carry a microphone.

Cole and Big A, along with Jake, the other two deputies, and three firefighters Ace trusted, would stand watch outside. Basically, everyone was hoping for a smooth operation but they preferred to play it safe.

Avery looked at the watch on her wrist, which she always wore on such assignments. *One hour to go until showtime.* She took a deep breath. At the same time, she reached into the inside pocket of her jacket and pulled out Miss Marple.

"Hello, little one. You get to join us today. Let's see how well Alberto can handle you on the dining room table."

"Avery?" Cole stood in the doorway.

"Yes?"

"Are you okay?"

She nodded.

"Then Big A and I will start doing our patrols."

"If Jake doesn't need anything more from you, that's a good idea."

"I'll ask him but I think he's done."

Cole stepped closer and raised his hand to touch it. At the last moment, he changed his mind and dropped it again. Instead, he asked, "Are you okay?"

"Yes. So far, so good." She rubbed her palms together before letting them fall loosely to her side again. "I'm a little nervous but that's normal for me, especially before a mission like this."

"I know that. It's a good thing, too. I always find it helps me to be more alert and aware. I would worry more if it were any other way."

She smiled at his clearly visible attempt not to act like a worried mother hen. "It'll be fine." She made a shooing hand gesture. "Now go and make sure there are no unpleasant surprises hanging around."

That brought a wry grin to his face. "Yes, ma'am," he said and saluted mockingly.

Alberto sat in the back seat of his rented limousine and glanced at the expensive watch on his wrist. Excellent. He was right on schedule. Together with two of his most trusted men, he had studied the area and the meeting place carefully. As it turned out, the Silver Lodge really did exist. The restaurant had excellent reviews. He had to hand it to Maria—Agent Wilkinson. She had style.

He was quite capable of acknowledging the strengths of his enemies. The place she picked for the meeting was known for its first-class food. Thanks to the preparations he had made, he would even be able to enjoy the culinary highlights.

He also confirmed Avery's claim she'd been kicked off the team and was currently unemployed. So her demand for ransom in exchange for his brother was credible. Of course, he had no intention of paying a dime for his no-good brother.

Leading up to the meeting, he would make his own arrangements to tip the balance in his favor. Agent or not, she had certainly made sure she didn't put herself in danger. Ten years in narcotics left their mark. You didn't just shake that off. He had put himself in her shoes, considered what he would do in her place, and determined his own steps. She wouldn't catch him off guard. On the contrary. If everything went according to plan, then tomorrow he would be rid of two troublesome agents and have his brother back.

He compared his current position with the map he had brought. Perfect. In half an hour they'd be there. He reached for the glass of champagne in front of him. Celebrations brought forward were the best.

Twenty-five miles farther, they drove across the county line and through Independence. He gave the chauffeur instructions where to turn. It was an old back road that ran almost parallel to the modern road that led all the way to Silver Lodge.

Here he had the driver stop once they arrived, of course. His two men got out. They would do their job while he waited in the warm car until it was time for the meeting.

On his tablet, he called up the restaurant's homepage. It was time to study the menu.

Cole felt a tingling in the back of his head. He had wanted to cancel the whole thing for several hours. Unfortunately, he knew all too well how his suggestion would be received. He scoured the forest that surrounded the lodge to see what was going on.

Except for the chance encounter with Big A, who was monitoring another sector, he hadn't seen a soul. He would rather be in the restaurant, in the middle of the action.

Suddenly, he heard a noise. Rifle at the ready, he turned to see a sleek black sedan driving up the narrow street. It stopped in the parking lot of the lodge.

Then, at first, nothing happened.

Seconds passed, turning into minutes.

A man got out. With the help of binoculars, he took a closer look. It was indeed Alberto, wearing a winter coat of Italian wool and a plaid scarf.

He slowly exhaled and relaxed. "The wolf has arrived. He is alone, except for the driver in the car," he spoke into the microphone on his chest.

His radio crackled. Then Big A spoke. "Explain to me again why the fire chief is sitting at the table holding hands with Valentina?" The tone of his voice made it clear what he thought of this split.

Cole laughed softly, "He's the mediator. And a former SEAL."

"Right."

"Jealous?"

"And how! Shut up!"

"*HAH*! It's only for show. Don't worry, big guy," Cole reassured him, clicking the off button.

Alberto walked toward the restaurant and disappeared through the front door.

The show would begin.

A twig cracked behind him.

Startled, he whirled around.

The world then went dark.

His senses strained to the utmost, Alberto stepped into the restaurant. While undoing the buttons on his coat—one had bought especially for the occasion, since it was never cold enough in San Diego that he needed such a warm garment—he let his eyes wander over the people present in the restaurant.

He spotted Avery at first glance. He took note of her position: she was seated with her back against the wall and facing the door at a white-covered table for two. That was the seat he would have chosen in her place.

On the other side of the wall a couple sat who seemed absorbed in their own world. An older woman sat reading a newspaper at the table, reading glasses on her nose, while a young man with an apron poured her coffee.

He stepped up to Avery's table. "Maria? Or should I rather say Agent Wilkinson? Or Avery?"

"I see you've done your homework," Avery said. "Except for the fact that I am no longer an agent, but I assume you're aware of that detail, too."

He tilted his head to confirm her assumption. Then he made a throwaway hand gesture. "Once an agent, always an agent."

Avery's face took on a hard expression. "Not if you go involuntarily."

Alberto studied her. He would not make the mistake of believing anything she told him. After all, she had successfully deceived him for several months. Not many managed to do that. She was good. Too bad she didn't work for him.

Both fell silent as another young man approached the table and brought them menus. "The special of the day is a rack of lamb in port wine sauce, with rosemary potatoes and carrots on the side." Eager to serve, he also poured Alberto a glass of ice water before taking his leave with an implied bow.

Avery had to stifle a grin. Toby certainly had good career prospects in the hospitality industry, should he ever find police work distasteful.

Alberto watched them closely and said, "I'm surprised to find two men working as waiters here."

Avery had been waiting for such an ideal opportunity. However, she had not expected it to arise so early in the conversation. Later would have been better, but in the field you had to be flexible. She laughed. "No wonder. The owners of the place are a gay couple. Naturally, they tend to hire young, good-looking fellows rather than pretty girls."

Alberto backed away in disgust at her words.

Avery tilted her head and studied him closely. "What's the matter? I thought you of all people would be okay with gay people?"

"Me? Why is that? I'm as straight as a man can be." His face grew redder and redder.

Avery mumbled an apology and took Miss Marple out of her pocket. Interested, the rat raised its snout in the air and sniffed thoroughly.

Ignoring the disgusted look on Alberto's face, she continued, "I know that, of course."

Thereupon he visibly relaxed. At that moment Toby came to their table with bread and foamy whipped butter. "Have you chosen anything yet?" he inquired politely.

"We need another moment."

"Was that one of the queers?" Alberto wanted to know irritably when Toby was out of earshot.

"No, that was not one of the owners. I don't know anything about the waiter's love life. I don't want to know."

"Probably better that way, too. And take that...that creature off the table!"

Seemingly contrite, Avery caught her rat and sat it on her lap, a little farther away, but still within sight of Alberto. Since the rodent seemed to help upset Alberto, he was allowed to stay. Miss Marple was not at all pleased about the relocation and fidgeted impatiently. After all, she had just decided on one of the rolls. Avery soothed her with a couple of kernels.

"That you are a ladies' man is well known," she said, resuming their conversation.

At her flattering words, her counterpart seemed to relax considerably. "You do what you can."

"No future Mrs. Monsanto in sight?"

"Oh, I'm in no hurry. There are so many beautiful women still waiting for me." At these words he let his clearly ambiguous gaze wander from her face to her breasts and slowly back up again.

EW. Was he flirting with her? She would drive that right out of him. "I would have thought in a family like yours, the demand for grandchildren would be high. And since Tony is obviously unlikely to honor his commitment, given his interests..."

"What are you implying?" He leaned over the table menacingly. "If you've got something on your mind, come right out with it, but be warned. Under the table, my gun is pointed at you." He was in control. Still.

Avery smiled amiably, a calculating twinkle in her eye. "Of course. I didn't expect anything else, either. Mine is, too."

His eyes narrowed to slits and scrutinized her. "Draw, then. At least for now. So I suggest you stop making reputation-damaging insinuations about my brother."

That 'for now' worried Avery a little, but she resolutely pushed it aside and focused on the task at hand. "What reputation-damaging innuendo? There's nothing wrong with him being gay."

Alberto looked like he was about to explode.

Hastily, she continued, "Besides, it's an open secret. Otherwise, he wouldn't be showing up at all the gay bars around San Diego. The FBI even has him on tape along with his latest flame."

Alberto pulled his pistol from under the table and pointed it at Avery for all to see. Out of the corner of her eye, she saw Ace make an effort to intervene.

She caught Valentina's gaze and shook her head. Valentina grabbed his arm with a firm grip and stopped him.

Only hesitantly did he let himself sink back into his chair. On the other side, Polly squinted anxiously over the edge of her newspaper.

"Your friends?" asked Alberto, gesturing from one to the other with the barrel of his gun.

Avery ignored the question and kept her eyes on his pistol.

"Now that's not very polite," she said, trying hard to keep control of the situation.

"I don't care," hissed Alberto. "Believe me when I say that all those queers who tried to seduce my brother are no longer a problem."

Avery eyed him coldly and leaned forward until the cold metal of the gun barrel pressed against the skin on her neck. "Is that why you killed them? To protect your brother? Then I've got news for you. Your brother picked up the men. Not the other way around."

"That is a lie. He was seduced, but they paid for it. Every single one of them had to pay with their blood. With every stab from my knife, I washed Tony clean."

"And the family name?"

"And the family name," Alberto confirmed, a little calmer again. Now that he had admitted everything, the tension seemed to fall away from him.

The man seemed to believe every word, Avery noted, stunned. She hadn't been sure how deep his delusions went until the very end. Deep, as was clear.

"Now, you call off your men and you lead me to Tony."

"I guess you'd like that."

"Please. Don't insult my intelligence. We both know you have no intention of turning Tony over to me for money." He paused and looked at her urgently. "Just as you know I have no intention of letting you go alive."

"Forget it," she said, but broke out in a cold sweat.

"Oh, I think so," Alberto said with an ominous grin. "At least if you want to see your teammate again. Or should I say, *childhood sweetheart*? You see, my brother was amazingly thorough a few days before he disappeared, and in an attempt to find you, he turned over every stone in this cursed town."

Avery turned pale. "You have Cole?"

"My insurance. Now take me to my brother," he demanded, pressing the barrel of the pistol against her head.

Inside, Avery was trembling, but outwardly she remained calm.

Slowly, she pulled out her gun and placed it on the table.

Ace didn't dare intervene. Even a surprise attack would be fatal to Avery as long as Alberto had the gun pointed at her temple. Valentina and Polly obviously came to the same conclusion.

They had to just watch as Alberto roughly grabbed Avery by the arm and led her out the door.

Alberto pushed Avery around the corner and slammed her head hard against the porch post. Dazed, she staggered. Without loosening his grip on her arm, he holstered the gun and pulled out an egg-shaped, camouflage-colored object.

Avery, still seeing stars, tried to wrest the hand grenade from him. Unfortunately, to no avail. Horrified, she watched as he pulled out the safety pin with his teeth, lunged, and tossed the grenade back into the guest room.

Filled with fear for her friends, Avery tried to break away. Without further ado, Alberto hit her over the head with the pistol. She almost went down; his iron grip kept her on her feet.

"Come on, come on now. We have to get out of here." He rushed her to the car.

At his sedan, he opened the door and pushed her roughly inside. He sat with her in the passenger seat and continued to point the gun at her.

"Get out of here fast!" he ordered his driver.

The latter complied with the request and started the engine.

CHAPTER TWENTY-FIVE

ACE, VALENTINA, AND POLLY had waited until Alberto disappeared around the corner outside. They didn't want to give him a reason to shoot Avery. As soon as they were out of sight, they jumped up from their seats and hurried toward the door. Just then, the mob boss appeared in the doorway and threw something at them.

Reflexively, Valentina caught the object. "A hand grenade!" she cried in horror. She took a swing and threw the hand grenade through the nearest window.

She looked paralyzed.

"Good job. Now let's get out of here," Ace said.

Valentina snapped out of it and ran after him, gun drawn, toward the kitchen, closely followed by Polly and the two deputies. No sooner were they out the back exit than the hand grenade exploded on the other side of the solid log building.

Fortunately, the lodge remained standing, but all the windows shattered under the blast wave.

Everyone threw themselves to the ground and tried to protect themselves as best they could from the falling glass and wood splinters.

When the ringing in her ears diminished a little, Valentina scrambled up and looked around for the others.

The driver pressed down on the gas pedal. Gravel splattered in all directions as he drove down the dirt road. "Where have you been hiding Tony?" Alberto harangued her.

Avery was aware that she was only alive because he was depending on her. So she would string him along as long as she could. She pressed her lips together and looked out the window.

"Now talk!" He pressed the barrel of the gun to her knee. "Do you like pain?"

No. Not the knee. She had no intention of dying today, nor did she feel like limping to rehab for a bullet wound in her knee. *Time for a more active strategy.* She tensed her body and threw herself with all her might toward Alberto, just as a loud bang sounded.

The hand grenade, it flashed through her mind and she glanced back. Behind them, the smoke next to the lodge rose ghostly above the trees.

My friends! she thought in horror. That look cost her precious time.

Alberto managed to put his hand to her throat and press her against the window. Desperately, she tugged at his fingers as she kicked her legs frantically.

Realizing she was no match for his strength, she reached for the gun in his other hand and tried to push it away from her.

Gradually, however, she ran out of breath.

Black dots appeared before her eyes. Two shots rang out. The driver flipped forward and the car skidded.

Alberto eased away from Avery to brace himself.

Gasping, she sucked the precious air into her lungs. Only slowly did she realize what was happening.

The limousine was speeding uncontrollably toward the woods. Her captor tried desperately to drag the driver, a tall, bulky man, onto his side. In vain.

Avery squinted past the two at the speedometer. They were traveling at fifty. And rising. Jumping out was out of the question. She saw the trees getting closer and closer and braced for impact.

Seconds later, that was it.

She was thrown back and forth on the back seat. She protected herself as best she could with her upper arms and legs. Finally, the sedan came to a stop with a loud crash and groan. Two gnarled pine trees, standing close together, had successfully gotten in the way of the vehicle.

Avery cautiously tested her limbs to see if they were functioning properly.

It was painful, and tomorrow she would probably be black and blue all over, but everything still seemed to work. At least her head had remained intact.

Cautiously, she looked around the vehicle. She saw a bullet hole in the driver's torso. No wonder he had lost control. Dead people were just very bad drivers.

Alberto had been thrown forward. He was lying with his head in the footwell on the passenger side.

Determined, she picked up the gun that had landed on the floor in all the commotion and tucked it into her waistband. She winced as the cold metal met an abrasion on her back. Tentatively, she tried the door. There was nothing to be done. It wouldn't move a millimeter. The only way out was obviously through the back window if she didn't want to crawl over the two men.

She pulled her legs under her and knelt on the back seat. Pulling the sleeves of her jacket over her hands, she banged on the glass. She hoped it was weakened enough by the two bullet holes that she could dislodge it completely. Finally, the hole was big enough. She grabbed the frame of the rear window and pulled herself out.

Two strong arms grabbed her under the armpits and helped her out of the car. When she lifted her eyes, she looked directly into Big A's worried eyes. "Hey there," he said.

"Thank you," she said in relief.

"You're welcome. Are you okay?"

"Yes. Everything is still on. I've been really lucky. How are the others? Did they survive the explosion?"

"Yes. Ace is organizing the fire department right now so the fire doesn't spread out of control."

"And Valentina and Polly?"

"Except for a few abrasions and bruises, both are fine. Miss Marple is also unharmed. Valentina found her in the kitchen with the bread."

Avery grinned. "Naturally! I can imagine that. Where is she now?"

"Valentina's taking care of her."

"Good, I was getting worried."

He pointed at the car. "Are those two guys still alive?"

"The driver is dead. Shot by...?"

"...by me," he confirmed. "I had to stop him somehow."

"Good job." She lowered her gaze to the tips of her shoes. "I don't know if Alberto is still alive. I didn't have the nerve to check his pulse."

"I'll check. Do you know where Cole is?"

"No! Until just now, I was hoping Alberto was bluffing. Apparently not."

"Bluffed with what?"

"He said something about having Cole as a hostage. I'm assuming he brought a couple of people with him for backup. I need to..." She glanced toward the car with the two men inside.

"Go ahead. Save your man. I'll take care of Alberto and the driver."

"Okay. Great. Thanks. Will do." Gratefully, Avery sprinted off. She looked from left to right. Nothing but trees everywhere. It was like looking for a needle in a haystack.

At that moment, Ace came down the hill.

"Did you find Cole?" she asked.

"Unfortunately, not yet," Ace said. "He could be anywhere."

"Crap, darn. Come on."

Ace grabbed her by the arm and began pulling her along with him. Only after a few feet did he let go of her. "I tripped over one of Alberto's henchmen."

"Did you get him?"

"Unfortunately not, he got away from me. I had to decide whether to give chase or come to your rescue." He pointed to a path leading down the mountain. "He ran that way."

"Let's go then. I really hope they haven't gotten too far yet. If necessary, I can also call up the helicopter with a thermal imaging camera."

"Let's try this way first. After all, the helicopter minutes are always expensive as heck."

The two of them ran. Stones came loose under Avery's feet and rolled downhill. Again and again she had to jump over roots and avoid dense branches. The path was almost unrecognizable in places. Obviously, it was no longer in regular use. One of her heavy boots caught on a withered tuft of grass. She caught herself again and kept running. To make matters worse, it was beginning to snow. Slowly but steadily the white flakes fell and blocked their view of the valley.

Some branches were bent. *Good. Seems Cole was able to fight.* As she continued to jump and slither downhill, her eyes ceaselessly scanned the surrounding area for more clues to Cole's whereabouts.

Panting, she stopped and listened intently for sounds that did not belong in the wintry forest. She cursed the snow, which was already beginning to swallow the sounds.

Finally, she heard something. Stones rumbled into the depths. The sound came from below and ahead of her. Apparently she had followed the mountain flank too far north. She adjusted her course and hurried in the direction where she had heard the rockfall. Forcing herself to a slower pace so as not to give herself away early by making her own noises, she worked her way down into the valley.

She caught sight of two people in front of her. One was dressed all in black and the other was his captive, being dragged by the collar of his jacket; the captive's hands were tied behind his back. The legs, however, were not. Whether that was an oversight or intentional, she didn't know. In any case, Cole had put up quite a fight. That explained why they hadn't gotten any farther.

Avery set off at a sprint. When she got there, she called out. "Freeze! Police! Drop your weapon!"

The man stopped so abruptly that Cole fell head-first to the ground with a thud. The kidnapper paid no further attention to his victim. He left him lying there and pointed a gun at his two pursuers.

"Don't take another step or I'll shoot," threatened Ace, who had caught up with them by now. "Your boss is in police custody. A little cooperation wouldn't hurt."

"He's what? Arrested?" cried the man in black.

"You heard me right. Arrested." Ace didn't flinch.

That was as far as he got. The man holstered his gun and fled.

Apparently, his loyalty to Alberto did not go so far that he voluntarily surrendered to the police.

"Doesn't look like he wanted to stay for tea," Ace noted humorously before setting off in pursuit. By radio, he let Jake know. Maybe he could intercept the attacker with the car.

Avery rushed to Cole, who lay motionless on the ground. Gently, she touched his carotid artery to see how he was doing. His pulse was regular, his breathing was also calm. "Hey, big hero, can you stand up?"

"I'd rather not," he said. "Got beat like a rookie. This is so embarrassing."

"If that's your only problem, you're doing fine."

"Never been so glad to see you," he murmured, making her smile as she pulled him up.

She pulled a knife from her pocket and cut the cable ties that bound his hands.

"Ah, finally, thank you." He spread his fingers a few times in succession to stimulate blood circulation.

Something silver flashed. He threw himself at Avery and rolled across the ground with her.

A gunshot echoed through the falling snow. Wood splintered beside them from the tree where they had just been standing.

They both scrambled to their feet and exchanged a glance.

"We'll get him!" Avery sounded very determined.

Grimly, Cole nodded. Side by side, they ran and climbed up the steep embankment at an angle. If they had judged correctly, they should be able to cut off the shooter.

"A few weeks on a tropical island with no shooting sounds wonderful," she groaned between breaths.

"I'm right there with you. How about Maui? Our honeymoon is still coming up, after all."

At his words, Avery almost stumbled. She caught herself at the last moment. Keeping her gaze fixed on the fleeing gunman, who was becoming harder to see in the thickening snow, she asked, "Oh, is it now?"

Cole took his time answering. "Yes. It is, Avery Carter. So, what do you say to Maui?"

"Maui?"

Finally, the distance between them and the man seemed to close. The attacker seemed to notice, too. More and more often he looked frantically over his shoulder, which cost him precious time.

When the distance was only a few yards, Avery gave Cole an amused look. "Yeah then, with Maui I can't very well say no."

Then she set off for the final spurt. With five big leaps, she had caught up with the shooter and jumped onto his back like a puma.

Both fell to the ground and rolled down the slope, wedged into each other.

Cole caught up with them. Maui was sounding more and more tempting. He'd best keep her locked in the hotel room for the entire two weeks so she wouldn't be tempted to single-handedly rescue a humpback whale or wrestle an octopus.

CHAPTER TWENTY-SIX

Around dinnertime, the whole group trickled into the diner. Avery longed for a long hot bath and her bed but as it was, all of Independence wanted to share in her investigative success. And collect their bets. Of course.

She leaned a little against Cole, who hadn't left her side since they had made the last arrest. Tony and Alberto's henchmen were behind bars and would be transported to California the next day.

Alberto had been transported by helicopter to a hospital in Denver. He was in a coma and it was doubtful he would survive the accident. Even better? Tony was picked up after his third visit to see Alberto in the hospital. They'd finally had enough to bring him in.

Jeff and Jarvis were relieved that the operation had been successful and that nothing bad had happened to either of them. Understandably, they had been struck first when they realized the extent of the destruction to their establishment, but since the insurance company would cover the damage, they had decided to take a vacation in Hawaii for the duration of the cleanup and repair work.

"For the fact that everything should have been top secret, a surprising number of people knew, don't you think?" Cole put an arm around her waist and gave her a gentle squeeze.

She winced.

Startled, he let go of her. "Sorry. Are you hurt? You said you were fine."

"Yes, yes. That's right. Scrapes and bruises don't count. But I still feel them."

Cole could have kicked himself for his own thoughtlessness. He was hurting too, after all, and Avery had taken a lot more than he had.

Miss Minnie walked by with a tray full of champagne glasses. He grabbed one and thrust it into Avery's hand. "Cheers. Wait for me here," he said.

"Okay. What are you up to?"

"I need to talk to Miss Daisy for a minute."

She looked after him in amazement but in the end she was too exhausted to rack her brains any longer about what he was doing. Tired, she leaned her head against the wall and closed her eyes.

"I heard you were the heroine of the day." Paula had stepped next to her.

Avery opened her eyes. "Oh, come on. Everyone was just doing their job."

"That may be so. Nevertheless, you not only stood your ground against Alberto, but also wrestled one of the henchmen to the ground with your own hands."

Avery chuckled. "You just wait and see. Tomorrow that will turn into three opponents, all as big as a house."

Paula grinned. "Sure. That's how legends are made."

"Finally. I've always wanted this." Avery laughed, even though it hurt her ribs.

"But seriously now. I'm glad you made it through everything in one piece. Honestly, I understand my brother a little better now."

"Hey. I thought you were on my side?"

"I am. But I can understand him. That being said? I think he's well aware of your abilities after today. No question."

Avery lowered her eyes and studied her battered ankles in detail. "We talked it out a few days ago. It seems like we both need to revise our opinions of each other."

"So you're back together?" Paula asked.

Were they? Probably so, if they were already joking about their honeymoon. She nodded sheepishly. "I guess."

"I knew it," Paula said.

Suddenly suspicious, Avery looked at her friend. "Why is this so important? Were you betting?"

"Of course." Paula grinned. "I do have to see that the betting fund is sufficiently filled. Christmas is coming up."

"Yes, yes. I'd just be happy if people here found a more exciting topic than my love life."

"Don't worry about it," Paula said. "They were more interested in me this morning."

"You? Really? What for? Did you adopt a grizzly bear?"

"*HA!* Now that would be nothing out of the ordinary but I'll let you find out for yourself. Thanks to social media, that shouldn't be hard for you. I'd better go now. My brother is coming toward us right now and he looks like he has big plans for you."

"Huh? Big things?" She didn't know if she could handle Cole and his big plans. She was pretty beaten up.

"I'll let you two lovebirds be," Paula said and rushed away.

As soon as Cole got to Avery, he said, "Drink up. We're leaving soon." He seemed a little nervous.

"We're leaving?" she asked.

He held up his right hand with a key dangling from his index finger. "The Honeymoon Suite at the bed-and-breakfast is ours for the night."

"Honeymoon suite? This isn't Maui, in case you missed that. There are more than a few palm trees missing. Plus, you left out an essential detail: getting married comes before honeymooning."

"*HAHA*. Don't worry, when we get married, you'll know. No, she gave me this room because it's the only room with a balcony and accompanying Jacuzzi."

Images of steam, starry skies, and bubbling water for her battered muscles filled her senses. "*UMM*...okay."

"We'll spend the night there tonight."

Not that Avery had anything to object to. A hot bubble bath, a hopefully naked Cole, and, if she could persuade Miss Minnie, a bottle of champagne, sounded heavenly. "Sounds good. When can we go?"

Surprised, Cole looked at her. "That simple? I was actually prepared to have to discuss this with you at length first."

Avery rolled her eyes. "I've never been averse to good ideas. Just dumb ones."

Brenda's voice rang through the microphone. "I have an announcement to make." She looked down at Leslie's and Shauna's heads. "Or rather, these two."

"I wonder if this has anything to do with Paula," Avery said.

"My sister?" he asked.

"Yes. She said she pushed us out of the Independence headlines today."

"Thank God. What did she do for it? Adopted a herd of Tibetan dwarf goats?"

Avery laughed. "I suspected a grizzly bear. She denied it."

"I guess we're about to find out."

The two girls climbed onto the makeshift podium and tried to adjust the microphone to their height. Stan came to their rescue.

Shauna nudged Leslie in the side. Leslie pressed her lips together and shook her head stubbornly. So, little Shauna took the lead. She pushed Leslie a step to the side and cleared her throat.

"Nate will have his hands full with that one," Cole said, laughing softly.

"I think so." Avery leaned back against him, anxiously waiting to see what was coming.

"As you know, our parents are in love," Shauna said.

Laughter filled the room.

Unsure of what that meant, Shauna frowned. "You know what I mean. They're kissing and stuff."

"And so," Cole said with a stifled laugh. "I'll have to ask my sister what's meant by 'and such'."

Avery gave him a friendly nudge with her elbow. "Shut up. I want to hear this."

Leslie seemed to have caught herself and showed compassion for her friend. She reached for the microphone. "What she's saying is that Nate and Paula are getting married. So not only did I get a new mom, but I got a dad and a sister at the same time. Isn't that the greatest Christmas present ever?"

The crowd broke into loud cheers. Many people clapped and whistles sounded, probably having to do with the good news...and some winning bets.

The two girls went wide-eyed as the commotion broke out and grabbed each other's hands. Paula went to the small podium and hugged them both. Mama Bear was on her way. Avery smiled when she saw it.

"Shall we go?" murmured Cole into her hair.

"In a moment. I have to say goodbye to George first and ask him to take care of Miss Marple."

"You do that. It gives me time to congratulate my sister and Nate."

"Good luck. Seems like all of Independence has the same idea."

Avery pushed her way through the many people. She saw George in the corner with a man she didn't know and seemed engrossed in conversation. Just as she was considering whether to interrupt them, Lily appeared at her side.

"Here's a brownie. They're from Aileen."

Avery's eyes lit up. "Really, for me?"

Lily smiled. "You just look like you could really use one."

"*Yesss.*" Avery bit into it with relish and closed her eyes. Aileen's pastry was pure pleasure. After she had consumed two bites and felt somewhat invigorated again, she opened her eyes and eyed Lily. "Is it a deceptive impression, or are you conspicuously often found around Aileen?"

The curvy brunette blushed slightly and lowered her eyes shyly. "No. Your impression is correct. We get along very well."

"I'm happy for you. You deserve a girlfriend who makes you happy."

Lily blushed slightly and looked to the side, embarrassed. "Thank you. It's all still pretty new to me. Not many people know yet, either." She squinted at Aileen, who was joking with a few guests.

"You mean it hasn't been shared on social media yet? Most people probably know. You know how it is in Independence."

"You really think so?" Lily bit her lower lip and looked around the diner anxiously.

"Really. You've probably only been spared so far because Aileen is related to the Diner Sisters. Maybe you'd best post an entry yourself. At least you'll have it somewhat under control."

"Good idea. I'll discuss it with Aileen right away."

"You do that. And thanks for the brownie. I really needed that."

"You're welcome."

Her grandfather was still talking, but she didn't feel like waiting now. When George's eyes fell on her, he beamed. He held out his arm to welcome her. "Here she is. The heroine of the day and my granddaughter, Avery Wilkinson."

She looked to the side, embarrassed, when he introduced her like that.

"Avery, this is Gianni de Luca. He bought land around here and is going to build a housing development."

She shook the man's hand and looked at him with interest. He was around fifty, with dark straight hair and a mustache. "Pleased to meet you. Are you building in

Breckenridge?"

"No. Here in Independence."

That astonished her. She hadn't known anything about it but probably she was just not up to date. Being part of such a close community was so familiar to her that she expected to be automatically up to date as soon as she was there. "Vacation rentals? Or for the residents here?"

"A mixture of both, I think. It's not set in stone yet. At the moment I'm in talks with the mayor and I'm looking for investors," he said smoothly.

Too smooth, in Avery's opinion. Her alarm systems flashed in her head. Or gut. Wherever her intuition resided. Maybe it was just the after-effects of the excitement of the last few hours, maybe not. In any case, she was too tired to think about it for long.

"Grandpa, can you come here?" She tugged on his arm. De Luca gave her a fake smile. "I'm sure you'll excuse us for a moment. I've had a very busy day and I want to say goodbye."

George looked a bit perplexed, after all she never called him 'Grandpa' but he complied and let her drag him behind the counter and into the kitchen.

"What's wrong?"

Avery peeked out by the crack in the door to make sure they weren't being overheard. "I'm not sure I like the vibes that guy's giving off."

"Don't you think you're being a little paranoid?" George asked.

"Maybe so, but promise me this. Don't invest anything in de Luca's business until I've checked him out thoroughly."

"All right."

"All right?" She had expected more resistance and already had several persuasive tactics ready in her head.

"Yeah, 'all right.' First of all, you'll have your reasons, and secondly, I decided not to do business with him after the first five minutes. There's something not right about him. I'll find out more so I can pretend to think it over."

Avery narrowed her eyes. "Please don't play detective on your own."

"Now you sound like Cole," he grumbled. "I already know what I'm doing. Who do you think gave you your famous sleuthing skills?"

That made her smile. When he was right, he was right. Still, she was worried about him. She realized, though, that she wasn't going to get anywhere there tonight, and gave up. "Okay. One other question: I'm staying at the bed-and-breakfast tonight..."

"With Cole?"

"With Cole, of course. With who else?" She rolled her eyes. "Can you take care of Miss Marple?"

"Sure. I'll just feed her and leave everything else to Smiri."

"Great. I'll see you tomorrow then."

"All right."

She reached up on her toes and kissed him on the cheek. "Thank you."

He stroked her cheek. "Don't mention it. Now go on. Have fun."

Avery laughed and left.

The snow clouds covered everything with a fine layer of snow in the afternoon and the whole area looked as if it had been dusted with powdered sugar. The harsh winter air heralded more snowfall.

The chances of a white Christmas were good and the night was starry. Lying side by side in the hot water of the spa, their heads resting against the cushioned rim and their hands intertwined, Avery and Cole looked up at the sky.

"If you could wish for one thing in your future, regardless of feasibility or potential income, what would it be?"

Avery turned her head toward Cole and smiled. "I'd like to start my own business in security. To do that, though, I need a team. Can't do it all by myself."

"Who are you missing from your team?"

She smirked and let her hand slide lightly over his flat stomach underwater. "Oh, I don't know? A former FBI agent with a knack for computers, maybe?"

"That's very fortunate. I might know someone," he said. "Is that all? Or do you need more people?"

Pleased he was honestly interested in her plans and didn't immediately dismiss them as impossible, she continued more seriously. "My goal is the private sector. I have no interest in any paramilitary contracts for the government. Those waters are too murky for me. What really interests me are cases where children need protection, or even entire families. But neither would I be satisfied with a pure bodyguard assignment. It's better to get rid of the threat. Of course, that would involve some travel. On the other hand, there would also be the possibility of relocating families to Independence. Thanks to our overly curious inhabitants, Independence is one of the safest places around. Of course, I would still have to discuss this point with the mayor, but I think she will like the idea."

"You seem to have given this a lot of thought already."

She smirked. "You know how it is when you go undercover. Hours of doing nothing, in other words, gives time to gather ideas."

"I've been carrying around a similar idea for quite some time," he admitted.

"Let's hear it. I'm curious." She bit her lower lip. "Maybe...?"

"Yes?"

"Maybe our ideas can be combined."

"Maybe, but hear them out before you offer to partner with me."

"Gladly. Fire away."

"Do you know the show *Leverage*?"

She took a sip of champagne. While the sparkling liquid moistened her still sore throat, she thought about the question.

"Isn't that kind of like a Robin Hood squad? A group steps in when people have been wronged and take the money or whatever back from the bad guys?"

Cole winced when he heard the Robin Hood reference. "That sounds so romanticized but yes, that's who I'm talking about. In my opinion, there is a need for such services, unfortunately. In normal circumstances, of course, the cases would be nowhere near as spectacular as they are in the series, but the result would be the same. So many people get ripped off every day, it's unbelievable. And while I couldn't care less if someone loses a million of their many millions, I care a lot about an ordinary person losing their pension."

"I can understand that. Then we definitely need more people. Trustworthy people. Things like this can't be done if you operate exclusively in the legal realm." Deep in thought, she furrowed her brow.

"That's right. *Gray area* is more accurate. And you said 'we'. Does that mean you could see yourself working together?"

"Absolutely." She turned her head so she could look directly at him. Her eyes sparkled in the light reflecting off the snow and water. Mischievously, she smiled at him. "Let's get right down to practicalities, then: do you have any money you can bring in?"

Cole laughed out loud. "That's what I love about you! You always get right to the point. The answer is yes. Sure I have. I've been toying with the idea of going into business for myself for a while, too. I feel the same way about the FBI as you do about narcotics. All the bureaucracy makes our work terribly inefficient. It frustrates me to no end."

"Then all we have to do now is get Big A and Valentina on board," she said with a happy glow on her face.

He set his champagne glass aside and repeated the same with hers, which he took from her hand.

"Let's drink to that."

"Later," he murmured. He slid his body over hers and lowered his lips to hers. After the first kiss, he lifted his head a little. "There are other ways to celebrate a successful day."

"Indeed," Avery said, giving herself completely over to her feelings. "That's the best ending of them all."

EPILOGUE

"Have you seen my lapel thing?" Taking two steps at a time, Avery sprinted down the stairs into the living room and looked around frantically.

George, already dressed in his finest suit and sitting in a large armchair reading the newspaper, looked over the rim of his reading glasses at his granddaughter.

"Wow. You look fabulous."

Avery was wearing an ice-blue dress. The straps were fastened at the neck. The top had a teardrop neckline and clung tightly to her torso. The skirt fell straight down in flowing panels above her knees.

"Yeah, yeah," Avery said, still searching for her flower arrangement that Lily had brought over earlier.

"No, really. Cole won't know what hit him if he sees you in it."

"He'll probably wonder where I hid my gun in that thing," she said.

"I wonder about that, too," her grandfather admitted.

She rolled her eyes and continued her search behind the kitchen counter.

George thought of something. "You don't mean that arrangement of dark red roses, oat ears, and some blue spiky flowers?"

Avery whirled around. "Yes, exactly that. The blue ones are thistles. Extremely appropriate for Paula, I think. It's just no use to me if I can't track it down in the foreseeable future. I have to be at Paula's farm in twenty minutes." She glanced at the watch on her wrist. "Wrong. More like fifteen. My Corvette is fast, but with the snow, I'm not sure I can make it in that short a time. So, have you seen the flower arrangement anywhere?"

George looked to the side guiltily. "It was there on the table earlier," he said unhelpfully.

Avery looked at the empty table. "So where is it now?"

"It could be that, uh, Miss Marple carried it off."

She stared at him in disbelief. "Miss Marple? And you let her?"

"Not directly. I just saw them flitting around the living room and was still thinking that I should probably put the flowers away."

"So, did you?"

"What?"

"Well, put them away."

He ducked his head a little. "I got distracted. Miss Minnie had called me to discuss some more details about the wedding."

Avery rolled her eyes in annoyance. "So you're telling me that because Miss Minnie desperately wanted to outdo her sister and secure the first dance with you, Miss Marple has now eaten my flower arrangement?"

"Uh yeah, something like that." At least he had the decency to look reasonably contrite.

"Geez..."

She walked over to the study and stuck her head in. Sure enough. There sat Miss Marple, gleefully eating the last of the oat grains. Smiri sat next to it with her head tilted and kept pawing at the red ribbon that held the whole thing together. *Oh, great.* "I have no choice but to send a floral distress call to Lily. Hope she can get me something new right away."

She grabbed her coat, slipped into her warm fur boots, the fancy shoes she had packed in a bag, and reached for her car keys. "At least try to show up on time for the wedding ceremony." She didn't even wait for his answer and slipped out of the house.

Outside, she stopped for a moment and took a deep breath of the crisp winter air. It was a beautiful morning. It had snowed a few inches during the night, making it feel as though one had landed in a winter wonderland. It was still early. The sun was just coming up, bathing the surrounding mountain peaks in a pinkish light.

At first, she hadn't understood why Nate and Paula had insisted on getting married in the winter. Spring would have made much more sense in her opinion. With all the glittering white splendor, she had to admit that a winter wedding certainly had its appeal.

The wedding ceremony would take place in the midst of all the animals and in the presence of all the relatives and the closest friends on Paula's farm. Afterward, they would continue to Jaz's place. Her converted barn offered enough space for all the curious acquaintances who would drop by. In addition, the laid wooden floor was excellent for dancing.

Paula and Nate wanted to do everything at the McArthy ranch, including the wedding ceremony, but they'd been overruled by their two daughters. A wedding without Dolly, Rufus, Lucky, the dogs and the cats was simply not a wedding. Half the family would be missing, they said. The two adults couldn't argue with that.

Avery understood the two girls. She also thought it was very appropriate to hold the wedding ceremony in the immediate family circle. She had been very surprised when Paula asked her to be the second bridesmaid after all.

"Tyler will come to the wedding with Pat and Ranger, but they've already mentioned that they won't be able to make it until the exact time of the wedding, since they can't get away any sooner. I do, however, want two bridesmaids to drink and laugh with before I tie myself to one man for the next fifty years."

"Seriously?" Avery answered.

"Yes, seriously. Next to Jaz, you're the closest to me. At least you know how to hit a target..."

"Unlike me," Jaz called from the next room.

"Right. You're steadfastly refusing."

"You know my karma is way too important to me."

"Yes, yes. She's still quite useful as a friend," Paula whispered confidently to Avery. "The woman is constantly accumulating so much good karma that I fully expect some of it to come off on me, too. And since my karmic account balance is constantly being affected by my big mouth, that's an advantage."

"I heard that!" Jaz said.

"I love you, too," Paula called back.

Avery had been pleased, secretly thinking she did have more in common with the women than she had first thought. "I'd love to. I'd be honored."

She gave herself a jolt and tore herself away from the beautiful scenery. She could marvel at nature just as well at Paula's ranch. Paula was probably cool with being a few minutes late, but Brenda and Jaz, who had organized the wedding together, were two perfectionists. Their nerves were stretched to the limit.

Avery folded herself into her Corvette, not at all easy with a skirt, and slammed the door.

"There you are at last," Jaz said and fell around her neck. Then she took a step back and said admiringly, "You look good. That color looks great on you."

"Thank you."

Normally she didn't care much for fancy clothes, as she believed they needed to be functional or fit well, like her favorite jeans, but she had to admit that the color showed off her dark hair excellently.

Paula came into the dining room still dressed in sweatpants and a tee-shirt. "Wow. Cole will probably want to join us in a minute. Well, maybe the priest will have time afterward."

Avery blushed slightly. "Oh, we're in no hurry to get married."

"*HA*. Just wait until he sees you in that dress."

"What is it with you all and this dress?" grumbled Avery.

"You never usually wear one, and it looks decidedly good on you."

"Well, first of all, it was very difficult to accommodate my pistol."

Jaz's eyes grew wide. "You're bringing a gun to a wedding?"

"I think that's great," Paula interjected. "Halter on the thigh?"

Avery nodded. "That's it, exactly."

Jaz rolled her eyes and set about opening a bottle of champagne. She had to get Paula to hold still for the next two hours while her makeup and hair were done. Relying on Avery probably didn't do much in that regard, listening to their conversation as she did. More likely, she was goading the bride into a morning jog. So there was champagne with the hope the alcohol would have a calming effect.

She gave everyone a filled glass. Brenda, who had just come in with Anna, the hairdresser—who would also take care of the makeup—also received a glass.

Anna declined with thanks. "Gladly later. First I need a sure hand. Otherwise, I can't guarantee an eyeliner."

"Very nice, your work ethic," Brenda complimented. "By the way, Avery? Lily called and said she'd bring you a new flower arrangement just before the wedding ceremony starts. Before that, she's helping Aileen set up the catering at the McArthy ranch."

"Super. I'm relieved that this is working out."

"Will you tell us what happened to the first flower arrangement?"

"Well, what can I say? Miss Marple seemed to have taken a fancy to it. In an unattended moment, she carried it off to another room and had her way with it."

Fortunately, everyone present except Anna belonged to Miss Marple's fan club and burst out laughing.

"Who is Miss Marple, then? A goat?" asked Anna.

"Miss Marple is my trained sleuth rat. She's trained for the police service and tracks down drugs and the like. In her spare time, she loves to eat for a living. Among other things, oatmeal."

"Oh, I see," Anna said. "A trained pet rat. Wow!"

"Are you coming to the wedding, too?"

"Not for the wedding ceremony but later for the party."

"Then you'll definitely get to meet her. My grandfather George is bringing her."

Anna didn't say anything else.

"We should start slowly. It's best if you sit here."

Paula looked doubtfully around for a moment. "Are you sure it's going to take that long? I usually don't need more than ten minutes."

"It's not like you get married every day. Chop, chop, now."

"You're pretty bossy for such a petite person," Paula said with narrowed eyes.

"I've heard that a few times," she said, grinning.

"Why do you think she got the job," Brenda teased. "I know my daughter, don't I? You would have tied your hair in a sloppy ponytail, powdered your nose, and felt like you were done otherwise."

"Would have been perfectly adequate," Paula grumbled.

"I'll go check on the girls," Avery volunteered.

"No way. They're probably stuck in the barn, busy driving either the dogs or the horses crazy with their beautification attempts. You've already got your dress on. I don't want to risk you getting dirty again in the meantime." Brenda stood. "I'll do that. In about an hour, I'll bring them both inside so they can change."

"Thanks, Mom."

Brenda winked at Paula. "Don't mention it. You know how I've grown fond of those two."

When Brenda left, Avery sat next to Jaz and Paula.

"So, how does it feel to be a future Mrs. Bale? That makes one less Carter in town."

"Don't ask. I can't really picture it yet. Tomorrow, Nate and I are going to Colorado Springs for a few days at the spa, sans kids. I'm super excited about that. No animals, no emergency calls to Nate's cell phone in the middle of the night, and no kids who can't sleep or have some other problem. Don't get me wrong. They're all wonderful but having a few days off is nice, too."

"Who's looking after the rest who are staying home?"

"Brenda. My mom is really a sweetheart."

Avery squeezed her hand. "You have a wonderful family in the first place."

"Thanks. You soon will too, if I judge my brother correctly."

"Oh, I don't know." Since the joke about the honeymoon on Maui, they hadn't talked about the subject. While it was clear how things would proceed professionally, they had once again had far too little time for personal matters. If she was honest, she hadn't felt like bringing up the subject on her own either. Maybe she was old-fashioned, but in any case, she had no intention of proposing to him. If she was going to let him get away with the occasional macho act, he'd have to darn-well ask her.

Jaz grabbed her by the wrist and said, "Was he an idiot? Do you want me to knock some sense into him? I have no sisterly loyalties to consider."

"Hey, me neither," Paula defended herself.

"Hold still," came Anna's immediate instruction.

Paula folded her mouth shut again, while Avery's remained open.

"You're going to beat up Cole? For me?" She didn't know whether to be startled or laugh out loud.

"Sure," Jaz said. "After all, I've trained with Pat long enough."

"Uh-huh, and what was that about the karmic account?"

"Oh, that would do some good," Jaz said.

Avery grinned. "So, I'm starting to get your understanding of how this karma thing works. I have to say I like it."

"She's not my best friend for nothing," Paula said.

Two hours later, Paula stood in front of the large mirror in her bedroom and had to swallow. Even she had to admit that she looked beautiful. Silently, she apologized for any ill thoughts she had harbored toward Anna. She had chosen a traditional wedding dress for the girls' sake. The dress had a round, wide neckline, tight, long sleeves of ivory lace, and a long falling skirt. For the party, she would change and slip into a dress similar to what her bridesmaids wore. Except hers was in a dark emerald hue, which set off her auburn hair beautifully. To go with it, she would slip into her much-loved cowboy boots but first, she had to struggle with the silky pumps. Oh, well. What one did not do for their loved ones.

Out loud, she thanked Anna, "It turned out really beautiful. I...I didn't even know I could look like that."

"Like a fairy princess," Shauna gasped. Leslie nodded vigorously.

"But you are also very pretty," Paula returned the compliment.

They both wore little dark red roses in their hair and the same dresses as Jaz and Avery, only in light blue for Shauna and antique pink for Leslie. Leslie hadn't dared touch the dress at first. She had been afraid of ruining the fine fabric. Only after repeated assurances that it wouldn't matter if anything happened to the dress had she reached for it.

Paula was really proud to be so beautiful. "I look like a real lady," she said.

Obviously, she had hit the right words. Anna beamed and said, "I'm glad you like it. That's the nicest compliment you can give me."

"Why don't you stay for the wedding ceremony?" Paula asked.

"Thank you, that's sweet of you but there are still a few of the ladies coming into the salon to get their hair done for the party afterward."

"Well, have a great afternoon then. Thanks! See you later."

"Bye." Anna packed up her things, and Brenda walked her to the door.

Leslie clapped her hands. "It's almost time now. Can we get out already?"

"Not yet. First, the men have to get into the barn."

"Right. What's taking so long?"

"Probably Nessy ate Dad's shoes," Shauna said.

Avery hoped she wasn't right. From the girls' varied stories, she knew Nate's Newfoundland dog was an outspoken shoe fetishist. She chewed up any footwear that came before her muzzle.

Finally, the sound of engines could be heard outside. The girls ran excitedly to the window.

"We'll lead them into the barn, okay?"

Paula laughed. "All right. When everyone is ready, you come back and get us, okay?"

"Yeah, let's do it." And away they went.

"I'd better go along and make sure the critters and kids don't run over each other," Brenda chimed in.

Paula grabbed her two friends by the hand. "I'm not really that maudlin, but somehow..."

"Stop! Don't you dare burst into tears now of all times," Jaz said, although she was visibly moved. "You didn't grit your teeth for two hours only to walk down the aisle like a raccoon at the last moment because of a few tears."

"At least I wouldn't have to worry about Nate changing his mind," Paula quipped. "Anything with four legs gets immediate care and attention."

"That's why you're such a good match." Avery squeezed her hand.

"Now go out and stand next to your wonderful husband and children."

Paula took a deep breath.

"Okay."

Later at the feast, Avery stood outside the barn to get some air after all the dancing. She was wonderfully full—not quite overstuffed—from all the amazing food Aileen conjured up. Of course, she ate far too much of everything, especially the dreamlike chocolate mousse that Aileen had made according to Paula's recipe.

The moon was full and shining in the sky. It bathed the whole area in a silvery light. She had just relieved George of his rat-babysitting duties. She reached into her thick winter coat and stroked her little friend.

"That was a lot of excitement, wasn't it?"

Miss Marple sniffed her fingers and curled up in the coat pocket again when she found nothing to eat.

"Oh, here you are," a voice behind her said.

She turned and caught sight of Cole. He had his hands buried in the pockets of his jacket and was eyeing her intently but maybe that was just the pale light of the moon.

"I didn't think anyone would notice my absence," she said. "Especially not you. You were pretty much the most wanted dance partner tonight."

For some reason, the Diner Sisters had chosen Cole as their favorite dance partner, along with Grandpa George. In addition, the Stone sisters had come home from college for Christmas. Even Rebecca Mirren, the internationally successful barrel racer, was there. And they had all been desperate to dance with Cole.

That was all well and good. She'd passed the time with Ace, Quinn, and Toby, danced with Jake and Sam, and, of course, with her grandfather, but at some point she'd gotten tired of seeing him with other women.

Cole came toward her. *No, she had not imagined the intensity he radiated.* Involuntarily, she took a step back.

He smiled. "You didn't seriously think I was going to leave you alone for the rest of the evening, did you?"

"Well, I..."

"I didn't want to hog you from the start, as after all you have other friends here, but enough is enough. Because you and I still have something to talk about."

Completely bewildered by his view of the evening, Avery couldn't think of anything better to say than to repeat like a parrot, "Something to talk about?"

"Yes. Flights to Maui don't get any cheaper. February is humpback whale season there. So what do you think?"

Avery's eyes narrowed to slits. She felt her blood pressure rise and it began to rush in her ears. Miss Marple, sensing her excitement, scrambled up inside her jacket pocket and anxiously stuck her snout an inch out of the collar.

"Cole Carter. If that's supposed to be a proposal, it's a downright bad one. If I tell Brenda, she'll laugh her ass off. Or spank you. Either one. The way you phrased it, I assume you're looking for a travel companion with benefits. There's a classifieds section for that kind of thing."

Cole had to laugh, but quickly stifled it when he saw Avery's evil eye. That's when he spotted Miss Marple. Glad for the distraction, he reached out to stroke her head.

"I guess I screwed that up pretty good, didn't I, Miss Marple?" he whispered to her, so that Avery heard it very well.

He reached into his pocket and pulled out a raisin. He handed it to the rat, which immediately disappeared with its loot back into the warm interior of Avery's coat.

"Don't think just because you charm my rat that everything is hunky-dory."

Cole laughed softly and belatedly turned it into a throat clearing. "Sorry. Do I have another shot?"

Avery crossed her arms and raised an eyebrow expectantly. "I'm curious about that. Your sister got decorated ponies, after all. So the bar is high."

"If you have fifteen minutes, I can organize a decorated pony," he said, motioning in the directions of Paula's horses, which had again been adorably decorated by the children for the wedding ceremony. "I don't know how intact the flowers may be, but still."

Avery didn't think twice and punched him in the shoulder. Hard.

"Ouch!"

She gave him a nasty glare.

He took a deep breath and stepped toward her. Once there, he wrapped his arms around her waist and rested his forehead against hers.

"Avery. I've already missed ten years by your side. Will you be my wife? Soon?"

When she didn't immediately respond, he hastily added, "If you don't want to get married here, we can do it in Vegas on the way to Maui."

Avery smiled. "Forget it. If we're going to get married, it's going to be here. I don't mind the timing. The sooner the better. After all, we've been pretty much engaged for ten years."

"Thank God," Cole said from the bottom of his heart.

"Now, finally, whisk me away to the dance floor. I have to tell about a dozen Independence ladies you're no longer available."

He did, and then the night was a blur of dancing, and music, and of endless laughter echoing in their heads and hearts. All was how it should be.

THANK YOU FOR READING!

Readers like you are my daily motivation to write.

If you enjoyed my story, it would mean a lot if you could leave a review on your preferred book platforms. This actively supports my writing, as it is one of the few ways for me as an author to draw attention to my craft.

If you are a NetGalley member, you can review advanced reader copies of my upcoming titles before they are released.

CONNECT WITH ME

I love hearing from my valued readers, so please reach out to me directly via email or social media:

 MAIL@VIRGINIAFOX.COM

 @FOX_VIRGINIA

 BooksVirginiaFox

www.VirginiaFox.com

JOIN ME!

Sign up for my newsletter to get insider information, and receive a FREE digital download of my Rocky Mountain Romances prequel, *Rocky Mountain Diner.*

Dive into a little romance, a dab of suspense,
and a whole lot of fun!

HTTPS://BOOKS.VIRGINIAFOX.COM/RMDINER_NOVELLA

PREVIEW

*DON'T MISS THE NEXT BOOK
IN THE ROCKY MOUNTAIN ROMANCES SERIES!*

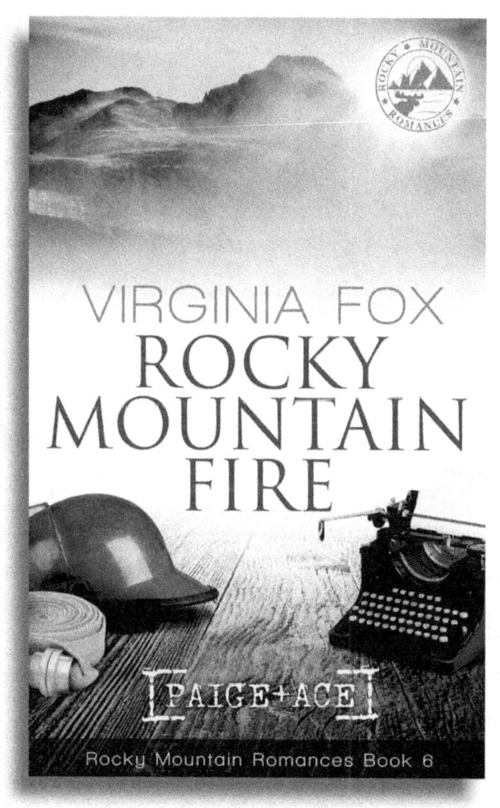

CHAPTER ONE

PAIGE PUT ONE ENERGETIC STEP in front of the other. Soon she would reach her destination for the day. All around her rose the majestic peaks of the Rocky Mountains. It was an exceptionally warm day for this time of year. March could be quite cold here in the mountains but today the sun shone from a blue sky, bringing with it a hint of spring. According to the locals, however, the good weather was not to be trusted. They good-naturedly made fun of her, telling her stories about snowstorms in May. Paige shuddered. During the long winter, those tales had depressed her quite a bit. She stopped to catch her breath and let her eyes wander over the panorama. Today, under the warming influence of the sun, the notion lost some of its terror. She might be in the mountains, but here, too, spring would arrive sooner or later, and she was already looking forward to the return of the hummingbirds.

Maybellene's bark snapped her out of her thoughts. She looked at the black ball of fur that had somehow, and completely without invitation, crept into her heart. Apparently, the break had lasted long enough, Paige thought, amused by Maybellene's tireless energy.

The schipperke dog had ended up at Kat Orlow's Safe Haven, the only animal shelter for miles around, last year after an odyssey with various owners. It was during Kat's efforts to rehabilitate the dog that they had met. For Paige, who had a panicked fear of dogs due to a bad experience with one in her youth, it had been a terrifying encounter, but under Kat's expert and patient guidance, as well as Maybellene's surprising and unwavering trust in her, she had managed to overcome her fear. Well, at least her fear of Maybellene. She still had an apprehension of strange dogs but her little shepherd kept the others at bay very reliably. Whether this was out of jealousy or because she sensed her owner's tension, Paige didn't know. The reason didn't matter. Just when she had destroyed almost every budding friendship with the people in Independence last year by a stupid mistake on her part, she had been very happy about the faithful dog.

Remembering the circumstances, she sighed and continued on her way toward the ridge. Her dog was happy that they were moving again and jumped like a bouncy ball between the large boulders from one small snow field to the next.

Although she had managed to make up for her mistake, the inhabitants of Independence were still quite cool toward her. Strangers didn't have it easy in this tight-knit society; tourists and newcomers were welcomed in a friendly manner, but then they found themselves in a kind of probationary period.

Without Kat's support during that time and Maybellene's company, she probably would have turned tail and moved away again. Lately, too, she'd been thinking more and more about whether that wouldn't be the smart thing to do. Start over again somewhere else. The lease on her Denver apartment, which she had been subletting since last year, was also about to expire. So she was free to do whatever she wanted. To do that, though, she'd first have to know "what" it was.

Unbidden, the image of a broad-shouldered, tall man slid before her inner eyes. Ace O'Neil. There had been an admittedly brief time when the chief of the local fire department and former SEAL had clearly indicated that he would be quite interested in getting to know her better. At that point, she had been too caught up in her own affairs to appreciate his attention. She had just lost her job as a newspaper reporter, which had led her to the mountains in the first place. Her head was full of lofty career plans, and she had let him run wild but only after the sight of him had burned itself into her subconscious. Later, when her whole world had collapsed and she had desperately needed a friend, or even the distraction that a lover brought, it had been too late. He had made it unmistakably clear to her on more than one occasion that he had no use for people like her. Maybe she really should make a fresh start.

She stopped again. Maybellene came running to her to find out what was the reason for the interruption of her walk this time. The dog was really tireless. She scanned the path toward the ridge. Ahead of her was a small section of woods in front of the trail that descended before the last part of the trail led up to the ridge. At least, if she remembered the map correctly. She was doing this hike for the first time today. Of course, she also had a hiking app saved on her phone but cell phone reception was more or less a matter of luck here in the mountains. She grimaced. *Luck.* Not exactly her most faithful companion, she thought self-pityingly.

"Not like you," she said to Maybellene, bending down to ruffle her fur. The dog, delighted at the sudden attention, raced off. Paige looked after her in wonder. What was she doing now? She seemed to be looking for something. Arriving at the first pine trees, Maybellene braked unexpectedly. The snow, which had become quite powdery due to the dry air, was spraying on all sides. The dog scratched the white splendor aside. Finally, she seemed to find what she was looking for. She stuck her head into the snow and jumped up again triumphantly, a pine cone between her teeth. With her tail raised high, she galloped back to Paige and sat expectantly in front of her.

Paige laughed. "You want to play?"

As if in confirmation, Maybellene spat the cone at her feet and let out a short, prompting yelp.

"It's okay, I get it."

She bent down and lifted the cone. With a flowing arm movement, she let the pine cone fly downhill. She had never mastered the fine art of long distance throwing; in this respect, she was a real girl. What a discriminating thought, she thought self-deprecatingly, but true of her, unfortunately. If she was going to throw things downhill, Maybellene at least had to try a little harder.

The schipperke raced after the cone, snatched it up with a joyful growl, and happily brought it back. That elicited a grin from Paige. She repeated the whole thing, breathing deeply of the fresh mountain air. Spreading her arms, she put her head back and stretched her face toward the sun with her eyes closed.

No. She wouldn't move away again and start over. She had friends here. Kat. Kat's mother. Even Kat's boyfriend, Sam Carter, had reluctantly accepted her when she'd accepted Kat's invitation and moved in with them, even though her big mistake had affected his sister. Paula and Leslie, the ones who had suffered, were now also friendly toward her. And she also liked the public relations work she had taken on for the Safe Haven better than she had ever imagined, although of course she sometimes missed the journalistic and investigative part. Plus, she felt it was an advantage that no one knew about her failed dream of one day becoming an important journalist. Heavens, the small town didn't even have a daily newspaper. It was just...She opened her eyes when she felt Maybellene's wet nose against her hand, and her useless longing for things that were missing in her life evaporated. The dog had obviously sensed her loneliness. Again. She crouched down and nuzzled the black bundle of fur.

"What would I do without you, huh?"

Enthusiastically Maybellene licked her across the face. Then she jumped a few steps away and barked. She apparently felt she had done enough introspection. Time to move on. Literally. If she really longed for a partner, Paige would do well to put the handsome fire chief, who by all accounts disliked her, out of her mind. After all, there were plenty of other attractive men in the area. Maybe one of the deputies would go out with her. Toby was cute, with his brown, unruly curls. Or maybe Morris? Morris taught high school chemistry and coached the field hockey team. Filled with new energy, she strode down the rocky path toward the woods.

She ignored the insistent voice in the back of her head that, unfortunately, none of them were Ace.

In the forest, the path led down slightly to a shadier part of the mountainside. She shivered and untied the jacket she had tied around her waist during the climb to pull it on. As she struggled with the zipper, her four-legged companion ran back to her and let out a low growl. The hair on her back had seriously stood up, and abruptly, Paige shuddered.

"What's wrong?" she asked in wonder. Not for the first time, she wished the little dog could talk. Not willing to let this ruin her hike for no apparent reason, Paige started to continue walking again. But she stumbled upon Maybellene, who immediately got in her way. Uncertain, she looked around in all directions. There was nothing there. *Or was there?* Stories of bears, mountain lions, and rattlesnakes, which were told with disturbing regularity at Rocky Mountain Diner whenever a new face appeared, came unbidden to her mind.

"Tourist eaten by a cougar," flashed the news ticker in her head. Did the tip about playing dead only apply to bears, or could the other animals be fooled by it, too? And had the bear also read the memo about playing dead? In moments like these, she wished she had accepted her dad's offer to go hiking with him more often as a child. After all, she was a city kid at heart. And now she was playing the great explorer here and basically had no idea how to behave, she thought with a good dose of self-irony.

She leashed the schipperke and wrapped the free end around her shoulder.

"Come on, we're going. There's nothing there."

Maybellene had a different opinion. With an astonishingly deep growl for her size, she made this clear. Another indication was that she put all four paws into the ground and refused to go in the direction she'd chosen.

After several feet, Paige gave up. It wasn't going to work that way, especially as it wasn't good for Maybellene's neck. Better to take her in her arms. She bent to pick the little girl up when the wind shifted. Irritated, she sniffed the air. Was that the smell of smoke? This far up? Memories of last year's forest fires came up. She turned in a semicircle. Sure enough. Now she not only smelled it, but saw dense, gray plumes rising from between the trees and disappearing into the sky. That had to be what her dog had smelled. She swallowed. What now? As a precaution, she took a step backward. And another. Should she try to find out where the fire came from?

Right. Then to attempt to extinguish the fire with the one liter of water she had in her backpack. She could already see the headlines in front of her: *Inexperienced Hiker Dies Trying to Put Out a Forest Fire With a Water Bottle.* Annoyed, she ran her palm over her face. Whether she hoped it would drive away the smell of smoke or get rid of that annoying habit of picturing everything in her head like news headlines, she didn't know. Unfortunately, it was of no use for either.

What was she supposed to do now? She wiped her sweaty hands on her pants and pulled her cell phone out of her jacket pocket. She probably had no choice but to alert the fire department. Say, to contact Ace. She grimaced. That was about the last thing she wanted to do. For that reason, her first reaction to the absence of a net connection was relief. Until her mind switched back on and she became aware of her precarious situation. The forest was on fire and she was in the middle of nowhere with no reception. She tried to remember where she had last used the GPS. That had been about three-quarters of an hour ago. Trying to suppress her rising panic, she memorized her surroundings before heading back.

After ten minutes, most of which she had covered jogging and hopping from rock to rock, she stopped, breathing heavily. Side-stitches plagued her, and her feet buzzed as if they were electrified. That was it—from now on, she would jog for half an hour every morning, and the delicious sweets she picked up at the diner or Sweets throughout the day were canceled. When she could stand up straight again, she checked the display. Yes. She already had a little reception here. She checked the coordinates via GPS and wrote them down with a pen on the inside of her wrist. Shielding her eyes from the sun with her hand, she let her gaze wander up the slope to assess the distance she had traveled. Now all she had to do was report the fire. She hesitated. Indecisively, her fingers hovered over her phone's touchscreen. Should she call Ace directly? She had his number. He had given it to her, not to mention forced it on her, while he was still talking to her. No, she decided against it. Emergencies of all kinds were reported by calling 911. The sheriff would then take care of coordinating the relief effort.

After a brief conversation with a very concerned Polly Miners, the former police officer who now managed the office work and apparently the emergency center calls,

Paige pocketed her phone again. Originally, she had wanted to wait here for the fire department to arrive but Polly wanted her off the mountain in case the fire spread quickly. Given the extreme drought that Colorado experienced most of the year, that was a legitimate concern. So she set about the descent.

Two hours later, Paige sat in the diner with Maybellene at her feet. The new café Sweets had tempted her with its delicacies, but it was still the case that Rocky Mountain Diner represented the heart and soul of Independence. If you wanted to be right on the pulse of current events, the diner was the place to be.

Paige was on her third espresso when Kat squeezed into the diner with her two mastiff dogs, Rocky and Nikita. Despite her tension, Paige had to laugh. One behind the other instead of side by side probably would have worked better but apparently, the two huge dogs were not to be convinced of that.

With a concerned look on her face, Kat hurried to her side and sat on the barstool next to her. The two dogs were intercepted by Maybellene at a safe distance of three feet, Paige noted with relief. She knew they were both totally sweet and overly friendly. It was just...they were big. Very big. With huge teeth. Of course, she knew rationally that it didn't make sense to not be afraid of Maybellene's teeth and be afraid of the others' but she also knew that she would only be able to control this irrational fear in mini-steps. Being alone in the same room with three dogs was a huge step for her. All the more she appreciated her personal bodyguard in the form of Maybellene.

"Are you okay?" Kat wanted to know.

"I'm fine. I was never in any danger, after all. I only smelled the smoke. That's as far as I got. Maybellene wouldn't let me get closer."

"Smart dog," Kat praised, petting the dog, who was now in the process of greeting Kat after making sure the other two were lying down at a proper distance from their mistress.

"Have you heard anything yet? Is the fire bad?"

Paige shrugged. "No. So far, no. I'm waiting for news, too."

Miss Minnie, who was just passing by with two fully loaded plates on her arm, pointed her chin toward the glass door.

"Here comes your info. And the bearer of the news is also so handsome," she concluded with a meaningful grin.

"Miss Minnie!" said Paige, embarrassed.

"What? I may be old, but that doesn't mean I'm blind. Anyway, it's the latest trend to take a young boyfriend."

The headline, *Cougars on the Prowl*, flashed in Paige's mind, accompanied by some disturbing images of Miss Minnie with her fictional lover. Determined to erase that image as quickly as possible, she shook her head.

Kat elbowed her in the ribs. "Something went wrong. Look at the expression on Ace's face."

Paige complied and almost flinched when she caught the scowl Ace gave her. *Jeez.* Someone was in a bad mood.

To Kat, she said, "You don't have to worry about that. When he's around me, he always wears that look on his face."

"I don't believe it. That can't be," Kat said.

Paige took a deep breath. "Believe it," she said, bracing herself as Ace stepped into the diner and walked purposefully toward her. She suppressed the urge to flee behind the counter and tightened her shoulders.

Ace stopped in front of her and just stared at her.

Finally, she couldn't take it any longer. "Is everything all right? Were you able to put out the fire?" she inquired anxiously.

"Your fire," he pressed out between clenched teeth, "was a controlled, permitted fire that someone had lit at his log cabin to get rid of old scrap wood."

"Oh!"

"*Oh*? Is that all you can think of?"

Paige shrugged.

He leaned forward until his face was very close to hers and she felt his hot breath on her skin.

Maybellene pushed herself between them and stared at him with her yellow eyes.

He backed away a little, but not much, and asked, "Has it not occurred to you to find out the origin of the fire?"

"I didn't know...and Mrs. Miners..." she began to defend herself.

"You know what? I don't care. You were obviously hoping to create your own headlines. Congratulations. You've succeeded. By tomorrow, thanks to Facebook, all of Independence will know that the fire department went out to put out a campfire. All I can say is bravo!"

With that, he turned on his heel and stormed out of the restaurant.

Stunned, Paige stared after him.

"What an ass," Kat was indignant.

Paige burst into tears. The tension of the last few hours, the many thoughts she'd had about her life. Everything together was just too much for her.

After some petting from Kat and Maybellene, she was ready to finally use the handkerchief Miss Minnie had brought her.

"But then why did Maybellene make such a fuss?" she finally brought out, sniffling.

"With her history, it could be anything. She's had so many different owners, and she's been treated badly more than once. Who knows what she experienced in connection with a campfire? Or maybe the owner of the cabin just smoked the same tobacco," she speculated. "There are all kinds of triggers for that kind of behavior but honestly, it doesn't really matter. You were out alone, in unfamiliar terrain, confronted with a scary situation, and you reacted."

When she had blown her nose, Miss Minnie came again. This time she had two small shot glasses with her.

"I think we can all use a boost."

Paige eyed the transparent liquid doubtfully.

"Put it down," Miss Minnie instructed her.

So she held her breath and downed the high-proof drink. This resulted in a coughing fit.

"You need more practice," was Miss Minnie's only response. She held out another glass to her. "Here."

Now it no longer mattered. She courageously emptied the second glass as well. She made a head movement over to Kat.

"What about you?"

"She's driving you home. She's not getting anything. If you're here by car, I'll get your keys now."

Paige shook her head.

"No, I didn't drive here. Sam gave me a ride to the starting point of my hike in the morning."

"Good." She patted her back. "I agree with Kat, by the way. You did exactly the right thing. Polly Miners and the sheriff agree. I don't know what crawled up our fire chief's ass."

Touched, Paige's face brightened.

"Seriously?"

"Seriously. There. Now I have to get on with it." Busily, she reached for a couple of glasses.

Paige looked after her. A warm feeling spread through her stomach. Sure. Part of it might have been due to the alcohol but her friends were responsible for the rest of the warmth.

To heck with Ace!

MISS DAISY'S RECIPES

Each recipe is calculated for four people, unless otherwise noted.

In addition to Miss Daisy, Avery and Paula have also contributed recipes this time.

Miss Daisy's Veal Cheeks Braised in Red Wine

This is a fantastic, warming winter meal.

INGREDIENTS

28 oz. organic veal cheeks

3 carrots, peeled and diced

3 stalks of celery, cut into small pieces

½ celeriac, peeled and diced

Onion, chopped

3 tbsp. olive oil

1 tbsp. butter

2 tbsp. tomato paste

2 cups red wine (e.g., Barolo)

1¾ cups beef stock

3 bay leaves

3 sprigs fresh thyme (or 1 tbsp. dried)

10.5 oz. shallots

1 tsp. sugar

Salt

Cayenne pepper

INSTRUCTIONS

Preheat oven to 350°F.

Season veal cheeks with salt and pepper.

In a roasting pan, heat the olive oil and sear the meat. Remove and set aside.

Reduce temperature and melt butter. Add onions. Saute for five minutes until soft.

Add the remaining vegetables and sauté for another five minutes. Towards the end of the five minutes, add the tomato paste and sauté.

Deglaze with the wine. Let wine boil down for another five minutes.

Add beef stock, meat, bay leaves, and thyme.

Cover and place in oven. After an hour, reduce oven temperature to 300°F and braise the dish for another 45 minutes.

At the end of this 45 minutes, add the peeled whole shallots. Stew for another 30 minutes.

Remove the shallots and the meat and keep warm. Take out half of the vegetables and keep warm as well.

Strain the sauce with the remaining vegetables and season with salt, pepper, and sugar. If the sauce is still too thin, you can thicken it with a little cornstarch.

Add the meat and shallots back into the sauce, and heat briefly.

Serve meat, sauce, and vegetables with polenta, mashed potatoes, or risotto.

Porcini Risotto from the House Recipe of Silver Lodge

*The secret to Jeff's risotto
is in the processing of the porcini mushrooms.*

INGREDIENTS

7 oz. porcini mushrooms, fresh or dried, chopped into tiny pieces

2 onions, chopped

1 clove garlic, pressed

14 oz. risotto rice

5 tbsp. olive oil

½ cup white wine

4¼ cups vegetable broth

¼ cup butter

½ cup Parmesan cheese

Sea salt

2 tbsp. olive oil

INSTRUCTIONS

If you use dried porcini mushrooms, soak them a few hours beforehand, then drain the soaking water.

In the risotto pan, sauté 1 chopped onion in 2 tablespoons of olive oil. Add mushrooms and garlic, salt a little, and saute. When onion pieces are soft, remove the mushrooms and onions from pan.

Add remaining olive oil and second onion; sauté until soft. Add risotto and sauté until translucent.

Deglaze with the white wine. Allow the wine to boil down quite a bit (beware: it burns easily at this stage).

Pour in broth until all rice is covered. Simmer for the next 20–30 minutes, stirring constantly. Whenever the liquid falls below half the contents of the pot, add more broth.

After 20 minutes, taste the risotto for the first time. To be perfect, the rice should still have some bite.

When the risotto is ready, add the butter, cheese, and porcini mushroom mixture. Stir well and serve with the veal cheeks.

Supplemented with a vegetable of choice, for example zucchini or even beet, this dish is also ideal for a vegetarian dinner.

Avery's Emergency Snack

Sometimes there just isn't time to cook.
This is Avery's emergency snack when she's shadowing someone
or so engrossed in a case that
she once again completely forgets to eat.

INGREDIENTS

Peanut butter

Apples

INSTRUCTIONS

Skin the apple and cut into slices.

Open the can of peanut butter.

Dip an apple slice in the peanut butter and take a bite. Continue until either the apple is eaten or the peanut butter is gone.

ALTERNATIVE FOR NUT ALLERGY SUFFERERS:

Almond paste, for example, is available in health food stores. Refined with very little salt and a little sugar or honey, it offers a pretty good substitute.

Paula's Special Chocolate Mousse

Since all the family members are addicted to this dessert,
Paula shared the recipe with Aileen
and asked her to make it for her wedding reception.

INGREDIENTS

3 eggs

6.5 oz. dark chocolate (50–60% cocoa content)

2 tbsp. water

1¼ cups whipped cream

1 pinch salt

1 tsp. sugar

INSTRUCTIONS

Separate the egg yolks from the whites. Beat the egg whites with a pinch of salt until egg whites are whipped. Place in refrigerator. Put the egg yolks in a large bowl and whisk to combine.

Break the chocolate into pieces. Add water and melt in a water bath. When the chocolate has melted, add to the egg yolks and mix well.

Using a mixer, whip the whipping cream together with the sugar until stiff. Mix the stiff cream into the chocolate and egg yolk mixture.

Gently fold in the beaten egg whites until you have a uniform brown mixture.

Chill for 1–2 hours. (It's best to put an extra portion in a small bowl and hide it in the very back of the fridge in case family members raid the fridge during the chilling period.)

BOOK CLUB QUESTIONS

1. Avery has a highly trained pet rat named Miss Marple. Do you think rats make great pets in real life? Could one really work for the FBI?

2. There's great hesitation between Avery and Cole. It seems it's always the wrong place and the wrong time for them to act upon their feelings. As they work together at times, do you think it's ever okay for coworkers to fan the flames of love?

3. Unrequited love is a big theme in *Rocky Mountain Secrets*. Why do you think the characters waited so long to act upon their feelings?

4. The serial killer targets young gay men. Why do you think they chose this demographic?

5. Townsfolk in Independence watch and bet on Avery and Cole getting married, mostly through social media. Do you think social media is good or bad for those in a pending relationship? Can it force them together...or apart?

6. The bonds of friendship are strong with the characters, especially those in Independence. How do you think this fact affected the story?

7. Do you know who Miss Marple might be named after? HINT: It's a famous literary character! Google is your friend!

8. Why do you think author Virginia Fox named Avery's pet rat Miss Marple?

9. Virginia Fox goes to some dark places in *Rocky Mountain Secrets* that the series hasn't previously explored. What did you think of the blending of genres? What other genres do you think might lend themselves to being blended with the Rocky Mountain Romances series?

10. Was there ever a doubt in your mind that Avery and Cole would end up together? Were there any other couples that surprised you?

ROCKY MOUNTAIN ROMANCES

Rocky Mountain Yoga

Rocky Mountain Star

Rocky Mountain Dogs

Rocky Mountain Kid

Rocky Mountain Secrets

COLLECT THE ENTIRE SERIES!

ABOUT THE AUTHOR

Author, mother, horse whisperer, and part-time healthy food cook, Virginia Fox is a woman who cares deeply about family, animals, the environment, and friendships.

Creative from a young age, she turned her love of books into a prolific career as a writer. Her German-language Rocky Mountain series saw every volume enter the Top 50 of the Kindle charts on day one of launch. Now the bestselling Rocky Mountain Romances series breaks onto the US scene.

Virginia Fox lives on a small ranch near Zurich with her family, her Australian cattle dog, and two moody tomcats. When she isn't writing, she delights in caring for her horses and cooking for her family. Discover more on her website:

www.VirginiaFox.com